April, 2011

Enjoy this
First Novel!

Christine
Anthony-
Grubbs

New House

A novel by

C. E. Anthony

New House

© Copyright 2011 by C. E. Anthony
All rights reserved.

Draft version IBSN: 978-1456449490, © 2010 by C. E. Anthony

Original version published by Lulu Publishing (www.lulu.com, ID: 938371),
© 2007 by C. E. Anthony

The poem, *"Man Making"* by Edwin Markham (also known as *"The Builder Grows"*) is in the public domain and is used under the Fair-Use guidelines of U.S. copyright laws.

This book or parts thereof may not be reproduced in any form, stored in a retrieval system, or transmitted in any form by any means – electronic, mechanical, photocopy, recorded, or other means – without prior written permission of the author, as provided by the United States of America copyright law.

International Standard Book Number: 978-1456449490

Published by The Hunter Group
Printed in the United States of America
Cover design by C. E. Anthony.

C.E. Anthony

To Patio, who inspired me, who co-authored the original version, and who was my faithful editor.

*To Mom and Poppie,
who taught us all to dream it, do it...*

...and to David – who believes I can.

New House

Man Making

We are all blind until we see
That in the human plan
Nothing is worth the making if
It does not make the man.

Why build these cities glorious
If man unbuilded goes?
In vain we build the world, unless
The builder also grows.

Edwin Markham, 1852-1940

New House

C.E. Anthony

PROLOGUE

23 November, 2057; World Government Building, Vienna

'This is damn, memory-making history,' Jack thought, as he peered over the wall of the press gallery. His skin felt electrified, and he couldn't stop grinning. 'This is award material, sure enough, and I'm here to see it, report it.'

As one of the newest members of the GINS reporting team, Jack Bannister hadn't lost his optimism and youthful excitement.

He turned to his co-anchor, "Damn, Mike, this is what it's all about; people coming together; making a decision that will affect generations to come. Democratic government."

The older man wasn't so thrilled. His cynicism was thick in his voice, "Sure, Jack. This is what it's all about."

Jack chalked up Mike's attitude to the fact that Jack had replaced him as lead anchor for GINS Mid-Central Area, and he turned back to the room. He touched the side of his wrist-mounted camera. It silently panned back and forth, reacting to voices below. When the Global Senate had been formed over fifty years ago, this room had always been full, topping three thousand easily. Today, the number of Senators in residence was a scant one hundred. The accepted norm these days was remote attendance – with giant glowing screens, capturing the world's Global Senators in their living rooms, offices and even on vacation. Jack wondered what brought these few to the building today. Maybe they feel what I'm feeling, and want to be here in person.

Ding, ding, ding. The murmuring began to subside. The Senate President slipped a remote microphone over her ear. "We will now reconvene." She waited a moment for the last of the voices to die, and then said, "First, I will re-read the question before this esteemed body; then read the outcome of the vote." She itemized the platform points they'd been arguing over for the last three weeks. Then with a deliberate pause, she looked around the room. "The decision of this Senate is two thousand and thirty eight, for; eight hundred and nine, against."

Jack Bannister felt his heart leap into his throat, and took a steadying breath. "My God! It's passed!" The tiny camera reacted to his voice and spun around, capturing his youthful, exuberant face. "The Global Senate has passed the Citizen Rule Law."

For the most part, the participants applauded; however, there were pockets of dissenters, heads together, frowning. 'Well, ' thought Jack, 'that's what a majority means, people. Someone has to be in the minority.' He didn't say that aloud, of course. That would be a career killer, and Jack was no fool. He was going places and this would take him there.

He turned slightly, as if to take in the room, but this time it was for the audience, knowing they loved this type of drama. "This brings a close to a difficult period in history, and opens new possibilities. My father used to talk about how in 2011 tyrannical governments began to be defeated with the rise of global networking. I remember thinking that it must have been an exciting time, one that could never be topped." He allowed his green eyes to slide around slowly to the camera, and he smiled lopsidedly, "But we did – today." Pause. Smile. "This is Jack Bannister at the World Government Building in Vienna on a great day for humanity."

He couldn't wait to get home and share all this with his fiancé. He packed up his gear and headed out, still filled with the excitement of the day.

23 April 2103 – forty-five years later…

Jack Bannister processed yet another funds transfer for his investigator. Chuck wasn't making a lot of progress and he'd been in Vienna for over a month. Jack needed more if these reports were going to make any impact.

Jack's wife, Amanda, came into the room, and handed him a cup of coffee. "Still no word from Chuck?"

"Just that fluff he sent a week ago. He keeps hinting that there is more."

"What are you looking for?"

"There's something strange with this new legislation, if we can only get our arms around it." Jack shrugged, "I'll just have to go with what I have."

Amanda adjusted the equipment. "Do you think anyone will pick you up this time?"

"I don't have much hope. If I can crack this, though, I might just get some notice, maybe even get back on top."

Amanda put her arms around him. "Sure, hon. You're going to come back."

They stood together for a moment; then Jack straightened up. "Let's do this." He took a sip of his coffee, rubbing his hand over tired eyes. He said, "System on, active link."

"Link open," responded the unit, and he saw the red confirmation light on the side of the camera, and his wife's reassuring smile.

"This is Jack Bannister reporting from Old Chicago on the Global Senate hearings going on in Vienna." He tried for some inflection, but it was hard. "Reports indicate that a majority of this Senate's Rotation will be spent gearing up for some new legislation which no one wants to talk about. All we know is that it involves the Scavenger situation. Outbreaks of vandalism and discontent are widespread all over the world; huge numbers Scavs are leaving the domes for the outside. And our Senators want to sit and talk. What happened to the shining dream – that perfect world our leaders offered us so many years ago?

"Will this new legislation provide a stronger arm to really help us? Or will it just be another excuse to do nothing?"

Jack paused, as he did when he was young, but now it was from long habit, and the audience – such that is was – adored him no longer. The pause lengthened and his wife waved her hand at him.

He drew a deep breath. "Our government's agenda should be addressing why we have Scavs to begin with? Why are so many of them leaving the domes, and more to the point, why are so many being murdered in the outworld camps?"

At the word "murder," his wife closed her eyes and shook her head.

He went on anyway. "Senators, wake up. Stop looking for band-aid solutions to a festering wound." He tried for a smile. "This is Jack Bannister reporting from Old Chicago."

Amanda turned off the equipment. "You didn't have to use that murdered Scavs angle again, Jack. No one can find any substance to that theory."

"It makes good copy. Besides, I know if I keep hammering away, something will break loose." He picked up his cup and swallowed the cold dregs. "I can't keep up these damn toothless reports. Chuck has to get something quick on that new legislation. I know it's all linked somehow.

Amanda went over and took his cup. "You can check on him later. Take a nap now. You look exhausted."

He knew his wife was right; even a simple report like that one made him tired. Or maybe he was just getting weary of the battle. He stretched out on his couch and closed his eyes, surrendering to sleep.

Twenty minutes later, a woman and her seven-year-old daughter were passing Bannisters' building, when a dull shudder shook the walkway. The woman dragged her screaming child across the street under a shower of shattered glass and old brick. Safely on the other side, the mother, wiping away tears and blood from her little girl's face, looked over her shoulder. The side of the building, precisely where Jack and Amanda Bannister lived, was now an ugly, gaping hole, still smoking from the explosion.

Almost at the same moment half way around the globe, Chuck Matthews was coming out of a nightclub in Vienna, arm and arm with a lovely, but expensive lady. Her laughter was trill-like and he wondered how long before it got on his nerves. On the other hand, he'd put up with a lot for someone who looked like this. He murmured something about the things that awaited her. She threw back her silvery-blond head, saying, "Ach, Chucky, meine liebe, you slay me."

The tongue-filled kiss that followed made him quicken his step. With their attention focused on each other, they stepped off the curb. They didn't see the lights. The hover transport smashed into them without slowing its speed, and disappeared into the night. People began screaming and running toward the couple, but those to arrive first knew it was no use.

1

Yumin Villanueva rolled over, twisting the cool sheets around her.

A smooth, male voice echoed through her rooms. "Wake up. It is 0615. Wake up now."

'Why was I getting up this early?' she thought vaguely.

"Wake up, now," the voice said again.

"Okay, I hear you," she mumbled into her pillow. The message continued. Min raised her voice, "Ivan, discontinue. I hear you." Silence cloaked the rooms and she drifted back to sleep.

Ten minutes later, "I can detect no activity. You must get up now. It is 0625. Wake up." The electronic voice repeated the message several more times.

Ivan, the Terrible – an appropriate nickname for her new I-VN 7000. This new Interface Voice Network was the very latest release in environmental organizers. "All right, Ivan, all right. Start the coffee." Again the message failed to terminate.

'That damn voice recognition.'

"Ivan," she said in a more distinct voice, "I hear you. Start the coffee; real beans today, not synthetic."

Min slipped from bed, rubbing her fingers briskly through her short, black hair. "Ivan, start the shower, normal cycle, medium hot." Dropping her nightshirt on the bathroom floor, Min slipped into her shower cylinder. The warm foaming stream swirled around her body and she let it do its work. The unit, after five minutes of foam, cycled into a mist. It felt so good that she said "Extend rinse" and the auto-light blinked, and the system asked, "Duration?"

She added another fifteen minutes; then, as she spoke the word 'Dry,' warm, swirling air surrounded her. When the unit terminated after a few minutes, she stepped out and pulled on a short bathrobe. She went to the kitchen where her food simulator held a steaming cup of coffee.

"Honey and Synthicream, Ivan," she instructed; then cradling the cup in her hands, she wandered over to her front window. The people who were emerging from their town homes were toting umbrellas or rain gear. Her workday usually started around ten, so she usually missed the morning rain cycle.

She glanced up at the sun. Its beams were piercing the steam-covered terradome almost a mile overhead and creating a myriad of tiny rainbows. It was beautiful, and almost made getting up at this ungodly hour worth it.

Back in her bedroom, she started dressing, saying, "Activate my news profile, Ivan."

"Please specify which news services," her system requested.

She sighed. She'd been so busy recently she hadn't taken the time to set up her preferences. Moreover, her old profile hadn't transferred correctly.

"Give me WIB, NCIB and LS," she said, then clarifying, "that's World Information Bureau, North Carolina Information Bureau and Local Services for Raleigh."

"I recognize common acronyms." *Did Ivan actually sound offended?* "Would you like text or human format?"

"Image KennyOne," then she remembered it wasn't there. "Give me the default male pattern, mid-twenties, reading headlines only. Store these parameters as Image KennyOne." She'd overwrite it later when she loaded her old profile.

A smiling young man appeared and began reciting the latest news headlines. She finished dressing and, as she walked back to the kitchen, KennyOne continued to deliver random news from each room. That was one of the great features about the I-VN 7000 – total environmental holographic replication. The system had real problems, though; programming bugs, which they should have corrected before its release. Besides not automatically inheriting her data, her new Ivan had an annoying argumentative tone, arbitrary defaults and an overall reluctance to take direction. She could probably reprogram these, but then she shouldn't have to, not for what she paid for it.

As she sipped her coffee, she let most of the headlines slip by, but a few articles caught her attention.

"KennyOne, play Garner riot, CNC bombing, and the Sandford articles, please."

The first article was a riot in Garner Center between a group of Scavs and Security Forces. Unbelievable scenes flicked by – dirty, angry groups being stunned, some striking back at the Forces, some curling up on the ground trying to fend off the blows. Eventually, the Forces subdued most who hadn't run away, and gathered them into vehicles. She thought she saw a couple Scavs who had become clients for reorganization. But that was crazy. Why would they become clients and then take to the streets again? It was such a waste.

The bombing of the Central Network Complex in Hilo, Hawaii, Pacific Region was another senseless scene. There were charred and blacken buildings, with a couple vehicles flipped on their sides. "While the buildings are all but destroyed, little damage was done to the actual network. Hilo Local News Service went out but the GINS switched to backup within a few seconds and little impact should be felt. Several groups are being investigated and arrests are imminent." She sipped her coffee thinking how funny the news reporting had become. Always "groups investigated...arrests imminent...cases closed" but rarely is there any follow up articles on who was arrested, why they did such a terrible thing. That kind of reporting went out with the 20th century.

The last article, however, she found most disturbing.

"A new Alexander Villanueva exhibition opened last week. Sponsored by the Sandford Gallery of Art, the exhibit is a retrospective of Villanueva's art from the earliest works to present. GINS reported that at least 2.5 million visitors signed onto the site in the first three days, and the numbers are holding through the week, breaking all records for similar shows.

"Hats off to Lumen Sandford for this inventive method for revisiting one of this era's most popular artists," cooed the brightly, smiling image. "Request your network to go to the

Sandford Gallery Archive section and specify Villanueva to view and download some of this fantastic art. Also, while you're there, check out..."

"Stop. End news," she said angrily. Revisiting? Lumen is acting as if Alex is washed up. And worse yet, he's taking the credit for Alex's art. A small slump and that stupid Lumen pushes retrospectives. She'd seen popularity cut off in mid-stride by just such a step. If people start thinking of her brother's work in the past tense, then it just might come true. She gathered up her things for the office, thinking that she should call him later.

As she left her condo, she paused a moment to make sure Ivan engaged the security. It seemed to take longer than the old system – or was she just imagining it? Finally the small green light next to the door handle turned to red. As she walked down her drive, she pulled up her hood and quickened her pace to the Maglev.

At the gate portal, she juggled her case as she retrieved a tiny, circular plastifoil from her folder and slipped it into the slot. She then laid her hand on the scanner.

"Error. Transport-mocur is required," the unit said.

"Whenever I'm in a hurry..." she said in frustration. She slipped the rejected mocur back into her case and repeated the procedure using the correct one. Why can't they consolidate these mocurs into one?

"Destination?" the system requested, as it scanned her palm.

"Neuse Station."

The Interfacer deducted the fare, popped it out and she returned it to her folder. Pushing through the gate, she joined the thousands of other travelers going into the city.

Alex Villanueva sat at the kitchen island sipping coffee and reading the news his counter screen. He preferred reading his news to hearing it ready by the avatars provided by the GINS network. One article caught his attention. It was by JR Hardy – he always had something radical to say.

BANNISTER DIES IN EXPLOSION

1 May 2103, 1300 LT, Special from JR Hardy (New Chicago IB) –

On 23 April 2103 Jack Bannister, a GINS reporter for over fifty years, and his wife, Alicia, were killed in Old Chicago when an explosion ripped through their flat. Those facts should have been the start of a story on Jack Bannister's life and career. However, what did the established news services report? "A Classé-riche woman, Ms. Carol Estefani, CEO of Zepher, Ltd., and her seven-year-old daughter, Lynnette, on vacation in the historic city, were injured when explosion debris showered them. Ms. Estefani and her daughter were treated and released, but there were two fatalities in the building." The official report listed it as just another accident, with no specifics on the cause of the explosion. Bannister, a popular newsman, and his wife, were mentioned only in passing, and nothing was mentioned about Jack's long and illustrious career. Jack, a long-time friend, was on the verge of uncovering a huge political scandal possibly tied to outworlders' murders. Could his death be linked in some way to...?*

Wow, Alex thought. *He's really grandstanding this time. I wonder if Hardy even knew Bannister.* Alex did remember the old reporter – and he had been well respected, but then nothing had been heard of him for years. *Typical of Hardy to make his passing something spectacular and mysterious.* He pushed the article into the trash zone on his screen and went to several articles on the Triangle Institute or Art reviews.

He was in the middle of a story on the Searcher VII mission, when he heard his daughter coming down the back stairs. He terminated his screen, knowing his peaceful time was at an end. With all her six-year-old enthusiasm and energy, AnneJuleé burst into the kitchen.

"Are we still going? Are we? You said we could."

"Of course. You and Adam wait for Mom after classes. She'll bring you to Consuelo's. We can go after we eat."

She put her arms around his legs. "You're snaggy, Daddy. I can't wait." As she heard her two brothers come in, she turned, saying. "Remember, we're going to the zoo today and then to Daddy's 'zibit."

Alex's sturdy middle child merely smiled. "Oh, good, Dad, I'd almost forgotten. I heard the new specimens are really slick. They have some Mars fossils that are really unique." Adam was much too serious for his eight years, Alex mused to himself. And as if answering his thoughts, Adam turned to AnneJuleé saying with a smug air, "And the word is exhibit, not 'zibit."

AnneJuleé frowned and muttered, "'zibit, 'zibit, 'zibit..." leaning against her father for reassurance.

"Leave her alone, Adam," James said as he sat down. "Dad, I won't be joining you. I have to go to the Crabtree Science Center to work on my digital laser project."

Alex was proud of all his children, but his eldest son was really gifted. He was years ahead of his level. His professors continually advanced him and Alex had been considering sending James to the St. Petersburg Institute. But he hadn't mentioned it to Karen. Heaven only knew what her reaction would be.

Amidst a comfortable chatter, Alex watched as his pride and joy ate their way through grilled cakes; none of them questioning the fact that their mother hadn't come down. He wondered briefly when it had become so normal to eat without her.

James made a quick swipe at his mouth with his napkin and slipped from the stool. "You guys have fun today. I'll be late tonight, Dad."

"Okay, but not beyond ten."

James waved a hand as he hurried out the door.

When Adam and AnneJuleé were finished, he gathered up their things for their daily trip to school. Adam was actually ready for home-based AutoEd Mentoring, but he wanted to give him one more year of interacting with children. He'd noticed that children forced too quickly into AutoEd did not always fit well into society. Once Adam had completed the First Level program, he would let him make the choice. And it's a long way off for AnneJuleé. So for now, this is my routine, Alex was thinking, as they walked the four blocks to the Preston Heights Primary.

"Bye, Daddy. Don't forget today," AnneJuleé said softly. She turned and walked up the building ramp with her brother. Her wispy blond head was already bowed, shyly, as she withdrew into herself.

Why does she do that? She's so vibrant around the family.

"I won't forget," Alex said to no one in particular, since the children had disappeared into the school. He smiled at the way they took his reply for granted. He turned toward home, lengthening his stride until he settled into a comfortable jog.

The man watching Casse Portland could tell she took great pleasure from her work. The slight woman ran her fingers caressingly over the wood spindle. She had an intense expression and was lost to everything around her.

She reached out for the sanding wand, gave the piece a few more passes. She removed it from the lathe and placed it with the three other legs. She then lifted a three-foot square of wood onto the workspace, and began moving the laser router around the edges to create a delicate double groove. She started humming something, and her chubby hips began swaying to and fro with the rhythm.

A strange feeling swept through him – erotic, yet tranquilizing. He was suddenly aware of every sensation – the woman's melody and the hypnotic drone of the tool; the sweet, pungent odor of freshly cut wood; the hot and musty air, which was raising moisture on his flesh. He was unable to move from his spot in the shadows.

He had done so many already – each one had been easier – yet this one, well, he was looking forward to doing a woman. That would be new. He absorbed in the energy of the moment a bit longer; then shook away the feeling.

His footsteps were silent on the sawdust-covered floor. But when his shoulder touched a chain hanging from the ceiling, he froze. A faint chaffing sound was audible overhead. He waited. She showed no reaction. Still, he waited. Nothing. He continued faster, reaching out abruptly and clamping muscular arm around her neck.

She was so surprised that she dropped the tool, reacting first with anger, but when the pain to her windpipe increased, she panicked. She clawed at his vise-like hold with pathetic efforts. He had always been strong, stronger than anyone he knew, so holding this slight woman was nothing.

He felt something wet on his hand and arm. He pulled her backwards so he could see her face. A steady stream of tears rolled down her face; her horrified eyes were dark dots in a sea of white.

A jolt of electricity shot through him. *God, this was exciting.*

Gradually, her struggling lessened and her eyes rolled back in their sockets. He let her loose and she slid to the floor. He stood looking down at her unconscious form. She wasn't dead yet and he needed it to look like an accident. They kept saying, accidents. He looked around for something.

The laser. It was skipping and cutting a macabre pattern in the wood. He reached for the tool and directed the laser toward the inert form on the floor.

Joshua Robertson had looked at the transport taking him to Somerville and had almost stayed behind. He'd traveled in many odd vehicles over the years. He'd even ridden in an antique wheeled vehicle or two – but this thing...*Good Lord!*

However, according to its driver, it still hovered at a decent pace. Matthew pulled himself into the driver's seat, adding in his educated, yet husky voice, "I'll get you to Somerville in no time at all."

Josh climbed aboard, settling into the ripped, dusty cabin, resigned to an uncomfortable trip. But it was worse; much worse. Before they had gone a mile, he realized the air vents were worthless, spewing out brown, foul-smelling air. And his meager attempts at conversation were quickly silenced; the SolarEngine created such a noise that you either yelled or kept quiet. Matthew chose yelling, keeping up what seemed like a 1000-decibel, one-sided conversation. Josh now understood his hoarse voice – years of competing with this old machine.

They'd been on the road for a couple of hours when suddenly, the huge transport settled to the ground, and the engine was hushed. "Be right back," were the words Matthew flung over his shoulder, as he jumped out and moved off into the bushes.

The lack of that overwhelming thunder made Josh aware how he'd been straining to keep his senses. His ears hurt, his throat was dry and raw and there was a painful throb in his temples. He climbed out of the cab, stretching and looking out at the misty peaks and deep blue valleys. The trees along the road had the soft, green fuzz of spring.

It wouldn't be long, he thought, until this valley will be lush and a riot of color from the azaleas and fruit trees. He loved the Blue Ridge area, but coming back also reminded him why he'd left. His family, the system, all so long ago. Another lifetime.

He had sold everything he owned, which at that time wasn't much, and had purchased a travel mocur. He had gone as far as it would carry him – the Pacific Area, as it turned out – and began working for food and lodging. It was tough for a time, but he'd found he liked the nomadic life, liked the luxury of being alone, being free from the network and trackers and all the chains the system entailed.

Josh heard Matthew returning and he climbed back in.

"Sorry, but nature always calls when I'm in the middle of nowhere," Matthew laughed, as he pulled himself up. He reached behind his seat and produced a jug of water. "Want some?"

"Thanks." Josh took the jug. The liquid was warm and iron tasting, but it was wet and was relief to his dry throat. "Are we almost there?"

"It's not far, now. We should be there in a couple of hours. I have one more stop." He started the engine, and, after a minute, the hover unit had the huge transport moving again.

"Do you…originate…round here?" Matthew yelled. "I hear…accent when you speak."

"Yes," Josh hollered back. "But it's been a long time."

Matthew shook his head, "What?" and motioned to his ears.

"Twenty years…left long time ago," he screamed again.

Matthew nodded and said something like "thought so…" and Josh resumed watching the ever-familiar landscape slip past the window.

"This used to be home," Josh said quietly.

Alex entered his huge, three-story house by the side entrance, taking back stairs, going directly to his room. He hoped to avoid Karen. As he changed, he could hear her moving about in the adjacent room. He was just about finished when she knocked softly, and walked in without waiting for an answer.

"I see you got wet, again," she said. "It doesn't make any sense that you jog when you know you're going to hit the rain cycle."

"I like the rain. It feels good."

"Does it?" she asked, sounding mildly surprised.

Alex stared into her beautiful face. He wondered what they'd ever had in common. Her words last night, so hurtful and cutting, had not betrayed any anger, only controlled censure.

She was now saying, "I'm not pressing you, but do you plan to work today?"

"I work in my studio every day."

New House

"No. You go to your studio every day. You haven't produced anything marketable in a long time. I know this is a touchy subject for you, but you've got to apply yourself." she persisted.

Instead of responding, he moved past her and into the hall.

"Alex, don't walk away. You have to admit I have a right to be concerned." She put a hand on his arm.

Even she thinks my career is over. He turned to face her, his face growing hot with anger. "Karen, you're driving me crazy. No wonder I can't paint with all of you hounding me. You, Lumen, the news services...none of you care why I'm blocked. You never ask me how I feel. All you care about are the GEMs and...the status." He pulled his arm away.

Karen stiffened and there was a flicker in her eyes that he couldn't define. "What are you talking about? Of course I care how you feel, but you're so remote all the time, I can't talk to you."

"Do you know how hard it is for me – trying to create and having nothing?" As he spoke, he saw the cynical look reappear and realized she was just manipulating him again. She wasn't trying to be sympathetic. *God, after all these years, Alex, you'd think you'd learn.*

She went on in her smooth, sympathetic voice, "You know that Lumen will be happy with whatever you do. Your name is what sells today, not the quality or substance of the work. People will buy anything."

"God, Karen."

"What? What did I say?"

"You really don't understand, do you?"

"For heaven's sake, Alex, it's just painting, not a new invention or something important."

"If you're so worried about us," he lashed, "why don't you produce an article of interest to someone outside of your tiny circle of friends."

He was shaking inside and was afraid she would see, so before she could respond, he turned and made his way up to his third floor studio. He closed the door and walked purposely to his stool, but didn't sit. He stood starring at the white cloth covering his easel, then began to pace around his studio. The intensity of his anger surprised him. Karen's taunts didn't usually get to him like this.

Then he realized that it wasn't her criticism that had made him react. He was afraid that she and the news services were right.

His gaze drifted around the huge room, at the shelves and cubbies filled with every medium, every form of tool. There was a corner dedicated to canvas construction, complete with an auto-stretcher and yards of canvasite. There were nine blank canvases waiting for his inspiration and dozens more half-finished works scattered about the room, but every time he picked up a brush, each stroke sickened him. He felt he was repeating stokes that he'd done a thousand times before. Nothing new. Nothing creative. Yet, in order to stay on top, he had to produce.

He pulled the cloth off the painting resting on his easel. It had the familiar theme, and demonstrated his talents, but no, it wasn't right. He looked around the room and examined several

New House

others. They were all without substance. In frustration, he threw the cloth back over the piece and left the studio.

2

The man had moved on to Brushridge three days earlier. Dry rot and termites filled the abandoned building he'd chosen for his encampment. He felt as if his skin was crawling, but it had to be. No one would come around; he could plan his next one without fear of detection.

They had not prepared him properly for this job, or what to expect. Initially, he was to exit for a few weeks. He was to pick his key targets and dispatch them quickly, which in itself was new for him. Up until this assignment he had been just an enforcer, only occasionally eliminating someone who got in the way. Now, though, they wanted an assassin, someone who could choose victims from set criteria. It surprised him how easily he settled into this new role. He found satisfaction selecting his victims and even more in the actual dispatch. There were times at the beginning when he wondered why he was doing this, but the more he did, the less he cared why.

So far he hadn't traveled far – no more than 2000 miles. Soon, however, he supposed he must push beyond the continent…maybe the Pacific Area or Asia. They might even want him to go to Eurafrica. He would welcome a chance to travel from this place.

New House

Hell of a place. Most of the glass was missing from the windows and a biting April wind flooded the area, kicking up the dust and cobwebs. *I need to get back to civilization for a while.* He rubbed his watering, bloodshot eyes and hunkered in a corner, pouring some coffee from his thermal carafe.

He'd viewed the optimages of the inhabitants more than a dozen times, but he played them again. There were about twenty families in the area; he could chose from several influential people. Borrelli looked like the best choice. Their house was over a mile from the main group, and he was always doing something in that barn of his. Some sort of garage. The father, however, was rarely out there without his son. Maybe he would give them two for the price of one.

Then he wondered what their reaction would be if he took out the boy. They might react as they did when he did that young man in Michigan. Hell, how could he have known the kid was a Classé-riche? He'd fit the bill and was living in a damn Scav camp. What kind of Classé-riche *chooses to live like that?*

He swore. It was stupid to worry about what they thought. They weren't out here. He was. He turned off the imager and poured some more coffee. *Damn, it's cold.*

Exiting the long path from his yard, Alex turned in the direction of the business district of Piedmont Heights. He'd spent another unproductive morning reading news and puttering around the house. Lumen had called and asked if he could stop by, so

Alex gave up and left for his agent's office. He could easily get it in before lunch and the outing with his kids.

His pace was leisurely, speculative. He'd never known a time when he was so unsure of his future. The only thing anchoring him was his children. And, of course, his parents – they always gave him strength. Tonight was another big family dinner at the estate in Umsted. His mother was up for another Global Senate rotation and Alex knew what to expect – a long evening of platform discussion, heated arguments, and some really great food.

The thought of family brought on the familiar sibling distress. Min was drifting so far from the family. She had always been a rebel, rejecting family status as far back as he could remember. She'd always fought against traditions, even scorning the name Villanueva. Lately, however, she'd been growing more defensive; more remote.

Then there was Angel, his younger brother. His gentle nature had been dissolving away into a moodiness that was as troubling as it was irritating. Alex wanted to reach out and pull them both back, but he didn't know how. Min. Angel. Karen. His art. Everything seemed to be out of his control.

As Alex passed the local Security Forces office, he heard someone yell his name. He looked around. Lt. Tami Donaldson came running down the steps in threes and hurried to catch up. A riot of unruly short, blond hair and bright smile, she hadn't changed much in the 25 years since their days at the Palmer School.

She fell into pace beside Alex, "I've got some playoff tickets to the Durham game Wednesday night. Can you join us?"

"Sure. I haven't been to a live game yet this season."

"Neither have I," she said. "These are great seats."

As they slowed for a cross street, Tami asked, "You're going to Connie's?" It was more of a statement than a question.

"Sure. But I have to make a stop first."

"That's OK. I'll walk along."

"I'm going to my agent's office." Alex waited for the usual reaction.

Tami made a face, "Lumen...right, then. Well, I'll see ya there." And her easy stride carried her on down the street.

Alex turned onto the side street and entered a non-descript building with simple lettering, announcing 'Sandford Galleries.'

Alex spotted Lumen in the back among a dozen or more crates, some open with packing material scattered around. Lumen guided his thin fingers over one of the sculptures, clearly admiring its form. He seemed to be aware someone had entered, and he straightened his emaciated body, exclaiming, "Alex! My good friend." He brushed his stringy black hair away from his face in his familiar re-focusing gesture. "And how are you today? It is so good to see you – very good."

"'Mornin', Lumen. How have you been? How is my show doing?"

"Very well, very well, my dear friend. It was profitable after only two days and the demand for your work has doubled. You are always popular." He waved his hand apologetically toward the crates, "My pardons, please, Alex. I will finish and be with you momentarily?"

"That's fine." Alex wandered around the room, which continually amazed him. Objects d'art were hanging on and leaning against the walls in no apparent order and with no style. The floor space also contained samples of his clients' sculptures, with narrow paths between the disorder. Yet despite the collection, there was very little of value out here. And security in these outer rooms was next to nil. These were authorized reproductions with the originals safely locked in environmentally controlled vaults somewhere below. Fortunately, few buyers saw this clutter. Most viewed and acquired their art virtually, seeing only an image transmitted from the elaborate studio next to Lumen's office. People generally didn't own original art any longer – the trend had been moving away from "hard art" for quite a while. Today it was holoart, something they could subscribe to briefly, or for just an evening or special event, then changing it whenever the mood struck them.

Alex paused next to a marble-like piece, two intertwined figures symbolically flowing into waterfall. "Who did this, Lumen?"

"No one important," he called from across the room. "He is not important. Now, these," his head nodded toward the recently uncrated pieces, "this artist...her work is very good. I have, as you see, just acquired some of her work for reproduction."

Alex turned back to the first artist's work. "Well, I like this better. It has a freshness that I admire."

"Truly?" Lumen exclaimed. "I must rethink him then, if you approve. But you..." his arms sweeping the area in another grand gesture – he was fond of dramatics, "...you, my friend, are still my best artist."

Alex was sure Lumen, the consummate salesman, said that to all of his artists.

His agent finally stood back so he could see the pieces better. Even though he hadn't physically uncrated anything, he brushed himself off and smoothed his already crisp attire. "Very good. Very good. We will start reproduction this afternoon." He walked over to Alex, "I have some new autho-repos for you to sign. Let me get them..."

"That can wait until later. What did you want to see me about?"

"Oh, yes, yes. The offer. You will be so pleased. Come."

Lumen paused outside his heavy, elaborate office door, allowing the retinal scanner's blue beam to do its work, and then he said his name. His office door slid quietly open, to the one place where his GEMs were carefully and generously spent.

"Sit, sit, my friend. Can I get you something?"

"No. I'm on my way to lunch. This is all very mysterious, Lumen. Why couldn't you just holo me a message?"

"A minute, only, my friend. I have a great thirst." He went to his glistening cabinet of heavy crystal and silver and made his selection. While Lumen needlessly supervised, Alex again took in the sumptuous office.

The walls, covered with a rich, dark green tapestry stood in stark contrast to melon and gold-stripped curtains framing a curved window bay. But the window was an illusion – there was no vista to the outside; too insecure. A holo-image of Bali at sunrise graced the window today. Occasionally, the scene was Earthrise from the Sea of Tranquility, the Aurora Borealis from the Hotel Nordica Resort, or some other favorite scene. The only concession to natural light was a single round skylight over his massive desk – four inches thick, and, Alex was sure, filled with sensors and alarms.

However, it was the series of small, high intensity spotlights that illuminated the real treasures – two Rembrandts, several small Monets, a grouping of five Timmerman inks, an early Villanueva, plus a half dozen or so pedestals supporting sculptures by Toppetti, Rodin, Crispin, Giacometti and Bonschevski – all originals. Lumen might spout trends to his clients, but deep down, he was a hard-art man. Alex always felt honored to have his piece displayed in this illustrious company, but also a little awkward.

Lumen walked back to his desk, sipping his drink. "Are you sure I cannot offer you one of these?" he asked, taking another long sip.

"No, thanks."

Sitting down, Lumen patted his imager, "This I had to give to you in person." He activated the unit and Alex watched as Karl Voltstadt, Chancellor of the Lake Ridge Art Center in New Chicago. The word "professorship" came up in the first sentences and Alex sat dumbfounded.

During all the soul-searching he'd been doing, not once had he considered teaching. While lower education was conducted via the GINS, the higher education, 5th Level and above, required personal guidance and generally fell to those with years of experience. It was truly an honor. Most people didn't get invited to teach at the university level until they were fifty or sixty, when they had years in their field. Alex was only thirty-three, and, while he'd been at the top of his profession for several years, he found it hard to believe that he would be considered for such a prestigious position.

When the message ended, his agent, barely containing his enthusiasm, said, "Well, my friend, what do you think?"

Alex didn't know what to think – full professorship in New Chicago. *Well, well, well...*

His agent, puzzled by Alex's silence, asked again, "What do you think? Is this not the most exciting offer?"

"I think it's very flattering, but it would take time away from my art. I'm not sure I'm ready to give it up yet."

"But my friend, you know, professors have ample time to pursue their studies. How can you hesitate?"

"I have a lot to consider. I know what an honor this is, and I know what a coup it is for you – not to mention your commission – but I can't just decide here and now." He stood up. "I'm late. I'll let you know soon."

Leaving his agent totally frustrated, Alex left and walked toward Consuello's Bistro & Pub to meet his friends for lunch, astounded by this turn of events.

Min reviewed the details of her proposal. It was odd, she thought, how the idea had developed.

At the morning's meeting, Director Tomaska had said, "The Global Senate has requested that all reorganization groups initiate a program to investigate what appeal Scavengers find in the hostile external world…"

The Director's new initiative was much like so many others launched by the Company, and Min hadn't paid much attention to it. But a few hours later, when interviewing one of her prospective clients, the idea began to percolate.

She knew the Company wouldn't approve an exit voucher for the Robertsons' request, but if she came up with a legitimate 'hook' connected to this latest initiative…well, she could gain an impressive number of new clients, and show a few people that she wasn't just corporate dressing. In fact, she wanted to extract a certain amount of revenge. Technocrats talked about Classé-riche snobbery; most of the technos she worked with had so many "chips" on their shoulders they could build a GINS network.

Moreover, the whole thing started with that strange request from Albert and Chrysta Robertson. They'd wasted no time in presenting it.

* * * * *

The Robertson's patriarch sat perched on the edge of the seat, rubbing his hands on his knees. Occasionally Albert would lock his unwavering and clearly hostile stare on Min. Chrysta, on the other hand, had arranged her plump body comfortably in the other client chair, smoothing her worn blue dress, as if it was

New House

expensive silk. When she was satisfied that everything was perfect, she sighed, and raised her enormous green eyes. "We want you to find our son," she blurted out.

"God, Chrys," growled Albert. "That's a great way to start."

"I beg your pardon?" Min thought she'd heard wrong.

Mrs. Robertson leaned forward, smiling wanly, "Our son. We want you to find him and bring him home."

Min almost laughed, but decided against it. "That's not the sort of thing we do here at the Socio-Center. You need the Security Forces if he's lost. Now how else…?"

"He's not exactly lost," Chrysta interrupted. "We just haven't heard from him in a while. We're worried." Her face looked anxious and her voice had a hint of a whimper. Min summed her up quickly. Manipulative; used to getting her own way. And clearly in denial of her age, with heavy makeup and youthful clothes. Time, however, had crept in around the corners, and when she smiled, she was almost ugly.

Min didn't quite know what to say. "I'm not sure you understand my role here. Perhaps if you let me explain my…"

Albert slapped his hands on the arms of the chair. "Chrys, you don't know how to deal with these people. Look, Ms. Villanueva, we've been to the Security Forces. They won't pursue someone who exits, especially not one of us. *Not their jurisdiction.*" He sounded tired, defeated yet still full of rage.

"He's gone outside?" *An Environ; obviously a teen outside the domes. Even more ridiculous.* Min decided it was time to put an end to this. "This is really not my job. I can give you the names of reliable agencies to trace runaways. I'm sorry, but I can't..."

"You don't fool me, miss," Albert growled. "I know who you are. You're one of them Villanuevas. Despite this techno job, you're really Classé-riche. You can do anything, get anything done."

In spite of her best efforts to control it, Min's voice became icy. "My family is certainly very influential, but that does not mean that I have access to anything I want. Nor, Mr. and Mrs. Robertson, can I ignore my job's responsibilities and go off looking for an Environ boy who's gotten lost."

Albert looked impatiently at his wife, then back to Min. "I knew this would be a waste of time. Let's go!" He started to rise, but wife reached over and touched his arm. He stiffened but lowered himself.

Chrysta smiled again – Min noticed that the ugly smile rarely reached her eyes, which were glistening? Fake tears? "I know it's not part of your job, but won't you at least try? He's traveled on the outside for most of his life and up until twelve or thirteen months ago, corresponded with us quite regularly..."

Albert interrupted her, "Well, I'd hardly say regular."

"Oh," heavy sigh, "well, maybe not regular, but just enough to know he was still alive. But it's been so long..." the tears actually began to spill over and roll down her chipmunk cheeks, "...well, if he knew how worried we are..." Her voice finally trailed off into her handkerchief.

She had to deal with some crazies in this job, but these two beat everything. Then in the next nanosecond – *oh, where's my* head. *Environs;* the focus of the Director's new project. *Why not?* Ridiculously, she found herself saying, "Okay, let's say I do look for him?"

Chrysta brightened, "Would you?"

However, Albert was more skeptical, "I assume by your tone that you'd want something in exchange?"

"You're very perceptive, Mr. Robertson. Yes, if I went and looked for your son, upon my return, you and your entire family would agree to become clients of our Center…whether I find him or not."

"Don't like that," he growled, shaking his head. "No. How do we know you've really looked?"

"Well, you'll have to take my word for it." She could see from his expression that he wasn't going to trust easily. "Ok, I'll return with some sort of evidence that I've tracked him. You understand, I may find him, but he might not want to return."

Albert sat back in the chair, clearly thinking her proposal over. "Okay, but the evidence has to be directly from him, a communication or something. We want to make sure, you understand."

"Ok, agreed. I'll bring you proof from your son, if he is still alive. If not, proof from someone that he is..." she didn't finish. "Either way, though, you bring your whole family in as clients."

He was still reluctant, but a tearful, "Please Albert," from his wife did the trick. He nodded briefly, and clutched the chair even harder.

Min was trying to formulate where to start. "Do you have any correspondence from him? Any clues to where he might be?"

Chrysta's eyes miraculously cleared of tears. She dug in her bag, "They're not recent. Over a year," she said, handing Min several old thermal ROMs.

"Do you know where he was last?"

"I think the last one – they're dated, you see – says something about the upper Mississippi River basin area. I can't remember where exactly."

After getting them to sign a promissory agreement, Min escorted them out, saying "I'll contact you when I return." Then she sat back down, wondering what she'd gotten into.

* * * * *

It was almost time to leave for the day, but she had a fairly descent proposal. She was sure that once she interviewed this kid, as well as a few others along the way, she'd get some interesting insight into the Environs' situation. She would also get the Robertson family to join a re-ed program. Two birds with one trip or something like that.

She dictated the final statement of her proposal, which, she noted, was more than a little vague. "By interviewing both types of Environs, defectors from the domes and the life-long outsiders," she finished, "I hope to detect a pattern which we can then address. Two weeks should be sufficient for the completion of this project. Transportation mocur is requested."

She looked at what she had dictated, made some changes and told the Interfacer to format it and send to the director's office. A couple of seconds later, the system announced

"Complete." Something would surely come out of this – a promotion, maybe; or at least a little respect. It was worth a try.

Alex picked up his pace when he realized he was running late – he had wandered aimlessly for a while thinking of the incredible offer, and eventually he found himself on a narrow, side street. Realizing the time, he cut between a couple of the high, thick stucco walls, over three streets, and came out adjacent to "Consuelo's Bistro & Pub." He traversed the colorful garden nested with tables, and went into the pub.

"Hi, Connie," Alex said to the short, red-haired man behind the bar. Many restaurant patrons, on first seeing Connie, commented that he did not look Latin, which wasn't at all surprising. Connie's real name was Conrad Luther Whitehall, a descendent in a long line of proper Englishmen. However, since he'd chosen Spanish and Mexican cuisine to dominate his menu, he rationalized that a Latin version of his name was preferable. "Have Robbie bring me a beer, will ya?"

Connie smiled and waved an acknowledgement, as Alex made his way through the inner room and went into the rear courtyard. The big table in the far corner held his lunch group, usually with five to seven gathering every day. Alex was one of the core participants and occasionally Connie would join, but only if they stayed past his busy hour.

Tami, at one end of the table, greeted Alex with a nod. Clem, Ellen, and Nan were on the far side, and were, at that moment, all listening to Michael, who sat with his back to the courtyard.

Alex took a seat next to Tami, and began sliding through the menu pages on the table screen, dragging his choices into the order window. Two large beef burritos, two cheeseburger baskets, a second beer and two cherry frizzles.

Michael looked at him in surprise, but it was Clement Wright who asked, "Really, Alex, you must stop this tendency to overeat."

Alex chuckled, "Adam and AnneJuleé are coming after class. We've an outing planned."

Ellen and Michael resumed a debate over new-wave art, which started, Tami said, as a friendly exchange. When their voices rose to a new level, Ellen whirled around to Alex.

"Come on, Alex, even you can see the advantages of holo-art, can't you? Defend me to this reprobate," she said, flinging her head toward Michael, her long, wild hair falling over her face. She pushed it back with an angry gesture, "Well?"

"Don't look at me. I'm still painting as they did in the 21st Century. Holo-art doesn't have the same meaning as owning an actual piece of art."

Michael said smugly, "See, our artist in residence agrees with me."

Alex could see that Ellen was beyond reasoning, and decided to switch to sports as a safer topic. "Did anyone watch the Atlas' victory last night? It was a terrific match."

"I saw it," Michael said. "Barker is one of the best challengers in the second division."

Tami shook her head, "With our luck, he'll be moved to a first division team and we'll be left without a good starter."

Ellen looked at the group, disgusted, "Oh, for pity's sake, let's not start on that bunch of gladiators." Unlike Alex, who didn't have any trouble mixing sports with art, Ellen Frederick possessed an artistic snobbery. She was an amateur sculptor who lived on her husband's professorship at University of North Carolina. From their huge home in Chapel Hill, Ellen made the trip to Consuelo's a couple times a week to eat with them. "What is it about those thugs that is worthy of discussion?"

Alex glanced at Nan, waiting for a reaction. As a retired gladiator, Ellen's taunts should have offended Nan, but she didn't notice. That was Nan. She had been top-ranked in her day; however, blows to her head, and a career-wrecking fall left her ten steps behind the rest. She could still talk about strokes, court strategy and season standings, but most of their conversation went right past her.

The conversation moved on to local politics, but out of the blue, Nan brightened, "The Arbor Atlas will never be as good as they were ten years ago." She must have spent the last few minutes coming up with something to add to the conversation. "There are too many teams today," she continued, blithely. "Not even Jimmy Barker can restore the Atlas to their former glory."

"My God, Nan, keep up." Michael had little patience with Nan. He shook his head, and turned his attention to the food, which had just arrived.

Almost as if on cue, Karen arrived with the kids. Tami moved down, leaving two chairs next to Alex. The two kids slipped in, chatting happily about their upcoming adventure.

Karen responded to several 'hellos' but made no effort to engage any of them in conversation. Clem, however, asked her something, and she leaned down to hear him better. She smiled and said something to him. Alex watched with fascination as Clem easily drew her out. She actually laughed and shook her head. At that moment, when she wasn't worrying about her appearance or thinking of her image, she was beautiful. Her silky hair caught the sunlight and looked like spun gold. She bent and kissed the top of Clem's baldhead.

No one suggested that Karen stay for lunch and she didn't linger, pausing only to turn to Alex, "I have some appointments today and I may go to an afternoon concert. But I'll be home in time for your parents' dinner." When she spoke to Alex, some of her beauty dissipated; lost, he supposed, in her animosity towards him.

"Fine," was all he said.

Min was just leaving to have dinner with a friend, when an *'Incoming message'* stopped her. "Receive message," she said.

The Director's image hovered over her desk, saying, "Min, excellent proposal. We suggest you select a gatherer to assist you, and work from the approved questionnaire downloading now. A minimum of five Remnant sites should give you reliable results;

therefore, we have extended your travel permit to three weeks, effective this Wednesday."

"Thank you, Director."

The image faded. Min was pleased that the Director had accepted her proposal, but she was also beginning to wonder. *A major project, complete with a gatherer and approved questionnaire?* Min sighed. Three weeks. She thought fleetingly of the engagements she'd have to break. She briefly glanced at the questionnaire, then told her system to power down, and left for the restaurant.

When Josh and Matthew had stopped in Denton for lunch, they'd picked up supplies and packages intended for three more settlements. It was after five o'clock before Matthew finally maneuvered his transport to a stop in Somerville. Josh knew they were somewhere on the Tennessee-North Carolina border, but he'd lost his exact position half way through the day. He slid down off the seat, stretched and walked up a slope to get a better view of the area.

A thick haze shrouded the distant valley and the surrounding peaks pierced threw it like dark blue islands. Just below he could see the corner of a clear, azure blue lake. *Lord, this is unbelievable.* Josh took a deep breath of the delicious air. It had been warm the last few days – unusually so for April – but now a brisk wind swirled around him, reminding him that in the mountains spring was slow coming. He put up his collar.

Josh watched as a big man strolled over to the transport, calling to Matthew. Josh walked back down.

"What have you got for us this week?" the man was asking; then he nodded to Josh, "Who's this?"

"This, Ramon, my man, is Josh Robertson. Hitched a ride with me from Beaver Gap. Josh, this is Ramon McGregor."

The two men exchanged a brief handshake, but Ramon held onto Josh's hand with growing interest. "Robertson? You mean Joshua Robertson, the one they call the Recorder?"

"I guess you could say that." Josh squirmed inwardly, withdrawing his hand. There were times when he longed for his earlier anonymous life. He shifted the conversation. "I've heard about your place up here. Thought I'd come over and check it out."

"That's fine. We love it. Mountains are great around here. Hey, you must be hungry. Matthew, get started and I'll send someone to help you unload; then we'll go to dinner. Meanwhile, I'll show you where to stow your things, Josh."

"Hey, look," Josh chimed in. "I can lend a hand too."

Matthew was firm. "No. Go on; dump your stuff. I can get the locals started, and I'll meet you in a bit."

"Good," Ramon smiled broadly. "That's settled." He walked off, and Josh fell in step beside him. "With the weather turning warm, we'll be getting more visitors, but there are still a few good beds. How long were you thinking of staying?"

"Not sure. Till you need the bed or I wear out my welcome, I suppose."

New House

Ramon let out a deep, welcoming chuckle, clapping his huge hand on Josh's shoulder. "Well, I don't figure that'll be soon." He paused only long enough to stick his head into a large barn-like building, where the aroma of cooking was prevalent. "Hey. Matthew's here! Needs help unloading." Josh could hear chairs scraping on the floor, but Ramon kept walking, not waiting to see who responded. He led the way beyond a row of small cabins, and came to another large wooden structure. "Well, here we are." He pushed open the door, letting Josh pass.

Josh looked around at the big, plain space. The room was open to the roof where slender windows promised slices of morning sunshine. There were six-foot tall partitions between the beds, and in each space, they'd added a table and lamp. Josh felt Ramon's eyes on him.

"I know it ain't fancy, but it should be comfortable." Ramon's tone wasn't apologetic. "We have tents, too, but I thought you'd like this better."

"This will be just fine. Which one's empty?" Ramon indicated three, and Josh chose one and dropped his bag.

"Come on." Ramon was off with his quick stride. "This way to the food."

Alex rested his arms on the patio wall, surveying the gardens where he'd played as a kid. The evening moisture cycle had just finished, and the setting sun flooded everything with its own special light.

"I never get tired of this view, either," said his mother, as she slipped in beside him. "You seem quiet this evening. Something bothering you?"

"No."

"I know you. There is."

"It's nothing that I can solve right now. I have some decisions to make, that's all. I'm not ready to talk about it. Dinner ready?"

"No. Besides, Angel and his girlfriend aren't here yet. So what have you been working on? Anything new?"

"Nothing significant."

His mother let the silence linger, understanding the words that he hadn't said. Finally, she rested her hand on his. "You'll hit on something soon."

He liked that she never pushed. *Then again,* he thought, as he looked at her strong profile, accentuated by the fading light and deep shadows, *maybe we just don't feel her pushing.* Somehow, she got the people around her to do what she wanted. Those who had worked with her over the years had commented from time to time that she managed with a velvet glove. He draped his long arm across her shoulders. "I love you, mother."

"Oh, don't get mushy," she said briskly, but she belied her words by hugging his waist. "Let's go see how dinner is coming."

A half hour later they were seated in the dining room – two uncles and their wives, his aunt, Grandmere, his cousin Phillippe and his wife Chauncey; even Uncle Will had flown over from London that afternoon. Only Alex's siblings were missing.

However, before the staff served the first course, Angel arrived, alone and with no apologies. Despite being clearly miffed about something – probably his girlfriend's absence – he joined the table discussion, and even seemed to pull himself out of the glooms, laughing at a couple of stories from Uncle Will. It turned into a great evening. He missed Min, though.

At that moment, Min was in her foyer, wondering why the entry light wasn't on. It was supposed to come on at dusk. "Ivan?"

"Do you require something?"

"Why isn't this light on?"

"Be more specific, please."

"The entry hall light. It's supposed to come on at dusk."

"You did not specify that parameter in your profile."

I don't believe this. "You have defaults – use them."

"I was about to activate, as my sensors detected diminished light." The hall light came on.

"Thank you."

"A specific entry into your personal profile will eliminate further confusion."

Damn, please give me my old system.

Min went in, dropping her portfolio in the hall, and stretched out on her sofa, thinking of the upcoming trip. *What have I done?* Then she repeated the thought aloud.

Ivan said, "Your query was not clear. Please repeat it."

"I'm not speaking to you, Ivan."

"I can detect no other presence in the area."

"Never mind. I was talking to myself." The quiet settled again; then she said, "Any calls today?"

"Are you directing this question to my message center or are you again talking to yourself? It is difficult to ascertain when I should acknowledge."

"I'm talking to you now, Ivan. Were there any calls today?"

"No incoming messages were received. If you would preface your inquiries with a designation, then I would know when you are speaking to me."

"Okay, thank you. Ivan, connect me to Alex, please," then added, "Alex, my brother."

There was a brief pause; then Ivan came back, saying, "Your brother and his family are away for the evening. Would you like to leave a message?"

"Yes, ask him to call me back." She then remembered that tonight was a family dinner, and wondered again, why she had no desire to join in. It was like waging emotional war every time they got together. She really loved her family, but she had always felt like an outsider. The one person she was close to was her grandmother. Grandmere's 90th birthday was coming up; she definitely wouldn't miss that gathering.

She changed her clothes and sat down at one of the five terminals in her condominium, inserting the old discs one by one into a converter. The correspondence between Joshua Alan Robertson and his parents surprised her a little. It didn't sound like the correspondence of a rebellious kid. There was eloquence

New House

in the passages, describing the skills he'd observed, the places he'd been. The date on the last transmission was fourteen months earlier. *Where was he when he made this?*

"Ivan, go back a few sections. There...stop." The passages mentioned villages along the western shores of the Mississippi River, and of some Illinois communities, but his last reference was a town called Dwyer.

"Ivan, display a map of Illinois, specifically the town of Dwyer."

"Dwyer does not appear on any listed coordinates. Please provide more details."

"Just store the coordinates for that region." It was as good a place to start as any, and once she got in the region, she was sure she'd find this Dwyer.

She read a while longer; then decided to go work on her latest project. She went to her spare room. Networking equipment covered a long table, but this was more than a simple Interfacer console. There were special power boosters, over a dozen odd-looking tools, and several small remote projectors in various stages of development.

"Ivan, HAM Imager 8." The smallest of the holo-imagers began to glow. "Display Sample 22, full color." Several basic geometric shapes glowed in the stream of light. She picked up one of the brushes.

"Magenta, screen 20%." As she 'brushed' one of the objects, a subtle change took place. "Cadmium yellow deep, 10% with 100% opacity fill." A few more stokes highlighted the side of the cube. A verbal command accompanied each pass of the brush – a change of color, hue or an increase or decrease intensity. Holographic technology had long since been the standard method for communications, business, sports and other areas of society.

However, this was different. A holographic art medium, which she affectionately called HAM, was a new tool allowing the user to 'paint with light.' The brush was an optical sensor, which allowed her to create, alter and enhance a holographic image through voice commands and Interfacer-controlled brushes. The image would never be a physical artifact, subject to environmental deterioration. It would remain forever in its purest, original form.

She hadn't set out to create a new art medium. Originally, in an attempt to turn her spare bedroom into a personal art gallery, she'd accidentally altered the holo-image of an old masterpiece. She was distressed at first; then surprised, and finally curious. Her scientific mind forced her to recreate the event. It wasn't until much later that the impact of what she'd done occurred to her. Her knowledge of holography and computer science, as well as her familiarity with art, had been all she'd needed.

Imagers had been in homes for decades; they were as common as mocurs. Even Scavs had them – they might not have decent clothes or enough food, but they had their imagers. And since the Global Interfacer Network ran everything in the domes and even some locations outside, her HAM would be an easy sell, at least technically. However, she was also no fool; she knew how the art world received new ideas. And, more specifically, Alex.

At the thought of her brother, she acknowledged another side to her anxiety. She had struggled to find her own position amongst the giants of the Villanueva clan. The HAM might be that way. On the other hand, it could be a monumental failure. While her family wouldn't condemn her failure, she would hate their pity.

Ivan broke into her thoughts, saying, "You have an incoming message. It's your brother, Alex."

"Thanks. Wait a minute. Terminate the HAM program first."

The simple piece of artwork disappeared, and the imager produced her brother's image. His elegant suit couldn't hide his tall, athletic frame. "Hello, Alex. Did you have a nice dinner?"

"Yes. We discussed Mom's Senate rotation and platform. It was a great evening – everyone was there. Grandmere said to say hello."

"I notice that they don't bother to invite me anymore."

"Good God, Min. You don't have to wait for an invitation from your own family. They probably quit calling you because you never come."

"They stopped calling because we always end up fighting. They think I'm wasting my life."

"Well, you don't really do anything to use that incredible brain of yours, do you?" He waved his arms in frustration.

She wished just once he could see what she was trying to do. She wished…oh, hell. This isn't why she called. "I don't want to fight."

He shook his head, rubbing his forehead as if a headache was forming. "Neither do I. Why did you call?"

"I'm exiting Wednesday for business. I thought I should let someone in the family know. In case anyone's interested," she added lamely; then wished she hadn't. She could see his anger flare.

"Damn it all. Stop feeling so sorry for yourself."

"I'm sorry. That *was* stupid."

"Very stupid." He was standing very quietly, his beautiful face a little sad.

"Yes, well...I'll probably be out for three weeks."

He looked surprised. "Why would your business take you outside? I thought your job was to counsel Remnants."

"It's the newest initiative of our company's director. She seems to think we can reorganize Environs, if we can understand them. I've volunteered to visit some of the encampments and do a study – you know, 'why they exit,' 'why they stay,' 'what's in the environment to satisfy them.' That type of stuff."

"Min, I've heard about the conditions in those places. It's not like camping in a global reserve – none of the comforts you're used to. It can be very dangerous out there. Once you exit...well, GINS can't track you in most of those places."

"I'll have my RIC, and I'll check in daily. I think I can stand it for a few weeks. If it becomes too unbearable, I can cut it short and re-enter. What have you been working on lately?"

He ignored her change in the direction. "It's an unnecessarily risk."

"For heaven's sake, Alex, I'll be okay," she shot. "I have a gatherer going along, so it's not like I'll be alone."

"It's just..."

"I didn't call for your approval, Alex. How are the kids?"

"They're great and stop trying to turn the conversation." Nevertheless, he laughed.

"Thanks for calling back. I'm tired and I want to do some programming before I go to bed. I'm having trouble breaking in my new Ivan."

"Min, you don't break in an Interfacer. You simply tell it what to do."

"Not this thing. He keeps trying to boss me around."

Alex smiled broadly. "Take care, Min."

"Sure."

Alex watched as his sister's image faded, thinking about the way she humanized her Interfacer. She'd never change.

The door opened and his wife walked into the den. "Was that Min?"

"Yes."

"What did she want?"

"She's exiting for a few weeks."

"Another vacation?"

"No, business this time."

"I don't see why she wastes her advanced degree on Scavs. It's such a waste – they're all so lazy."

"Leave it alone."

"You feel the same. I've heard you say as much to your parents. In fact, just tonight..."

"Drop it, will you?"

"Oh, sure, you criticize her, but let me say one word and you rush to her defense. You know she's wasting her life on a bunch of people who'll never achieve anything better than a gatherer, or worse, a security cop. God knows, we have more than enough of those."

Alex didn't respond; and he let the dig about Tami pass. He was just so tired of arguing.

She stood very still for a moment waiting for his reply; then said quietly, "It's a great pity I cannot get the same loyalty." She seemed to be studying him. Finally, she turned and walked off.

3

The weather had turned a lot colder. The man crouched silently on the small hill behind the Borrelli house, waiting for darkness. A lilac thicket afforded him a little visual cover, but nothing could shelter him from the wind, which was pushing ugly clouds in from the northwest. *Even if this does blow up a storm, it will be easier when it's dark.*

The infra-scan showed the heat images of three figures sitting at a table. The wind cut into the audio, so he heard only parts of what was being said.

"...about done, son?" The father.

"Yeah, just finishing up...was hungry. That was great, ma." The figures began to move away from the table.

The larger figure – which he identified as Sam Borrelli – went over and put his arms around the female. The two figures then began to move around in a rhythmic manner, "Yeah, it was a great m... *(crackle)* ...bout dessert, woman."

"Get out, you sil..." Laughter. She pushed him away. "...clean up."

Someone said something, which the wind totally blew away. The two males then emerged from the side door. They traversed the short distance to their barn and resumed their work.

According to his chronometer, the local time was 1534. There was still too much light. He secured the collar flap around his neck, pulled his woven cap tighter over his ears and settled back.

As darkness spread over the sky, the storm blew itself out. In the distance he could see the glow of lights from the house and barn. As the evening wore on, the lights in the big house went out, so only the light in the Borrellis' barn was visible. He rose and made his way down the hill and across the yard. *Have to work this one carefully. Don't want to tangle with two at once.*

Through the window, he could see the father leaning over the engine. *Where's the son?* Then he saw the father look under the frame of the transport and speak into the pit. *Good. The son's under it, out of the way.*

He waited until he was sure they were engrossed in their work; then eased through the door, covering the short space quickly. Sam Borrelli seemed to sense something and started to turn, just as the man struck the soft joint just below the father's skull.

"What...?" was all he got out. The bigger Borrelli fell against the vehicle and slid to the floor.

"Dad? What's the matter? Who's there?" The son reacted quickly, pulling his way from under the transport, but he was not fast enough and the younger man joined his father. The man looked down at the inert figures. He was used to pushing people around and starting trouble, but nothing like what he'd been doing out here.

He went over to the row of LBF cylinders he'd discovered in an earlier search. He hadn't figured why they'd be storing this much volatile fuel, but it served his purpose. He touched the valve readout button to the first container. *Twenty-five percent.* Not enough. He repeated the procedure until he found one nearly full.

As he lifted it, he accidentally bumped the valve and some of the liquid got on his hand. He wiped it off quickly, but the subzero substance still numbed his hand to the bone. With his good hand, he lifted the heavy vessel, catching it under his arm.

More careful now with the fuel, he made a trail from the cylinders to the transport, encircling the two men. A final trail flowed from the ring to the door, and as he left, he dropped the cylinder. He backed up about ten feet, and snapped a small vial. Holding it at arm's length until it glowed a bright orange, he flicked it into the fuel stream.

A smokeless, blue flame licked and ate the fuel greedily. He turned and made his way back to the hillside thicket. At one point, he thought he heard a cry of pain, but he couldn't be sure.

Minutes went by, but only one wall was showing any sign of fire. Suddenly, it came – what he'd been waiting for. The initial explosion ripped apart the top of the barn and one wall. Two more explosions interrupted the night, then a fourth, as one-by-one the LBF cylinders heated beyond their limits and the expanding fuel erupted.

At the first explosion, the woman had come from the house, screaming and waving her arms. She ran all the way around the building. She seemed to be looking for a way in. *She's stupid,* he mused to himself. *She's going to make it three if she's not careful.* He watched her sink to the ground, as she seemed to realize the futility of her efforts.

There was not much of the original structure left, only a skeletal shadow. The explosions had also leveled a small nearby shed. Many of the windows in the house were shattered. His attention went again to the woman. Her screams were growing louder and louder, as shock and hysteria gripped her.

The flames lighting the sky ranged from a brilliant orange to a hot blue-white center. It was beautiful, spectacular. He wanted to watch longer, but the explosions, not to mention the fire, would bring people soon.

The echo of *"Oh, God, oh my God. Sammie, David...Oh, God..."* followed him as he made his way over the ridge.

Min was enjoying her breakfast at the Hilton Imperial's second-floor dining room and scanning Joshua Robertson's correspondence for a fourth time. She was revising her original picture of him. She originally thought him to be a runaway youth – perhaps in his early twenties – but doing the math, she now figured he was much older. He'd been out there over twenty years. Even if he exited when he was a teen, he would have to be at least in his late thirties. Based on what she'd been reading, though, she figured he was in his mid to late forties. He sounded extremely intelligent – a surprise for a Remnant – and had a maturity acquired with years.

New House

A commotion in the courtyard made her glance out the window. She had a clear view of the Grand Fountain where a number of Scavs were demonstrating. As security officers tried to break them up, one protestor climbed onto the edge of the fountain, yelling and waving his arms. The more security tried to get them to leave, the more violent they became.

Several trucks with heavily armed officers arrived, rounding up everyone who hadn't fled.

Suddenly, her great idea didn't seem so great. *What have I gotten into? These people don't want help – they fight us with every breath. And Environs have to be even worse.*

She pushed her plate away, and it was immediately whisked up by the auto-server. She poured another cup of coffee from the carafe and looked again at the scene below.

She couldn't imagine what Environ encampments must be like. Despite the fact that Joshua Robertson sounded intelligent, he was still a rebel – like those lunatics in the courtyard. *God! What are we coming to?*

For a couple of GEMs she would quit this trek right now and go home. Nothing had gone as expected from the start. Yet, her stubborn part, which always got her in trouble, forced her to stay. She laid her plastifoil on the table's 'Bill Pay' area and waited for it to scan the transaction. She then went in search of Belinda Carroll. It was time she and her gatherer got going.

Alex could see Adam on the other side of the field, pushing his way through the opposition. They were in the playoffs, the final game before their break. Both teams were playing harder than ever, adrenalin running high in an effort to be number one.

"Hi, Dad." James climbed up to Alex's row.

"Hi, there," Alex said, sliding over a bit. "Didn't think you'd make it."

"It was close, but I wouldn't miss Adam's final game for anything." He brushed an arm over his face, flushed and damp from running. "I forgot the time and had to hustle. What's the score?"

"Adam's team is up by 3 points, but that Roanoke team is good."

They watch the two teams scramble for the ball, up the field and back, neither making any goals. There was a lot of kicking and shoving; then a Roanoke player suddenly took a swing at one of Adam's teammates, catching him squarely on the chin. Within seconds, a dozen small figures were wildly throwing punches and bloodying noses.

Alex resisted his fatherly impulse to run out on to the field and rescue his son. It wasn't necessary though, as the umpires were already interceding. Adam went to the sidelines with a cut over his cheek; a girl was bleeding from her lip. *Minor stuff, but enough to make Karen renew her objections.* James had never been really into sports, but Adam was soccer-mad.

James echoed Alex's thoughts. "Boy, will Mom ever zeek out when she sees Adam."

"We'll take him to the derma-lab before we go home. Your mother doesn't have to know."

"Good thinking. But aren't you worried about setting a bad example for your sons? Lying to Mom and all?"

"We aren't lying. We're just not mentioning it. That's called omission."

"Small details." Yet James' smile indicated that he would keep the secret.

An hour later, they were in the hospital's crowded waiting room. A technician walked into the area, "Adam Villanueva?"

"Right here," Alex said. "Do you want me to go with you, Adam?"

"Awe, Dad..." He marched off without looking back, following the attendant down the hall.

"I hate this, Dad."

"I think most people dislike this, with all the sickness, and dying – what's to like?"

"It's not that. This..." he waved his arm. "It's demeaning. We shouldn't have had to wait. You should have told them who you were."

Alex looked at James. "What good would that have done? Others were more seriously injured than Adam. You wouldn't want them to suffer, just because you don't want to wait, do you?"

James looked at his dad as if he was going to say more, but just shook his head and was silent.

Twenty minutes later, Adam came back, a brave grin on his face. The only evidence that he'd suffered an injury was a trace of red and a little swelling under his left eye.

"How was it, kid?" James asked, as he punched his brother's shoulder.

"It was okay. Just a tickle." He would never admit that it hurt.

"Come on, boys. Let's go home."

"Hey, Ramon. Look out!"

A stack of hundred-pound bags of oats suddenly tipped over, pushing Ramon backwards. "Oh …hell" was all Josh heard before Ramon was nearly buried.

Josh leaped off the truck and two other workers scrambled over.

"Lift, dammit, lift," Pete Granger yelled, dragging the sacks off. He had a strained, anxious look, "Ramon, can you hear me?"

Another man – Josh couldn't remember his name – was also calling to his friend. "Ramon, we're coming. Hang on."

"God! Stop…yellin'," was the muffled reply from beneath the remaining sacks.

"Hurry it up," Pete croaked.

As they lifted the last sack, Ramon rolled over. "Give me…a…oh, damn." He took a deep, stabilizing breath. "I'm not…dead…just…winded." He managed a smile, looking up at his friends. "If you could…see your faces…"

"You sure you're okay?" Josh asked.

"I guess." But as they grabbed his arm to pull him up, he recoiled violently. "Ahhh…Brad…wait."

Ramon was perspiring and his breath was coming in short gasps. He folded his arm quickly back into his side. "I think...pulled something."

Pete was all business. "Brad, go for Doc Simone. Marco, help me get him up."

"You know, guys, I think I'm just bruised. You don't have to get the doc."

"Shut up," Pete said as they helped Ramon the rest of the way to his feet.

Ramon's wife, Margie, hurried over when she saw them, full of gentle, but efficient, concern. "What's happened? Ramon, honey, you okay?"

"I think he might have broken something." Josh said. "We should probably get him to his cabin."

Later, sitting around the McGregor table amongst dirty dishes and coffee cups, a small group was discussing Ramon's condition. Margie had made sure her husband was comfortable, before preparing dinner for their friends – Pete Granger, Simone and Mike Carlyle, Brad *something*, Marco Yin, and Marco's wife Emily. Simone had taped up Ramon's ribs, put a patch on a forehead cut and had given him some medicine for pain, but was having trouble making him stay down.

"He's so stubborn," Margie said with a brief shake of her head and deep chuckle. She got up to get the pot of coffee.

Simone was a little grimmer. "Well, he's cracked a couple of ribs and if he's not careful, he'll do more damage. I don't think he has a concussion but I don't want him up and about for a while."

Pete held out his cup for a refill. "Brad and I will stay a while to make sure he stays down."

"I can stay, too, if you want," Josh offered.

"Well, we may have to sit on him," Brad smiled, "so your size will come in handy."

Josh leaned back and mused over the warmth at the table. These people were strangers, but he felt unusually close to them. This place would be harder to leave than most, but he knew himself. He'd get anxious soon and want to move on. For now, however, he was enjoying himself with this comfortable, friendly group.

By 11:45 a.m. Min and Belinda had arrived at Exit Portal 107. This was clearly a human exit portal only. The station had only a small air lock – for no more than 10-15 people – and a luggage conveyor. The Hilton has sent their luggage and equipment on ahead to the Auto-Park.

Belinda placed her left palm on the scanner, its pale red light glowing for a second before turning green. It had collected her DNA code from the invisible thin bars in her palm. The system requested her destination and duration of her exit. She responded; then turned to Min. "Your turn, Ms. Villa-nueva."

Belinda had been continually mispronouncing her name, saying the hard double-L. Slighted irritated, she said, "Belinda, my name, as I've told you, its *vee-ya-nu-ava*. If you can't say it right, please don't even try."

Belinda looked as if she didn't care how Min pronounced her name. She simply said again, "Your turn."

Min looked at the reader. "It's not mandatory. I think I'm going to pass this time." She rubbed her palm. She'd always resisted these things unless it was absolutely necessary. This time it wasn't.

"You should always register; otherwise, they won't know where you are." Belinda said.

"They can track us outside any time we turn on our RICs, so what difference does this one make."

Belinda shrugged her shoulders, "It's just sensible."

Sensible? That wasn't the word Min would use – sinister, ubiquitous, insidious maybe. While she understood the reasoning to track the movement of some people, doing it every minute of every day was excessive. Whose business was it to know every intimate detail of our lives?

It all started in the late 20th Century, with satellites and GPS positioning. When the COPI – or Certified Omni-Personal Identifier – began sixty years ago, it seemed harmless. Infants born in the domes began having an invisible bar code embedded in their palm for their protection. It all sounded so noble. Soon billions of scanners around the world could read those same harmless bars. Now the COPI contained all the personal, physical, ancestral and financial information for the majority of dome residents. Some still believed COPIs were an invasion of privacy, but their voices were getting quieter every year. Unfortunately, Min was one of them.

She started to explain her feelings to Belinda; then thought, *what was the point?* She'd never understand.

Min pushed through the first set of doors. Belinda joined her in the air lock, just as the standard announcement began. "Please hold the railing and secure all belongings." The doors slid shut.

Min glanced at Belinda. Was she anxious? "Have you never exited before?" No response.

A thundering rush of air pulled at their hair and clothing for a few seconds, then it calmed and the voice announced, "Pressure neutralized. You may exit."

Belinda appeared to be more relaxed, but she had her face upturned, as if to catch something that eluded her. "What is that aroma?" she asked.

"You probably smell those flowers." An ordered row of brilliant yellow daffodils and multi-colored hyacinths lined the walkway.

"Yes, I recognized those, but there's something else, something I can't identify."

"You've never been outside, have you?" Min asked again.

"No. Never."

"You probably smell the external environment."

Belinda seemed to take this in, then for the first time look genuinely amused. "I can't believe there is so much difference in the air quality. It's almost overpowering."

"I've always liked it. It's a great change from the sterile stuff we usually breathe. Some people never adjust to the outside."

Then Belinda focused on the sky. "Oh, my goodness – it's so blue."

"If you think this is blue, you should see it in the mountains. Then there is the blue-black of space. That's really beautiful." Min paused, realizing this person, with her limited education and experience, could not appreciate anything she was describing.

By this time, they'd arrived at the Auto-Park waiting area, tripping the entry sensor. "Identification, please – name first, then vehicle type and duration."

"Villanueva, two-passenger auto-van, three weeks."

"Acknowledged! Your unit is not ready. Please have a seat."

Ten minutes later, their vehicle pulled up. The rounded, cream-colored cab had been coupled to a gleaming, green van unit about twelve feet in length. The accordion neck, which linked them, was a darker shade of green, giving the impression of a stubby flower on its side. It was the ugliest vehicle Min had ever seen, yet it would provide them some conveniences, and more importantly, a state-of-the-art security system. *Alex would feel better if he could see this.* Then, as Min looked at the silly thing again, she thought, *maybe not.* She was laughing to herself, as they climbed into the cab.

Min took in the pilot's seat. "Profile the mirrors, seats and controls for the current driver," Min said to the van's system. The unit made minor adjustments to accommodate for Min's height. "Store as Pilot One." She turned to Belinda. "We'll set yours when you pilot."

"You're going to trust me with this monster? I've never piloted something this large before. Just a small hoverer."

"Not to worry. It has an override." Min again addressed the unit, "Start hover-mode." It took a moment for the air to raise the vehicle. Min read in the approximate coordinates for Dwyer and they began to move forward. "Engage autopilot," she said, and leaned back to relax.

By 12:40 p.m. on Thursday afternoon, local time, Min and Belinda were traveling west to the last known location of Joshua Robertson.

The terse, high-pitched voice emanating from the man's RIC said, "We're satisfied, but..." There was a noticeable pause, but without an image, without an expression to read, the man could only guess what was coming next.

His RIC was similar in size to standard units, but its similarity ended there. This one had maximum security protocols, blocking and scrambling anyone from tracking his signal. Even if someone did trace his I-VN 6500, he had multiple access ports that would rotate through dozens of dummy locations before connecting to his RIC. He was virtually invisible.

"We're not getting the response we wanted. Not nearly enough."

"I'm just doing what you told me to do."

"Yes, good, but..." hesitation again. "Everything must escalate. They must feel vulnerable; feel the need to return to the safety of the domes. Understand?"

"I understand you. If you want me to escalate, I will. But they may not all look like accidents."

"We've been thinking about that. Maybe our first thought about all accidents wasn't the way to go. A more defined threat may be more to our purpose." Another pause... "And don't let so much time elapse between them."

The man said simply, "My next one should be in a day or two. I'm already in place and have him picked out."

"Good. Remember. Stir things up."

"Yes." The man tapped his earpiece, terminating the call. He stowed his RIC and looked around at the drab countryside. It was still brown and ugly from winter. He vowed to take a vacation after this was over; to go somewhere hot and green. He took a large gulp of coffee – it was cold. Tossing it away, he climbed back into his compact terracraft, and drove on.

On Friday, Josh spent two hours doing something totally out of character – relaying his life and travels to a group of children. He had declined initially, but Rita Harper was a hard woman to resist in many ways. As it turned out, he was gratified when his young audience responded with "Oohs" and "Aahs" to his tales.

When he was through, Rita turned to her class. "Do you have any questions for Mr. Robertson?"

A boy with straw-like hair stretched his hand into the air. Rita said, "Yes, Peter?"

"Mr. Robertson. What's it like living in the domes?"

Josh was thrown off guard. When he didn't respond, Peter went on. "Can you breathe good in there? Where do you get air from? Are there buildings and cities and stuff?"

Another boy behind Peter chimed in. "What is the dome made of? What if it got a crack in it?"

Then, the big question came from a soft voice, asking shyly, "Why didn't you stay there?"

"Whoa, kids. One question at a time. Peter, you first." Rita turned to Josh, expectantly.

Why the domes? Why hadn't they asked their teacher? Or others in their group? Josh looked at the nineteen faces staring at him.

"The domes manufacture and filter air, and if the dome cracks, it has a self healing surface which closes it. They have homes and buildings and cities. Life in there is similar to yours, only people out here have more freedom. That was one reason why I left."

"Freedom?" Several children called in unison.

An older boy about fourteen said surly, "We don't have freedom."

"Well," Josh went on, "you may not realize it now but you do." He was feeling a little irritated, "It's very complicated. Haven't any of you been in the domes?"

"I have," brightened a girl from the back. "We went to visit my aunt a long time ago. I don't remember much."

New House

Rita must have sensed Josh's discomfort. "I think we've taken enough of Mr. Robertson's time. Say thank you."

There was a somewhat uniform, "Thank you," then they began to stir. Rita dismissed the class and turned to Josh.

"Sorry about that. Most of them have never been to the habitat domes or they left when they were too young to remember. Even the agridomes must seem like shiny stars on the horizon. Naturally, they're curious."

"Doesn't anyone tell them what it's really like in there?"

"Better than anyone, you must know we all closed doors when we left. We respect each other's reasons and ask no questions. Perhaps the children instinctively know that. You're a stranger, so they felt, I suppose, they could ask you. Haven't you run into this sort of thing before?"

"No. This is the first time I've ever done this."

"Then I'm honored." She began to pick up some tablets lying on her desk. "Are you staying for the In-Memorium celebration on Monday?"

"Yes, I'll be here for awhile."

"Good," she said, loading the word. "Do you need any help getting settled?"

He moved toward the door. "No. I don't have much. But why don't you meet me for dinner." He didn't want to waste time – after all, she *was* beautiful.

For quite a while the air coming into Min's vehicle had the sour smell of damp earth and decay, as she steered it south along the banks of the Mississippi River. She had switched the auto-van to manual a while back, and was feeling the exhilaration of controlling the vehicle. Without exact lats for Dwyer, she couldn't use the GPS lock and had gotten lost. Finally, with somewhat conflicting directions from a couple of locals, Min brought the vehicle to a halt. They were on a rise overlooking a community, with a sign proclaiming "Dwyer."

An antiquated solar generator plant droned a welcome as they moved into town. *That can't be their only power. How do they live like this?* She felt she'd been thrust back a hundred years.

She looked at the coordinates on the GPS screen and discovered it was a match for an old town called Placid, Illinois. Now she understood why the system couldn't locate it. The inhabitants had given their town a new name when they resettled it. She stopped in front of what looked like a food depot, turned off the engine and let the giant settle to the ground. "Wait here a minute," she said to Belinda.

Inside, a huge woman balancing dangerously on a step-stool paused as she entered. "Morning. What can I get you?"

"Nothing, thanks. I need some information."

The woman's eyes narrowed. "You ain't another one of them Candle folks, are you?"

"Candle? What is that?"

"The Silver Candle? Always nosin' around."

"No, I'm with the Triangle SocioCenter, a re-organizational agency in Greater Raleigh Domes."

"Well, what do you want with us?" She went back to stocking shelves.

"We'd like to conduct some interviews – talk with families in your area."

"You don't say. You'd better clear it with our brassers, before you start poking around."

"Brassers?"

"Yeah, them that knows stuff. You know – the rule makers."

"Your leaders, you mean? Where might I find them?"

"Old man Merriman is one. Pat Wedmark, Donna Blackman...oh, just go up to the Hall. One of them is always there this time of day."

"Where is the Hall?"

She climbed down and brushed off her hideously flowered dress. "For Pete's sake, I haven't got time to stand around chatting. Go up the street to the first block and turn left. It's down that street – a big green building...can't miss it."

"Could I ask just one more question?" Min smiled.

The woman turned around with a look of bemused resignation, her bosoms responding to a heavy sigh. "Okay. One more. What?"

"Do you know a Joshua Robertson?"

The woman's face relaxed. "The recorder fellow? Sure. He came here winter before last. Was a nice young man."

"Was? He's not here now?"

"No, no. Was only here a couple of months; left..." she seemed to push her brain to its limits. "Oh! I can't remember when, but there was still snow on the ground. Not this winter, you see, last one. He used to come over in the evenings and drink hot rum with me." The guarded look returned. "What do you want with him?"

"I have a message from his parents. Do you know where he was going when he left?"

"Can't say. Might have told someone else, but not me. He was more of a listener than a talker, if you get my drift."

Back in the vehicle, Belinda had taken out her RIC and pulled up the questionnaire on her small processor.

"Better wait with that, Belinda. First, we have to talk to their leaders – brassers they're called around here." Min grinned to herself. It seemed silly that people, who rejected order for chaos, would choose leaders. Maybe, though, one of them knew of Robertson's whereabouts.

The Hall was right where the old woman had said, but green really didn't describe it. The gray, exposed boards had a few remaining patches of olive green. The steps to the porch were new, but Min eyed the porch's roof with misgivings. Inside, the smell of dusty, old wood assailed her nostrils.

Several people were occupying the tables, and a thin fellow staffed the counter along the left wall, busily writing in a book. As they approached, he glanced up, his gaunt face melting into an enormous smile. "Mornin', ladies."

This was more promising than the old woman. "Good morning. I'm Yumin Villanueva and this," she waved a hand over her shoulder, "is my associate, Belinda Carroll."

He extended his hand across the counter. "I'm Pat Wedmark. Howdy do. How can I be of service?"

"We're doing a survey of Environ encampments and would like to interview some of Dwyer's families."

"Not to correct you so early, but we call ourselves Preservers. You won't get very far with the people by calling them Environs.

"Sorry. Preservers, yes. Thanks. A women down the road said we should clear our project with someone here. Are you one of the...brassers?"

It seemed impossible, but his smile grew. "Well, I guess. Brasser is a fancy word for those of us who kind of keep things running."

"Well, how do I go about getting started with our project?"

"Lord, I don't know. I suppose you could post something over there." He indicated a couple of old HD screens. "People come in here and read the bulletins almost every day."

Min looked at the screen, shaking her head. "I don't think that will work; take too long. Couldn't you hold a meeting or something?"

"Nope, won't work either," Patrick said, shaking his head. "You'd still have to wait for folks to read about it."

"Don't tell me. Over there on those screens?"

Patrick Wedmark chuckled, "'fraid so."

Min turned to Belinda, who was standing mutely leaning against the counter. "Do you have any ideas?"

Patrick Wedmark went on, "I must warn you. People don't take to dome people."

"I was just thinking," Belinda said, addressing Wedmark, "If you came along with us to make an introduction, they would know we mean no harm. Maybe they'd be more willing to cooperate."

Wedmark looked from Min to Belinda brightly. "What have I been thinking? Tomorrow is Saturday. Our In-Memorium breakfast is tomorrow. Everyone'll be there."

Belinda looked at Pat Wedmark, speaking slowly as if addressing a half-wit. "In-Memorium is on Monday."

He seemed unconcerned. "Oh, we know that." He laughed. "We celebrate for the whole weekend, starting Saturday morning." He turned to Min. "You can come and we'll give you a little introduction. How'd that be?"

"That would be wonderful." With this hopeful prospect, Min and Belinda moved their van to an out-of-the-way location, and began making a meal. Min didn't want to push the Joshua Robertson question now. She'd pick her time when she got a better feel for the people here.

New House

4

Josh withdrew his arm from beneath Rita's red tangle and clasped his hands behind his head. This was the third night he'd been with her. She was passionate and energetic, as well as beautiful. The sex was great but, as with so many others, he saw no permanence; no forever after. He would never succumb to a woman the way his father had. Over the years, he'd watched his father diminish under his mother's greater will. That will never happen to him.

Rita stirred and it was clear, as her hand began stroking his body that she wanted more. He felt himself harden with excitement and was more than happy to oblige. As the dawn began to creep into the room, though, he slipped from her bed, resolved to leave soon before this became a habit.

Min was fascinated. Thaddeus Merriman stood before them like a grand, old professor, his frosty white hair tossing in the cool breeze, his beautiful deep voice rising and falling as if he were reciting a poem. "...as a reminder of the importance of this holiday..." he was saying. "...gives us the opportunity to revive our commitment to this life."

There were over one hundred and fifty people lining the tables, straining to hear his words, all of them silent, except for an occasional crying baby.

Min found it hard to grasp. These people have goals, commitments, leaders...*why leave the domes if you just bring along the traditions and rules with you?* The life inside was so much easier and enjoyable...and state-of-the-art. Every piece of equipment she'd seen so far was at least fifty years old. *Why would they choose to live like this?*

Merriman was finishing up. He said something about their stomachs growling so loud that he couldn't hear himself speak. There was laughter and a patter of applause. Then he looked toward Pat Wedmark. "Do you want to introduce them or shall I?"

"I'll do it." Wedmark rose and came around to the head of the table. He introduced Min and Belinda, explaining where they were from, what they would like to do, and that they would be in the Hall tomorrow morning. He encouraged all to participate.

"What do they want from us?" "Tell them to go home."

Pat seemed a bit flustered. "They don't mean harm..."

"I don't see why we should cooperate with them." The protests were coming from everywhere.

"Folks, please..."

A woman at the next table stood up and waved her arm at Min and Belinda. "I've had all I can stand from them. I came here to get away. I won't talk with them."

New House

"Well, Trudy, you don't have to. But," Pat raised his voice to take in all of the tables, "I don't see where it can hurt. We give everyone a chance out here, remember?"

There were a few more ripples of hostility, but quieter now. Pat Wedmark seemed to have a substantial influence over his neighbors. "Well, good," he said, seemingly satisfied, "let's eat."

When Pat moved to the food table, Min followed. "Mr. Wedmark?"

"I told you...Pat."

"Okay. Pat, could I ask *you* some questions? Someone said you knew Joshua Robertson, and well, I have some questions about him."

Pat's face broke into his familiar grin. "Josh. Sure. He stayed with us a couple of months. But he left a while back. It think it was a year ago December; just before the year end. What d'you want with him?"

"Do you know where he was going, what his plans were?"

"Well, I'd have to think. I'm sure he told me." He closed his eyes; then shook his head. "Can't recall exactly. Give me time to think on it. Maybe my wife will remember."

"Sure, all right," Min said, smothering her impatience.

"It's going to be a bit crazy today. Why don't you stop by our house later? That way we can talk, and I can find out why you're interested in Josh. Say, for dinner?"

"That would be fine. Where do you live?"

"Point that funny looking vehicle south on Main, then west on Creek Road. We are in the last house before the river. Can't miss it. Why don't you and Mrs. Carroll come around seven o'clock?"

"I'll be there; but Belinda probably has some work to do." Min eyed the tables laden with food. "I might not be in the mood for eating, though."

He laughed, and nodded his head in agreement. "See you then."

Alex was in his den, staring down at the backyard. It was empty of activity and the house was too quiet. The kids had wanted to go riding this morning, so they spent the night at his parent's house. *This is how it will be when they leave…just me and Karen and the silence.* He would probably leave then, but not now. Not now, when the kids needed him. Maybe when they were a little older.

He was also worrying about the staleness of his work. The worst thing for an artist is to feel like you've painted it all, and there was nothing left.

Hell! Shake this off, Alex.

"Monitor," he said, absently. "Resume the morning news, audio only." A voice started rattling off articles on local politics, including a reference to his mother's upcoming Senate assignment…an article about the space stations…a company had been forced into bankruptcy…Michael Kemp had returned from Paris.

Funny, how the media reports Michael's movements, as if, somehow, people needed to know what Michael Kemp was doing. Michael had been part of their lunch circle for over three years – one of the flashy elite – yet Alex really didn't know much about him. His mind wandered for a bit until a name struck a chord. Jenkins...

"Monitor, stop and go back to the beginning of that article."

"The final report on Jerry Ray "Buddy" Jenkins was filed yesterday by the Security Forces," the voice droned. *"Not accepting the original findings, Dr. J.R. Jenkins, Director of the Roanoke Valley Center for the Arts, has been using his considerable influence to keep his son's investigation active. As a courtesy to Dr. Jenkins, the S.F. had initially investigated the outworlder accident, but finding no explanation for the death, they ruled it accidental. Buddy Jenkins died over two months ago in a fall near the Environ village of Sand Cliff, Michigan. He had left the domes over a year ago for reasons unknown, and had no plans to return, according to the young man's family."*

"Oh, my God."

Dr. Jerry Ray Jenkins, Sr. had been Alex's teacher, mentor and friend since his early days as an artist at the Triangle Institute of Arts, and Alex hadn't seen him since he and his family had moved to Roanoke Valley two years ago. Buddy, his only son, had been a generation younger than Alex, but they had always gotten along. Buddy had been very talented and promising. *What on earth was he doing in an Environ encampment?*

"System, place a call to Dr. Jenkins."

The connection went through. Jerry Ray had always been a powerful force, exploding with life. Now, despite the forced cheerful façade at the sight of his old student, he looked small, sunken and lost.

"Jerry Ray, it's been a long time."

"Alex, my boy. Yes, too long."

"Jerry Ray…I just heard. God. I am so sorry."

At the mention of Buddy, his façade crumbled. "Yes," he said quietly, "yes. Thank you."

This suddenly didn't seem like a good idea. His friend drifted off somewhere in his memories, which was good as Alex didn't know what to say. Finally, after letting a few moments pass, he asked, "Is there anything I can do?" *Lame, Alex. Very lame.*

"You can come up here so we can talk properly."

Alex hadn't expected this. "Sure we can get together soon."

"No, I mean, how soon can you come. I need to talk to someone or I think I'll go crazy."

Alex could see the panic in Jerry Ray's manner. "Tomorrow? I can come up after lunch."

"Good." The man sitting in front of him wilted with relief. "Tomorrow. Yes, good." His friend's image dissolved. Alex leaned back in his chair, perplexed. *What on earth?*

As expected, Min wasn't hungry when she sat down to the Wedmarks' table. She nibbled politely, declining Kookie's offer of dessert.

"Oh, no, Mrs. Wedmark. I have to stop."

"Now stop that. Pat's mother is Mrs. Wedmark. I'm Kookie," she said, clearing away some of the dishes. "I'm sorry your friend couldn't come."

"Yes, well. Belinda was sorry, but she had to finish up some things." Mid didn't mention the fact that she hadn't asked Belinda and she far from a friend.

Pat got up and replenished their coffee, the children disappearing as if on cue. Turning to Min, he said, "Now. What d'you want with Josh?"

Kookie brightened. "Josh? Josh Robertson? Oh, you know him? He stayed here a while back."

"Yes, sweetie, I told her. She's trying to find him." Pat leaned back in his chair, folding his arms across his chest. "Can't help wondering why?"

Min stirred some honey into her cup; then looking up, smiled. "It's nothing sinister, believe me. His parents are clients of mine and haven't heard from him in a while. They gave me a message to deliver personally. The last correspondence was from here, so this is where I started. Anything you can tell me would be helpful."

"Well," Pat said, leaning forward again. "He talked about a lot of places, but I don't remember anything in particular. What 'bout you, Kookie?"

"I do remember him talking about Morgan, that camp up on Rock River."

Min's face must have showed her confusion – and Kookie laughed. "Sorry, Kentucky."

"You're right," Pat said, brightening. "And there was also Beaver Gap – that's in Tennessee," he added, clarifying for Min. "But I don't remember if he said where he was going. He usually stays in one place for quite a while, though, so besides him being pretty famous, you won't have trouble finding him."

"Famous?" One aspect she hadn't imagined. "No, I didn't know. What's he famous for?"

"He is a Recorder. He's putting together a complete log of skills; putting down the old ways, ya know."

"No, I didn't know."

Pat continued, "Like my weapon making. He was particularly interested in that, what with public weapons outlawed in the domes. Also, the pearling process. He liked that one, too. He spent days down by the beds."

"Pearling?"

"The process of making cultured pearls. There've been oyster beds in this region since the early twenty-first century. The Orient beds failed about then and we became famous for cultured pearls. The Merriman family has kept it going all these years, though not so much call for them anymore." Then Pat's face brightened. "Ya know something? Merriman's family has never been in the domes. They settled this area. He would be a great subject for your study. Someone else would be Jeff Capshaw or Susan Har…"

"Whoa, boy," Kookie laughed, as she affectionately slapped her husband's bony shoulder. "Take a breath. More coffee, Min?"

"Yes, please." There was something surprising in this small kitchen with its worn floor, antiquated microwave and Freon-based cold storage. While their speech and mannerisms were very colloquial, these people seemed normal and happy. She hadn't expected that. But she also didn't want to get too familiar. Min stood up.

"I appreciate your kindness."

"When you get time, come back; I'll show you my work," Pat said.

"Obsession, more like," laughed Pat's wife. "He's out there more than in here."

"Well, if you were nicer to me, I'd come in more," he said to his wife. She really punched him this time.

Min slipped away, and as she drove back, she thought about Wedmark's description of Josh. A very complicated man. She didn't know who she was looking for now – rebel or historian, drifter or man on a mission.

The man had just ended another frustrating call from his client; nothing was ever good enough. He was beginning to wonder if he should go out on his own. If he broke out and got a reputation, he could pick his clients and not be stuck working for stupid people. This assignment – this would be his last with them.

He slipped into his vehicle and moved over the field in the direction of Thomas LaFleur's metal shop.

Alex's father, John Villanueva, stood in the middle of the library, with a snifter of brandy, musing over his youngest son. "Angel, how do you expect me to take you seriously when you talk so wildly? You're more likely to destroy everything we've worked for instead of improve it."

Angel shook his blond head, frustrated. "We're not trying to destroy the system – we are trying to correct what's wrong. No one seems to *do anything* in these rotations."

Alex walked over and put his hand on his brother's muscular shoulder, saying softly, "Easy, boy."

His father tossed off the brandy and replenished it, sitting in one of his deep, winged-back chairs. "Angel, you cannot want our system to go back to when the big-money men, politicians and the media ran things. Be serious."

"No, we don't want that, I am very serious, Father."

His father's head turned in Alex's direction, his left eyebrow rising ever so slightly. "Alex, you seem awfully quiet this evening. What do you have to say about all this?"

"Sorry, Angel, you do come up with some wild ideas. Sure, we have things that should change. Every age has them. But you are proposing to do away with the very foundation that makes our system run so well."

"The System!" Angel was almost screaming. "The System *is* the problem. It runs everything, does everything for us. We don't have to think anymore," Angel said stormily, gray eyes flashing. "Don't you see that?"

The argument was an old one. Their father was growing impatient. "Angel, drop this. If you don't have anything constructive to say, then let's rejoin the family." He stood and, without waiting for his son's reply, walked to the door. Clearly, a dismissal.

Angel looked far from through, but instead flopped into a chair. "You go."

"Suit yourself. You coming, Alex?"

"In a minute." When his father had left, Alex turned to his brother. "When will you learn? Ranting at Father gets you nowhere. What's with you lately? You've been moody and combative."

"Why shouldn't I be troubled? Don't you see what's happening?"

Alex waved his hands in his brother's direction, "It's just like you to dramatize everything. Change happens in small steps. I know it's not a perfect world, but you don't make change by bashing people over the head."

"Unbelievable. You sound like the *royal frigging Senate*. You coast through life believing all the shit they dish out. Perfect world? Hell. I sometimes think the Environs have the right idea."

"Oh, please. Give me a break. First Min goes off on a trek to find the meaning of Environs; now you're admiring them."

Alex walked to the door, "Are you coming? If so, don't keep arguing and upset mother. She hates it when the family bickers."

"All right, but you can't shut me up. The Candle knows what they are talking about."

Alex stopped at the door. "Candle? What's that?"

Angel looked suddenly embarrassed. "Nothing. Forget it. Let's go." He pushed past Alex into the hallway.

"Angel, what are you into?" Alex asked, but didn't get an answer because their grandmother was approaching them.

"I wondered where you two had gone," she said, linking her arms with her two 'boys.' "We're having dessert in the media room so we can watch the light display. Please come."

All conversation between the two brothers ended.

Min was surprised at how much information they accumulated from the Dwyer Environs, despite their initial hostility. Many still flatly refused to have anything to do with '*them.*' In the end, however, a large number did talk with Min and Belinda, probably because of Pat's encouragement and support.

On the side, Min continued to ask about Josh. Everyone clearly remembered the man; there were many varied descriptions of him. Few, however, remembered exactly where he was going, though there were a lot of suggestions.

At one point, Belinda asked, "Who is this Josh? I've heard you asking about him. What has he to do with this project?"

New House

Min had been prepared for this question. "Josh is the son of one of my clients. He was once part of the system, but has been out here for years. I thought he might make an interesting side focus."

Belinda shrugged it off.

After loading her vehicle's navigator with Josh's most likely locations, Min and Belinda set out early on Thursday morning for Effingham, Illinois, the nearest one.

As it was, her quarry was not there, and hadn't been since last spring. Belinda had started pulling out equipment and was talking to someone about getting permission to work.

Min walked up, saying, "I think we'll only stay a half day here. Go ahead and do a few interviews. I have some things to do. Let's meet back here around one o'clock. Do as many as you can."

"What!" Belinda said surprised. "We come all this way – there were many camps we could have tried – now we're just here for a few hours? What's going on?"

"It's complicated. At any rate, we're leaving this afternoon."

"You know, Ms. Villanueva (she mispronounced it again), I'm getting tired of your high-handedness. You ignore me, talk down to me, neglect me...leave for hours and let me do all the work. You..."

Min cut her off. "You're wasting time. I'll be back at one." Min walked away leaving Belinda smoldering with hostility.

5

Wednesday morning Min and Belinda arrived in Beaver Gap, another possible location, but still no Josh.

"He was here a few months ago," one helpful man said, "but he's long gone."

"Do you know where exactly?"

"Sure, Somerville. Up there in the Blue Ridge. Near Fox Lake, ya' know?"

Min had been staying just a few hours in each of the camps, but decided to pacify Belinda a bit.

"Why don't we stay here overnight? We've been travelling hard and could use a break."

Belinda didn't seem to appreciate the gesture; she just began pulling out the equipment.

Min was glad they were nearing the end of all this. She couldn't take much more of her gatherer.

The next morning, after Min had gotten nearly coherent directions, they were back on the road. Belinda was maintaining her silence, neither acknowledging Min, nor fighting with her. Min reasoned that they might get more work done if they weren't fighting, but the silence was almost worse. The quiet, however, allowed Min to speculate more on the enigmatic man she was chasing.

The Jenkins' home was as Alex expected – art and treasures lining the walls, comfortable furniture filling each space. There was staleness in the air, though, as if time stood still. Dust had accumulated on all surfaces.

Jerry Ray sat in his armchair, nursing a large glass of golden liquor. "I've tried to get someone to listen. I've been convinced it wasn't an accident from the start. Monica and I have been pounding on doors, but I haven't been able to get anyone to listen." He took a large gulp, allowing the liquid to slide down his throat, his blood-shot eyes betraying tears. "But the S.F. is so stupid. They ruled it accidental. Alex, if you could have seen him. His neck wasn't broken in a fall. It was crushed."

"If it was so clear, then why?" Alex believed the old man was close to a nervous breakdown.

"Why? They dismissed us as grieving relatives – an irrational father and sister. Even though Buddy started his life in here, he ended an Environ. He lived outside the system, so he wasn't worth an investigation. The S.F. doesn't have tolerance or the time to expend on their deaths. The only reason they followed up at all was who I am. Otherwise…" His voice trailed off.

"Jerry Ray, why was Buddy out there?"

From his pinched expression, it was a painful question. "Damn it, Alex. Don't you think I've tried to figure out that one?

I can only tell you what he told me. He said besides all the privileges, his life didn't have any meaning. I guess he was looking for something else." He got up wearily, and poured some more whiskey. "He started a theatre out there. Did you know that? He could have done that here. He was never a natural talent like you, but he was showing promise, if he'd only tried." He sat back down. "He'd written a play about a nineteenth century activist, S. B. Anthony. I still have his script, all of his scripts – they gave me all of his things. They are here...somewhere..." He looked around as if they would materialize. "He had been working late, they said, when..." As with the call earlier, he slipped into his private thoughts.

Alex sat quietly and waited for him to return. After a few moments, his eyes refocused on his guest. "Sorry. Been doing that a lot lately. Thank God for Monica; she keeps me sane. Alex, I still can't believe he's dead." He stood up quickly. "Do you want something to eat?"

"No, thanks. I'm fine." Yet Alex was talking to the air. Jerry Ray had already gone into the kitchen; Alex followed. "Jerry Ray, I need to get back to the City tonight. So please don't fuss."

"Why don't you wait until Monica comes home? I expect her soon. Did you tell me what you wanted for dinner?" He seemed glad to have something to do.

Alex decided that to rush off and leave him alone was impossible. "Yes. I'll stay to dinner. Just let me make a call."

Monica came in as they were sitting down. She began more coherently to relay their suspicions. By the time they had finished, it was too late to return home, so he agreed to stay.

When Alex's head finally hit the pillow, he replayed the dinner conversation in his mind. *Certainly, it was very interesting and entertaining, and totally unbelievable.*

Both were convinced Buddy had been murdered, but neither had a clue as to a motive. The Security Forces had made their ruling and close the case, but it was also clear they'd not bothered to do much investigating.

Monica and Buddy had talked often. He'd told her about a growing fear in the outworld communities. So bad, in fact, many were re-entering the system. "Better to be safe than free," Monica had said, as they'd pushed away the last of their meal.

He couldn't imagine anyone willingly leaving the system, much less reluctantly returning. It was absurd. Alex rolled over in the large bed. *Absurd.*

Min found Somerville, and finally discovered her quarry. Somerville was less of a town, and more a camp, with tents pitched all around a clearing. There were four wooden structures nestled at the heart. A woman, pointing to the largest of these structures, informed Min that Josh was there. She parked their vehicle near it, and Min got out. Belinda remained in the cab.

"Will you wait here?" Min asked.

"Go. I'm only here to serve."

Min shook her head. *God. I'm so glad this is almost over.*

Min approached the log structure, and stopped the first person she came to, asking for Josh.

"Josh, man," he yelled. "Lady wants you."

She had prepared herself for an extraordinary individual, one who matched the intense words that she'd been reading. Not this scruffy man, who strolled over, saying, "You looking for me?"

"You're Joshua Robertson?" Surprise and doubt was thick in her voice.

"Yes, as far as I know. My parents have told me that all my life, so we'll just have to take their word for it."

"I'm sorry. It's just that I'd formed a somewhat different picture. For one, I thought you'd be younger. You're..."

"Hey, let's not get insulting, especially when we've just met. I'm not that old, you know."

"Can we start over? I'm Yumin Villanueva. Min," she added. She extended her hand only to lose it in his enormous grasp. "Your parents are – well, clients of mine. Or I hope they will be. They wanted me to…"

"Clients? Whoa. Slow a bit. Have you eaten dinner? We just finished, but I'm sure we can scrounge something." Before she could answer, he dragged her into the building, calling out, "Michelle, Brad, can I get some food over here?"

"I have a companion with me. She's outside," Min looked toward the door. "Her name is Belinda and she's probably with our vehicle. And, if you actually want an answer, yes, I am hungry."

Josh threw his head back, laughing, and went off in search of her 'companion.' Suddenly weary, Min sat down at one of the crude tables. She hadn't really thought what she would say to this man. She felt stupid, babbling at him like that. Great first impression!

A shy teenager with stringy blond hair served Min a bowl of thick soup and a slice of bread. When Min thanked her, she stammered something like, "it's no…nothin,' ma'am."

"Are you Michelle?"

At that, her eyes rolled in Min's direction and a dimple caressed her cheek. "Yes, ma'am. Michelle."

"It's a pretty name. Michelle, could you get me something to drink?"

"No need," Josh said returning with two cups of a steaming, but suspicious-looking brew. "Hot tea with rum," he said. "It gets cold up here at night. This should warm you. Now, between mouthfuls, please tell me how you know my parents."

"Well," she started, cautiously taking a spoonful, "where do I begin? First you should know I work for a social re-organizational company in North Carolina." Min waited for the expected veil of boredom or cynicism that usually came with that pronouncement – but it didn't come. Instead, he sat there with a slight smile, sipping his tea. A good start, so she pushed on. "Your parents came in for what I thought was a standard interview, but it was anything *but* standard."

"That doesn't surprise me in the least."

"You don't care for your parents." Min said almost to herself, not a question, just an immediate impression.

Josh looked up from his cup, "Now why in God's green earth would you say that?"

"It was just in your tone."

"Ah, yes, well...but then, we digress."

"Yes," she mimicked. "Well, instead of wanting to join a program, they wanted me to find you."

"So here you are. I find it amazing that you just up and run all over the country looking for me just to do this kindness for my parents?" He was clearly annoyed.

"I didn't just 'up and run all over the country.' I had a clear plan based upon your letters."

Now he was mad. He stood quickly, his gray-green eyes flashing. "They gave you my...God!"

"Your mother did it to help me locate you. I'm sure she didn't..."

"My mother..." he said, with disgust; then he mentally gathered himself back together and sat down. "Go on. I suppose there's more?"

"We made this bargain." *Yikes,* she thought, *that sounds so shifty.* She immediately tried to explain it so it sounded better. "If I look for you, they'll join a program – all ten of them. It would be a big opportunity for me." *Oh man, this is getting worse.* "Anyway, here I am."

"It makes sense why you're here. You are here for profit. What doesn't make sense is why'd they wanted to find me? Is there something wrong at home?" Min noticed the question held only mild curiosity.

"Nothing they shared with me. It's just that your mother hadn't heard from you in such a long time." She felt she should say something nice about his parents, but she couldn't remember anything she liked about them. "She was worried, I guess."

"I doubt that."

Min was getting a headache. She soaked up the last of her soup with the bread. "Look," she said through chews. "I was just supposed find you and pass along their message. That's all. By the way, this is great soup. What is it?"

"Snake."

Min's eyes flew to his face in surprise. His face was serious, but a gleam in his eyes gave him away. "Oh...I almost believed you."

"No, it is really," he said seriously.

Min wasn't sure whether to believe him or not, but he was apparently enjoying her discomfort. Laughing, he rose, "Let me see what's keeping your friend."

Moments later, he returned with Belinda and a second bowl.

"Hi. Did you get lost?" Min attempted a normal tone, but she hated making small talk with this horrid woman.

"I was working. I wanted to get in some interviews before dark." Belinda turned to Josh. "Do you have sleeping facilities here? I'm getting tired of that van."

"Sure. However, it won't be anything as nice as that. We sleep on cots here, or floaters."

"That will be okay."

Josh turned to Min. "Do you want somewhere to sleep too?"

"No."

He nodded, as if he felt the undercurrent between the two women, and went off to make sleeping arrangements for Belinda.

The Maglev swept silently through the connector tubes on its route back to the Greater RDU Domes. Alex was hardly aware of the trip. Jerry Ray had presented him with a new dilemma.

"Alex, I can't really find peace until I know why Buddy was killed. For me, Alex, please find out who killed my son."

Me find out who killed Buddy? The S.F. had already closed the case. He wouldn't know where to start.

He stared out the train window, past the clear tube to the countryside beyond. Why would anyone want to murder a young man like Buddy? It didn't make sense. Buddy didn't have any GEM credit or property to steal; he didn't possess sophisticated knowledge that would make him a threat to anyone. Yet Jerry Ray and Monica were sure he had been murdered.

Murder? It was such a foreign word. It was something reported occasionally on the broadcasts, but never touched anyone he knew. Now it was right in front of him –if he believed them, that is.

He'd told Jerry Ray that he'd mention it to his S.F. friend. With the mention of the S.F., Jerry Ray's spirit sunk again.

What else could I have said? What can I do? It wasn't that he didn't want to help; he just didn't know where to start. He might say something to Tami; maybe not.

New House

A young blond girl in the seat just ahead of him turned and smiled. He smiled back. The intrigues of last evening began to fade. The little girl reminded him that, if he hurried, he could see AnneJuleé ride in her equestrian event.

Alex made his way through the crowds toward the street. Someone pushed up close behind him and suddenly a large arm blocked his way. A male voice, very close to his ear, said, "Keep your nose out of things that don't concern you."

"What?" Alex started to turn, as the arm was withdrawn, but the owner of the voice was swallowed up by the crowd.

Min and Belinda were compiling data. Finally Min said, "I'm sick of this. We cannot spend the rest of the trip fighting or not talking."

"As far as I can see, your part of the trip is over. You found what you came out here for."

"What are you talking about? We just barely started this trip."

"You know what I'm talking about. It's that man, something about that man."

"Alright, yes. One of the reasons I came out here was to find Joshua Robertson. For his parents. There is nothing wrong with that."

"Depends on why."

"My motives are none of your business."

"This is my career. Not a *hobby*."

Min scrutinized her face. "What have I done to make you dislike me so much?"

"I dislike what you stand for. To dislike you, personally, I would first have to know you, and I have no intentions of doing that. Let's just finish and go home."

"Fine!"

It's just like my mother, Josh thought, *sending some stranger running all over the country to track me down.* He'd escaped her clutches, but she was still trying to manage him. It had been her fault that his family had never joined him all those years ago.

All those years ago...

Josh had arranged everything. He had traveled several times to an agristation to relay messages to his family. He'd even managed a vid-call to tell them the final details. It was rewarding seeing his father's excitement.

"It's beautiful, Dad. Perfect land for whatever we want to do. It's in the Prairie-Mount Area – Montana – above the Flathead Reservoir. You'll love it."

"Give us a few months to get things in order here. I'll contact you when we are ready to exit."

Eight months had passed without word from them. He'd gone again and again to the agristation, waiting for word. Finally, one day it had come.

"Here you go," the manager had said, as he'd activated the console. "I figured this is what you've been waiting for."

Yes, the message – but not the one he'd expected.

"Sorry, Joshua," his father had looked deflated, defeated. "Your mother says Tenya's expecting and she will need us around as she starts her family. I know how much you wanted this, but it can't be. Not right now, at least."

Josh had known what really had happened. His mother had put a stop to their plans. She dominated the whole family. Not him, though. No! And he'd never go back to where she could get her clutches into him again.

Then, without warning, his mother's image faded and Yumin's appeared. Min, she'd said people called her. He liked that...Min. What was it about her that was so appealing? She was cute, but that wasn't it. Rita was beautiful, and exciting, yet she hadn't filled his mind like this. He pictured Min again, the way she moved, the way her thoughts fired those great, dark eyes.

Whoa, Josh, bad road to start down.

Then he wondered what she was doing.

Madge spoke crossly to him. "Joshua, I wish you'd stop daydreaming and take these."

"Sorry, Madge. What?"

"I want you to take these linens over to the new family who arrived this morning." She dumped a load of blankets and towels in his arms. "Please," she added, with a wrinkled smile.

"Yes, ma'am." Josh said meekly, and started towards the door. Before he was ten feet outside, he found himself looking for Min.

Min had been given permission to use the dining hall midmornings or late afternoons. There weren't that many people willing to talk to them, though. She tapped her RIC earpiece and recorded a few final thoughts on the last interview. She had kept it on local for the entire trip so far, and wondered if she should check in. She was just about to, when she felt someone near. She looked up. Josh was standing about three feet away, holding an armful of blankets.

"What exactly do you do?" he asked.

Taken aback, she recovered quickly. "That was what I was just thinking. What do you do out here?"

"Not fair. I asked first."

"Well, I help Remnants get reorganized."

"Lord, I hate that word. Remnants. Like leftovers."

"I didn't invent it. You're squaring off against the wrong person. I try to help those people."

"How? Reorganize? What does that mean?"

"Oh, for heaven's sake. I get enough of this from my family. I don't need it from you."

"Sorry. I just want to understand what a 'Remnant Reorganizer' does."

"Any answer I give you will start a fight. And I'm tired of fighting." She returned to her recording, ignoring him.

"You asked what I do. Do you still want to know?"

He seemed determined to tell her, so she sighed, "Yes, I suppose."

"Well, to put is simply – I record things. Arts, trades, crafts, human skills which otherwise would be lost."

"Why?"

"Why not? It's better than staying in the system, being reorganized by social do-gooders, who only want to make themselves feel good." He seemed to lay the words in front of her like a gauntlet, his face somber, his eyes fired with battle.

She refused to continue bantering words with this outworlder. *Who the hell did he think he was?* She glared at him, then stood and began to pick up her equipment.

He came closer, "I'm sorry. I didn't mean it like that. We just see the world differently."

Min muttered, "Not important."

"But it is important."

She smiled, "It's okay, really. I've been working all day, and I'm tired. I think I'll go back to the van."

"Are you coming to the dining hall later?" He fell into step with her.

"No. I'll just fix something and go to bed." Before he could say anything more, she quickened her pace. She didn't look back but knew he was still standing there with all those silly blankets, watching her walk away and, for some reason that bothered her. It was kind of creepy.

6

Alex was by himself in Consuelo's courtyard waiting for Tami. He'd reached his house feeling unsettled by the stranger at the station. The next morning he was still feeling anxious. It hadn't been the words, but the tone and the physical contact, which had conveyed the threat. Why would anyone bother? Had they gotten the wrong person? And if not, what had he done or said that would make anyone feel at risk? He could think of only one thing and that really didn't make sense.

"Hi. We missed you the last couple of days." Tami said casually, as she sat down. "Where have you been? What's up?"

Alex poured some beer and handed the glass to Tami, then drank deeply from his own before speaking. "Thanks for coming."

"How could I not come? You sounded so mysterious."

"I want to ask you for a favor."

"Anything."

"Don't be so quick to agree. Wait until I tell you what I want."

"I won't kill anyone for you," Tami smiled.

"I don't need anyone killed, but I'd like you to check into someone's death. I wasn't going to ask you. In fact, I'd made up my mind that Jerry Ray was imagining things, but then the guy at the station, well...I think someone doesn't want..."

"Alex, slow up. What guy at the station?"

Alex rubbed his forehead. "Sorry." He described the disturbing evening in Roanoke Valley and the warning on the trip home. "If it hadn't been for the last part, I wouldn't have thought much about it."

"Sorry to eavesdrop, but I was wondering what you two were doing out here." Michael had come into the yard, and sat down at their table. "What mysterious guy are you talking about?"

Tami looked mildly annoyed and Alex wished Michael miles away. "Michael," Alex began, "it's nothing. Some weird guy at the station."

"Don't give me that. I heard enough to know what you were talking about. It's the Environs' deaths, isn't it? Or, at least one in particular – Jenkins, wasn't it? You mentioned Monica. She told me about her brother's death. It was tragic, and I remember thinking at the time there was something bigger going on. Later, I was convinced of it, especially when I heard about the others."

Both Alex and Tami turned to him, and almost in unison said, "What others?"

After supper, Alex went to the den. "System, scan the news services for stories on Environs deaths, eliminating those which were clearly natural causes or where a killer has been identified. I only want accidents or unsolved murders." Then as an afterthought, "Include missing persons, too."

Earlier Michael had relayed stories about people he'd known who had exited, only to return after a few months, recounting descriptions of horrible accidents.

"Everywhere you go," Michael had whispered like a conspirator, "you hear about people dying violently. As expected, the S.F. dismissed most without investigating. The rumblings were that someone's deliberately killing Environs."

Tami had smiled at Michael's sense of the dramatic. Alex might've been inclined to dismiss him, except that Michael always seemed to know news reports long before anyone reported them officially.

Alex's I-VN was taking a long time, so he asked, "System, do you have anything yet?"

"Currently, I have 3179 occurrences."

Alex realized he'd not narrowed his parameters enough. "Stop. Limit your search to the North Central and Eastern Areas, and for only twelve months."

The monitor flicked for a few nano-seconds; then said, "Given your parameters, I now have 1044 occurrences."

"Go back one year with the same search criteria."

The system came back with, "There are another 173 which fit your profile. Do you want to view the articles?"

"Yes. And save the search criteria." Over eleven hundred questionable deaths and missing persons in 24 months and he'd only scanned two areas. He noted that the number was larger in the past year than in the prior months.

The list was unemotional and statistical, a formal account of deaths outside the system. He absorbed the data with apprehension. The list reported the method of death or, if missing, the place where they were last seen, home location and any reference to relations still in the System. He came across Buddy's name, and again he remembered his old friend's desperate attempt to make sense out of it. Most of the deaths were violent, but as he perused the screen, there didn't seem to be a connection. It was all so random. If there was a link, it was not obvious. Then he realized that he was assuming there was some plan or plot connecting them, and felt a little silly.

His I-VN came back with another list. "My scan has detected additional names that fit your profile. Would you like to see the details?"

"How many are we talking about?"

"There are eleven additional names."

"Only eleven? Let me see the list." The names made even less sense, especially one – Jack Banister. He remembered Hardy mentioning his death in a report a while back, but to put such a distinguished reporter on this list was absurd.

"System, why include Jack Banister?"

"Your search was for violent, unsolved deaths related to Environs. It fit your broad parameters. Banister's articles over the last ten years frequently mentioned the Environ population, and more recently, he had been investigating Environ deaths."

"Are the remaining ten also of this category?"

"Yes."

"Display details."

The details were like the others, except these people all lived within the system. He now had more questions than when he started. He was tired. He told the system to close and save the file.

It was late and Josh was helping Min complete interviews. They weren't making any progress, however; they kept arguing over the questions. He couldn't understand why such an intelligent woman could be so obstinate and obtuse.

"Just record the damn answers," she flared. "Never mind whether you think this is relevant or not."

"You're losing your temper, again," he said, smiling. He liked stirring the coals.

"Yes, I am. You aren't really helping. Please go away."

He pursued his earlier tact. "You'll learn nothing from these questions. I could give you some that would get useful responses."

"That's it. Go away." She snatched the equipment out of his hands and sat back down, just as the next woman came up for her interview.

"I'm sorry. We'll do it your way." He smiled his most engaging smile. That should do it, he thought.

Min's eyes were still burning, but as she looked at him, he could see the anger fade, and a reluctant smile grow. "Okay. But shut up."

New House

Alex was relieved. When Min answered, she was sitting at a table, surrounded by a meal, looking relaxed, calm, and unaware of all the violence he'd been reading about. He was suddenly angry that he'd been worrying about her. He said in a sarcastic tone, "Have I interrupted your dinner?"

"You have, but that's okay. What's up?"

"You're not alone, are you?"

"No. Just a sec." There was some interference on the holo-imager as she walked outside. Then the image settled back down. "Okay. You can talk now. What's up?"

"I've heard some disturbing things about the camps and wanted to see if you were all right. Are you all right?"

"Oh, for heaven's sake. You can see yourself."

"Well, yes. You look safe. Where are you?"

"Somerville, Tennessee. But don't look for it on any map."

"Min, I've been hearing about a lot of unexplained deaths out there. Have you heard anything?"

"Well, yes. There's been talk about accidents, and some ghoulish individuals like to chatter on about murder and plots. But, generally, no one's paying much attention to them."

"Some are. The stats show a great number of outworlders have re-entered – more than usual. I worry about you being out there."

Min laughed. "It's rough, so people naturally seek the system when things get bad."

Alex told her some of the things he'd learned, especially about Buddy and the stories Michael had recalled. With satisfaction, he saw her face become serious. They talked some more and she said, "Okay, maybe something bigger is happening, maybe not. At any rate, I'm coming back soon, so you don't have to worry. I have a little more to do. I'll probably be back by the weekend, no later than Monday."

"Good. Make it earlier if you can, okay?"

Josh stretched out on his bunk. He wondered if he'd provoked Min too much. She seemed to be avoiding him. He was always sorry when he did it, but she made him so angry. She was so rigid in her ideas – her wonderful system – she wouldn't listen to anything. Yet despite the arguing, he looked forward to being around her.

He'd heard some people in the dining hall say that she would be leaving soon, probably the first of next week. *Maybe that was good. She disrupts my life too much. I've hardly done any work since she came. The sooner she leaves, the quicker I can get back to normal.*

The next afternoon he ran into Min sitting with Agnes Millhouse. Min was asking those ridiculous questions, while the elderly woman sorted bits of metal into various piles for her kiln. She was answering Min's questions with a smile, as she might humor a small child. Josh's voice broke into Agnes' description.

"Is she grilling you too, Agnes? Watch it or she'll have you back in the domes."

"Do you mind? This lady is interviewing me."

"Could I see you when you're through?" he asked Min. "I'll be in the dining hall."

Min glanced up, nodded and went on with her questions. A half hour later, she joined him for coffee. "What's the matter?"

Now he didn't know what he wanted to say. "I just haven't seen much of you. How's it going?"

"Almost through. I'll be leaving tomorrow morning."

"Tomorrow?"

"Yes, we have everything we need. Besides, I talked to my brother last night. He's worried about me. He's heard talk about a lot of deaths out here and would like me to come back."

"What? You do what your brother says?"

"No. I'm just finished with my project."

"I know there have been a lot of accidents, but we expect that out here. We don't get any protection from the sweet farce." When he saw her questioning look, he clarified, "The S.F. Sweet Farce."

"Well, my brother thinks there's more to it."

"What does he do? Is he a detective or something?"

Min slowly stirred her coffee. "No. He's an artist." She looked up challengingly.

He laughed and threw up his hands. "Don't flare at me. I have no objections if he wants to play detective. There's nothing to find."

"What if there is something to them? Don't you ever consider past the immediate...?"

"Hey, don't start. It's too great a day." He suddenly remembered the ROM that he'd made for his parents. "I have something for you. Close your eyes."

"You've got to be kidding."

"No. Close them, or you won't get it." When she did, he took her hand and put the ROM into it. She opened her eyes, looking at it in surprise, then up into his face. "That's your ticket to ten new clients. It's a correspondence for my parents."

"Thanks," she said, uncertainly, and put it in her pocket.

"Are you really leaving tomorrow?"

"Yes, of course."

"What are you doing tonight?"

"Eating, going to bed early."

"May I eat with you?"

"Do you mean, will I join you for dinner or can you join me for mine?"

"Either." He moved slightly and the sun flooding through the window caught her in the eyes. Those beautiful almond-shaped eyes, with their dark pupils flecked with gold. He was such a sap for eyes.

She put up a hand to shield the sun. "Ok, seven in my van. But I warn you, my cooking is only slightly better than my temper."

New House

Alex was wading through some more data on the Environs' cases, when he heard a small tap at the door. "Daddy, can I come in?"

"AnneJuleé, you're home early. Where are the boys? How did you get home? "

"I 'membered the way and came by myself."

Even though it was only a few blocks, Alex found himself getting angry with all the people who should have been looking out for his daughter. He pulled her onto his lap. "Honey, I think it's good that you did it all by yourself, but you shouldn't come home alone."

She looked stubbornly at him, "I'm not little any more, Daddy."

"Well, you're home. Never mind. Just don't do it again, okay?" When she didn't answer, he prompted her again, "Okay?"

"'kay," she mumbled.

Just then, the door slammed, "AnneJuleé? Are you here?" James's voice was raised in panic.

"She's in here," Alex said as calmly as he could.

James appeared at the den door. "You wretched little girl," He was shaking. "I could strangle you."

"James, where were you? She came home alone."

"Don't be mad at me, Dad. I went to her room to get her and they had dismissed her class early. She just left. I ran all the way, hoping she was here."

"Well, she won't do it again, will you?"

"Said so," AnneJuleé pouted.

James flopped in chair and stared at the big holo-imager, "What are you working on?"

"Nothing. Just looking at some data." He told the system to power off the screen.

"That was some pretty awful stuff. Who are those people, Dad?"

"No one. Just some outworlders."

"God, Dad. Why on earth are you interested in those people? It's enough that Aunt Min has to embarrass us by working with Scavs; don't you get into it, too."

The hatred in his son's voice surprised Alex. He sounded just like Karen.

"Well, it's nothing. Let's go outside for a while."

At six thirty, Min heard Josh tap on her van door. She had been regretting her invitation for hours, now it was too late to back out. She took a calming breath, then straightened her cream shirt, and ran a hand through her short hair. "Come in."

"Don't you lock your door?" he asked without any hint of formality. "I thought you were so worried about all our violence."

"You're early. And no one's bothered me – at least not until now."

He started to retort. "No, I promised myself that I'd behave. What's for dinner? Dehydrated or powdered protein?"

"You're getting snake stew."

He let loose a deep laugh. "Did you know that you're wonderful?"

She stiffened, not responding to his comment.

"Something does smell good," he said, moving to the stove.

"It really is stew – with Agnes' help. Nothing processed in there. It's not quiet done, though. Sit. Want something to drink?"

He went to the tap and poured himself some water, and slipped into a chair. "What's the matter? Don't you like being told that you're wonderful? Personally, I think it would be great to be told that. But, then, I'm not you. Would you prefer to be told you're impossible? You're that, too, you know."

She was getting another headache. "Why do you always do this? Just once I'd like to talk with you." She saw him open his mouth to answer. "No, don't say it. We don't talk. We fight. We argue. We throw clever witticisms at each other, but none of it bears any resemblance to normal conversation." She put a plate of raw veggies in front of him. "Munch on this and shut up."

She added a few spices to the pot and served up two plates, placing them on the table. "One negative comment and you get it in your lap."

"Yes, ma'am." He dipped his spoon in and took a bite. "Hum, delicious. Surprisingly good. For a working girl, that is."

Min rubbed her eyes, letting out a heavy sigh. She retrieved the bread from the heating element, sliding into the chair opposite Josh. He was watching her closely – too closely – and she looked at him. "Please stop staring. It's unnerving. Just eat."

"I'm sorry. You just look so totally out of character. I guess you don't do much cooking back home?"

"No. I have a very efficient I-VN 7000 with a cooking program. I'm too busy to worry about preparing food; and then I eat out a lot." She took a bite and realized something was wrong with it. "Oh, this is awful. Don't eat it. I must have left something out."

"No, it's not that bad. Do you have some salt?" He reached over and picked up her plate, along with his own, and dumped both back into the pot. He turned, waiting. "Well...?"

"What are you doing?"

"I need salt."

"Ah." Min retrieved the container from the shelf. "Is that all?"

"No, do you have some spice, or onions, or some flavoring?"

"I don't know. Look in there." She pointed to a cupboard with various containers.

After adding several items, and bringing the whole thing to a boil, he tasted it again. "That's better." He allowed it to simmer a bit more; then loaded up the plates.

They sat back down and started over. "How's that?" he asked.

"Better."

They ate in silence for a few minutes. "You seem very comfortable cooking."

"Why shouldn't I? I do it all the time. We don't have the luxury of 'cooking programs' out here."

She refused to rise to his bait. "No, I wouldn't expect you to have."

He raised his brows. "Nice parry."

She just smiled and asked him some neutral questions about his travels. They finished the meal that way, easily avoiding any topic of conflict.

As Min rose and started loading the dishes in the incinerator, he exclaimed, "What! You throw away your dishes?"

"They are combustible and biodegradable," she started to explain, and then looked at him. "But you already know that." She turned back to her task, and he came over to her. He didn't touch her, but he stood so close that she could feel the heat from his body. Her breathing became a bit labored.

"May I stay?" His words were whispered so softly that she wasn't sure she heard right.

She turned and found herself looking up into his face. She could see the lines around his mouth and eyes. His olive skin in the artificial light looked sallow and there were dark shadows under his glowing eyes. "I don't even like you."

"I'm sure I don't like you. You stand for everything that I wanted to leave behind. You annoy the hell out of me. Half of the time, I want to shake you. The other half I want to do this." His lips touched hers gently, but then, as his arms slid around her, he pressed harder.

Min felt a quiver run through her body and she put her arms around his neck. As she responded, his tongue parted her lips and his hands began to stroke her back, lightly at first, then with more intensity.

Suddenly Min broke away. The impracticality of the situation erupted into the moment.

"What's wrong?" He took a step back.

"I don't know."

"Min?" He whispered in that soft voice.

"Oh, please. Don't do this to me."

"Do what. This?" He started to reach for her again. His breathing was short and rapid, and as close as he was, she could almost hear his heart pounding.

"I don't want you complicating my life."

"But life isn't neat and orderly. It's only that way when there is nothing interesting in it. Don't pull away because you don't want to upset your order; that's just stupid. You have feelings for me, I know it."

"I'd expected that kind of response from you. If it's orderly, if it's part of the system, then it's stupid. I like my life. It's just the way I want it."

"Can't you let down your guard for just one instant? You might find something better."

"I can't … no…" she stepped back so he couldn't confuse her any more. "No."

"I see." The tension between them was so physical she could almost touch it. Then he seemed to surrender. "Well, that's clear enough." He went to the door. "Thanks for supper."

"You're welcome." The door closed silently, and she used all of her will power not to call him back.

The next dispatch had taken only a couple of days to plan. LaFleur was a giant and, while he had no doubt that he could take him, he didn't want to get into a physical confrontation with a dispatch. Instead, he chose a snap-vial of NR2. Pop and you get a nice little nap.

The foundry noise was so deafening that he approached LaFleur from behind easily. Holding a protective cloth over his own face, he tapped the big man on the shoulder, and delivered the gas into his face. LaFleur blinked, coughed once, blinked again and went down, heavily, noisily, without any grace.

The man waited for the spray to dissipate. He leaned over the huge limp ironworker, binding the muscular wrists with a strong rope. The method of dispatch had become clear the minute he saw the foundry. He reached out and grabbed the chain hanging from the derrick overhead, and looped the large hook easily through LaFleur's wrist bindings. The man climbed the steep stairs to the ramp walkway where the derrick's controls were located, activating the powerful engine. The huge crane lifted LaFleur off the floor, and as the sleeping form cleared the railing, it twirled and swung over the open caldron.

The man checked the setting on the zeron ray. Even a low setting of the ray could keep metals and other compounds in a constant liquid state. *Hot enough for flesh and bones.* He walked back to the rail to wait.

Fifteen minutes later, Thomas LaFleur groaned, his head lolling to one side, finally opened his eyes. It took him a few seconds for his mind to clear. When he realized where he was, a primordial scream ripped from his throat. His eyes became blue dots surrounded by white; his coppery skin glistened with sweat. LaFleur flung out with his feet trying to reach the rail, but he was too far away.

But this is wonderful, the man thought, as his blood surged through his veins. The more LaFleur fought, the more excited the man became.

LaFleur screamed, "Let me go. You're insane. Stop this, and let me go."

The man smiled. "Yes, I'll let you go." He reached for the lever on the crane. LaFleur relaxed, but then realized at the last instant what the man really meant. LaFleur screamed something incoherent, as he plunged into the molten metal and, with a '*glub*,' disappeared. Released from the derrick, the chain slipped free and followed the form down. It traced a design on the surface briefly before catching fire and disappearing with the body.

There had been nothing left this time. Clean and very neat. The man was clammy and his heart was racing. He licked the salty moisture from his upper lip, and left the building.

Min sat on the train, starring at the passing scene without really seeing anything.

Back in Somerville she had said her goodbyes and thanked those who'd been friendly and cooperative. When she'd finished, she had returned to the van. Josh had been there, waiting. She hadn't realized it, but she had been looking for him. "Morning," he'd said as she walked up. "You all set?"

"Yes. That's what's nice about the van. Nothing to pack."

"Of course…well, goodbye. Have a safe trip back."

"Thanks. Take care of yourself."

"Sure, I'm good at that." He'd started to walk away, but turned back. "And, by the way. I'll be here through the end of the week. Next week I'm going on to Mount Bryson, North Carolina."

"Why would…?" Min had started to ask.

"Just in case...for...whatever." His smile had a way of totally undermining her resolve. "Just in case," he had repeated.

Belinda was already in the cab; Min climbed into the driver's seat. He had stepped backwards, getting out of the way.

"Thanks. Did you want me to relay that to your folks?" Min asked through the open window.

"No, please don't. And Min?"

The engine had started and the unit began its ascent. "What?"

"I think I love you."

Damn you, I don't want you to love me. I don't want any of this.

The Maglev slipped quickly through the countryside, making the short trip from the mountains down into the Piedmont Valley. By eleven a.m. Min was sitting in her condo looking at the familiar rooms, feeling like a stranger.

Josh still couldn't believe what he'd said. The words had just slipped out, as if belonging to someone else's voice. In the first place, he was quite sure he didn't love her. Then he'd seen her face – the surprise and disgust – *Well, dear boy, you blew that one.*

Josh suddenly found himself alone; not physically, but in all the ways that count. He'd said goodbye to thousands of people over the years, some were women he'd known intimately. It had never bothered him to leave them. There had been the blond in...where had she lived? West Florida? Alabama? Well, somewhere in the Southeast Area. Moreover, he couldn't even recall her name. It would probably be like that with Min. *Five years from now, I won't even remember her name.*

Ramon had told him about a new family who had moved into the dormitory, and he went over to lend a hand. He would just forget Min. That's all. A sure way to do that was to get back to work.

Alex leaned back into the soft cushions and wondered what was wrong with his sister.

"Min. Could you pay attention? I'm trying to tell you something."

She paused shifting around the six small figurines on her table, and looked directly at him. "I am paying attention. I'm just a bit restless."

"You can say that again. You haven't been still since I came in."

"I've heard everything you've said. You visited Jerry Ray and found out that they think Buddy was murdered. Don't you think that's typical, trying to place blame? It gives people comfort to believe someone else is responsible when all they have are questions."

"Yes, I thought so, at first. However, when we heard what Michael had to say – you know Michael? Well, he only reinforced what I'd heard from Jerry Ray."

"We? Who else do you have involved? You're not seriously pursuing this?"

"I promised Jerry Ray and Monica that I'd look into it. Tami's running down some things."

"Tami? You didn't! She could get into real trouble if she gets involved in an illegal investigation. Whatever made you?"

"She offered. She's as convinced as I am."

"Why is this so important for you?"

"Well, there is something else." he said, finally.

"What?"

"Someone accosted me in the train station and gave me a warning." He felt a little silly. He'd only told Tami and Michael, and it still sounded overly dramatic.

Min came over and sat beside him. "A warning? What kind of warning?"

"Only to stop prying into things that weren't my concern. He wasn't specific, but what else could he have been referring to?"

"Alex, you should stop. If someone is threatening you..."

He finally seemed to have her undivided attention. "Don't you see, Min, if someone is afraid that I'm involved and cares enough to send a warning, it proves there is something to all this." He set his cup on the table and shook his head. "Knowing that there's something going on is not the same as knowing who and why."

"You've handed it off to Tami. Just let it alone. She's trained for this stuff. You're not."

"I can't stop."

"Why not?"

"When Buddy left the system, he and his father never reconciled." As he spoke, Alex remembered the pain in his mentor's eyes. "I just can't, that's all."

"Did Buddy find what he was looking for?" Min said softly.

"Monica seemed to think so. I don't understand it."

"I think I do," she said, almost to herself.

Alex was aware of a change in his sister.

"I'm not sure that I can describe it to you, Alex. Environs aren't at all what we've been led to think. They're rough and crude. They waste their time preserving skills we think are archaic and unnecessary, but they take pride in what they do. I don't totally understand them, but I have to admire them. The people I deal with in here are different from those outside. Dome Remnants have given up. The Environs haven't."

"Well, I don't understand any of it," he said. "Choosing to live in such primitive and uncivilized conditions?"

"You're right, of course. It's very primitive, but not uncivilized. Everywhere I went I saw order. It's as if, by instinct, they need structure. They have schools, communities, leaders. Pat Wedmark was a Dwyer leader; brassers they're called. Then there was Thad Merriman, as civilized and educated as you and me. He was wonderful. If you could have heard the speech he made to..." She trailed off, realizing that she was rambling. "Well, they make an impression, that's all."

"Okay, okay. It's clear that they won you over." Alex had not remembered his sister being this intense about anything in a long time.

"I'm not going to run out and become a Preserver, if that's what you're implying. They do get to you." She looked at him, "I think I understand your willingness to get involved."

"Tami is going to look into some of the official case reports."

"You know, getting her to ask questions is one thing. That alone could get her into trouble. If she starts looking at case reports that are not her domain, she could get suspended – or worse."

"I know. When she so readily agreed, I actually played devil's advocate and told her just that. She said she wanted to, and could justify her involvement if she needed to. When I pressed her about what she meant, she just said not to worry. She should have some of the reports tomorrow, especially the Jenkins file."

Min rose to her feet and went to the window. "Where did you say the last death was?"

"I don't know. I have a list of all the dates and locations at the house. Do you want to pull up my file and see?"

"Yes, I would. Ivan, activate…"

"Actually, I was thinking of first taking you to lunch. How about it?" He was so glad that she was back, safe. "When we come back, we can look at my data."

"As long as it isn't Consuelo's, you're on."

"Hey, what's wrong with Connie's? They have great food."

"Sure if you like Latin-Irish. Don't you ever get tired of eating there?"

"It's more than just the food. You know that. It's tradition."

"But daily?"

They left her condo and wandered down the street, still arguing where they'd have lunch.

7

The previous night, there had been a soft knock on Josh's door. He'd been surprised to hear the door open and to have Rita slip under the covers beside him. He had been avoiding her, not just when Min had been in camp, but also after she'd left.

"Hi," she'd whispered. "Haven't seen much of you lately."

"No. I've been busy."

She had seemed to sense his hesitation. "What's wrong? You do want me, don't you?"

It had been true; he had wanted her – or to be more precise, he had wanted the physical release and was attracted to her. But now, he wasn't sure. The idea had crossed his mind that he was a bit crazy. A beautiful, willing woman, with passion to spare, wanted him and he had hesitated.

"Rita, it's late and I'm really tired."

She had reached over and tried to caress the side of his face. He'd laid his hand over hers, stopping her. "It's that other woman – the one from the domes, isn't it?"

"No, Rita. It's just that I'm tired."

"Suit yourself." She'd stood up again and had pulled on her robe. "Good night, Mr. Robertson. Sleep well."

Now, running by the lake path in the crisp morning air, he pounded away the tension from the previous night. He came to an old ruin. He guessed it had once been a stately house based on its ghostly foundation. The proud front stoop and huge chimney defied time and he dropped onto the damp steps to rest, enjoying the spectacular view of the lake. The sun was still low, and its rays skittered across the surface like a dance. A hawk dove towards the water. It brushed the surface, soaring skyward with breakfast, leaving rings on the water's surface.

The scene, for whatever reason, made him think of Min. He knew she would have enjoyed it. They would have shared it – momentarily, at least – but would have fallen into an argument about something.

He had never liked women around him for long. They were best in the dark, full of passion and little talk. In the daylight, he tired of them quickly.

He'd never slept with Min. In fact, while he'd thought of making love to her, that hadn't been the prevailing thought driving him to seek her out each day. She had a quick humor and wit; but was equally aggravating with her stupid ideas about that senseless life she lived. She was...*God!* He had to stop thinking about her. She was gone and that was it.

"So leave me alone," he shouted, startling some crows into flight. He took comfort in the fact that she would soon disappear from his mind. Her image would eventually loose definition like the ripples on the water. He'd get back to his peaceful life. On the run back, he decided it was time to check on transportation to Mount Bryson.

Tuesday morning, Min was sitting at her desk trying to compile her report. She had called the Robertsons to tell them she'd located their son. If they could come in, say, Wednesday, she could give them the ROM he'd sent. Yes, Chrysta had said, they could come Wednesday morning.

She re-read the last few lines she had dictated, and told the system to delete the last paragraph. She wasn't really focusing; she was remembering yesterday afternoon with her brother.

* * * * *

When she and Alex had returned from lunch, Min had given Ivan authorization to admit Alex's voice commands. She turned to her brother. "Go ahead, make the link."

Alex recited a series of phrases to access his private files, and soon they were listening to the data on the Environs.

There was more than Alex had remembered. "Monitor, stop. Back up to the first new story about Environs and display as text only – no narrative."

She and Alex sat side-by-side on the sofa, reading the new data displayed on her large vidscreen. As always, the information was sterile.

"It reads like a report on the weather, than people's deaths."

Alex said, "Yes, that bothered me, too."

Min noted that occasionally some were expanded, a reporter sensationalizing for the readers' enjoyment. She stopped the screen. "Monitor, replay that last article."

BLAZE LEAVES TWO DEAD

12 April 2103, 0900, BRUSH VALLEY, IL (Bloomington, IL local services)

Two Environs died when the garage where they were working exploded in flames. The blaze lit up the sky for miles and burned all night. The bodies of Samuel Borrelli, 35, and his son, David, 14, were recovered from the hot ruins Friday afternoon. Borrelli was known to store fuel in the garage. While Cora Borrelli, wife of the deceased, insisted that he was never careless, the Security Forces from Bloomington ruled the deaths accidental. No autopsies were performed on the charred remains, an S.F. contact said Friday. Clearly, a good example of the hazardous life outside the domes.

"That's horrible, but it sounds accidental."

"Yet it parallels a number of other stories that I've heard. Jerry Ray said the same thing about Buddy – he was sure something was wrong, but the S.F. refused to pursue."

"Alex, this doesn't sound at all like Buddy's death. Buddy died in a fall; these two died in a fire. Buddy was alone; this one had two victims. Nothing is similar."

"For pity's sake, Min, you know what I mean. Stop being obtuse. It's the same *type* of story. In fact, so is the next one."

17 March 2103, 2200 LT, LAKE HOWARD, KY (Lexington IB) –

A 38-year-old woman, Casse Portland, was killed when her laser tool malfunctioned and cut her to death in the Lake Howard Environ camp. Friends found her body in her workshop. The Lexington Security Forces reported that it was a regrettable accident and recommended the encampment take precautions to avoid such incidents in the future. S.F. closed the case, saying there are no grounds for further investigation.

"That one doesn't seem like it could have been an accident at all. I mean, how could a tool cut someone to death like that?"

Alex was already onto the next one. "Min, look at this. Hardy is stirring things up again..."

MORE ENVIRONS TO DIE?

15 April 2103, 1300 LT, Special from JR Hardy (New Chicago IB) –

An article from the Bloomington local services reported the fiery deaths of a man and his 14-year-old son in Brushridge, Illinois. And once again the local S.F. dismissed the death as an accident. This analyst can't help but think that there is a connection linking all of the violent so-called accidents involving Environs. How many Environs must die before the Security

Forces take some action? Is their inaction merely because these people are outsiders?

"You're right. He doesn't really know anything – just likes to get people riled up. The more sensational, the more the news services grab it up." She halted the text, standing up and pacing the room. "What do we really have, though? I can't see any pattern."

"Damn, Min, maybe there isn't anything to find."

"No, you said it yourself. Why would someone approach you if there wasn't anything to worry about? We might get farther if we knew more about the victims." Min turned and looked again at the last articles still displayed on the screen, "Ivan, prepare an analysis of the articles. Find out who the victims were. Specifically, where they were born, what they did for a living, who their relatives were? List all references to the victims and their families and look for any connections between these people."

"Ivan, add when and where they exited, or if they were outworld born."

"Good thought. Have we left anything out?"

Alex thought for a few minutes, but shook his head. "I can't think of anything else. But this should give us a good start."

I-VN came back with a question of its own, "How many generations should I list on their lineage?"

"What do you think? Two?" Alex asked.

"Yes. Ivan, only list two generations."

"How would you like the information displayed?"

Min sighed and glanced at her brother. "See what I mean. He's so anal."

Alex smiled. "System, just list the details in a table."

They both leaned back to wait. Min recounted some more stories about her trip, carefully avoiding reference to Josh. She wasn't exactly sure why.

Finally, Alex stood up, stretching. "This is taking too long. I'm going home to fix dinner for the kids. Let me know when it's finished."

"I'll have Ivan send it to you."

"Thanks." He planted a light kiss on her cheek. "See ya."

By the time Ivan generated information, it was late and she was tired. She glanced briefly at the columns, looking for something, but her brain wouldn't cooperate. She went to bed, but not before having Ivan send the data to Alex.

* * * * *

Now in her office, she re-read her report. It still sounded as unexciting as it had the first three times.

Avery won't see what point I'm trying to make. He'll read this and declare the trip was a waste of time. While she had been impressed with Environs – *Preservers,* correcting herself – there was no way to communicate what she had experienced out there. She remembered some of the stronger individuals. *What a contribution they would make to the system.* And yet, no. She couldn't picture any of them in the domes.

The craziest idea is that someone would bother to hurt any of them.

Just then, her comlink buzzed. "Yes?"

"Yumin, could you come and see me for a few minutes?"

"Of course, Avery, but I really wanted to finish this report first."

"It will only take a few minutes. I want to clear something up."

Min walked down the hallway to Avery Bascomb's office. She was surprised to find Belinda there. Avery was clearly angry.

"Belinda has been giving me some very disturbing information, Yumin. Is it true that you had some other motive for exiting? That you neglected your duty to the project in order to complete some personal project?"

"Do you want to hear what I have to say first before you court-martial me?"

"I haven't made up my mind. I just want to hear what you have to say. Please sit down."

"No, thanks. I'll stand. To be honest with you, there was another reason I went out, but it wasn't personal. Simply by locating one Preserver, I expect to add ten new clients to our base. I did locate him and will complete the contracts this coming Wednesday.

"As to neglecting my job – absolutely not. I have all the information the Committee has requested. And in compiling my data, I'm discovering some conclusions. Avery, you shouldn't listen to someone who has set herself against me from the moment we exited." Min turned to Belinda, who had not even looked at her. "I don't know why you're trying to make trouble, but we should keep our quarrel between ourselves and not involve the Company. Don't you think?"

Belinda clearly didn't think that at all. She continued to look at Avery. "I still maintain that she didn't fulfill her responsibilities to the Company. The last three days, she spent almost the entire time with that *man*."

"There was a good reason for that."

Belinda finally turned and glared at Min. "I'm sure."

"Joshua Robertson has traveled to hundreds of settlements – over twenty years worth – and has more information in his head than...well, he was very valuable. He has excellent insight into the reasons people exit." Her heart was pounding and she forced herself to calm down.

"You didn't look like you were doing research when you were with him."

"Enough!" Avery growled. "It's obvious to me that you two have a personality problem. I'll wait until I read the reports. I assume you'll each submit your own version. Now get out of here. I have work to do."

"You'll have mine by this afternoon, Avery." Min left without again looking at Belinda.

Alex reached over to his palette and dipped his broad brush into the dark alizarin crimson. Sliding the bristles slightly into viridian green, he blended the pigments together, adding a bit more of the green until it was right. He transferred the color to a smaller brush and applied it to a section of the canvasite, making that section recede into the shadows. When he was satisfied, he picked up a second brush and chose cadmium yellow and raw white. Using the same method of mixing and dabbing, he brought his imagined sunlight into the scene. He sat back, swiveling slightly on his stool.

This will make seventeen paintings finished. Lumen will be mad with excitement. The current piece was one that he'd started months ago. Originally, the figure scaling the mountain had been no one in particular, but now his younger brother's rebellious and determined face was bringing the picture to life.

There was a knock on the door. "Come in," he said, not turning from his task. He assumed it was one of his children coming to ask a favor. Instead, he heard Karen's voice.

"I dislike bothering you, but I just heard the strangest thing from Janine. It sounded too ridiculous, but..." She stopped abruptly. She had noticed the finished pieces around the room. "You've been busy."

He waited for some reaction of pleasure, but her eyes narrowed suspiciously. "You didn't tell me you've been working so diligently."

"Not so much diligence; just finishing a lot of pieces that have been nagging at me."

"But there must be a dozen new pieces. I haven't noticed you up here that much. When did you do them?" She walked to a chair, but instead of sitting, she stood behind it and gripped the back.

"What is it, Karen? Do you want something?"

"What's going on? Janine told me something and I told her she was crazy, but now, looking at all of this, I'm not sure."

"What did you hear?"

"Have you accepted a professorship at the Lakes Art Center? Janine said she heard you'd be starting in the August term."

There was a dangerous tone in her voice. Alex was accustomed to her coolness, but this was different. With deliberate slowness, Alex laid his brushes aside and stood up. He hated confrontation and the next few minutes were not going to be pleasant. He turned to face her. "No, I've been *offered* a professorship. I have not accepted it. I had no intention of deciding without discussing it first."

Her eyes darkened. "When? When did this happen?" Her voice cracked.

"A week or so ago. Lumen told me, but frankly, it slipped my mind."

"And if I hadn't heard the rumor, exactly when would you have told me?"

Usually Karen walked away before her emotional facade broke; but she was past that now. As Alex watched her, he could see she was finding it difficult to remain calm. He didn't want to discuss it like this, but she was intent on pursuing it. He was surprised at the naked fury in her eyes and could feel his own anger growing. "So much has been happening, I just haven't thought about it. Why are you so angry?"

"I can't believe it. It's all true and *I didn't know*. My friends know; your family knows, *I'm sure*. Your agent knows –

but I'm left in the dark. I don't know what's happening in my own home. All my friends are laughing at me."

"I'm sorry you found out the way you did, but really, Karen, all this fuss just because I didn't tell you right away."

"I can't believe this," she repeated. "I'll never live this down." He noticed she hadn't mentioned the offer itself.

"Well, now that you know, what do you think?"

She looked up, startled. "You aren't serious?"

"The offer is real. I'd like to consider it."

"Why?"

"Karen, you can't dismiss this so easily. I would've thought you'd be pleased. The position is very prestigious, not just for me, but for you as well. Just think, I'd be teaching at a major university."

"It's out of the question. You're too young for starters."

"What has my age to do with it?"

She shook her head. "We can't move to New Chicago. We're established here."

"I haven't accepted anything."

When she didn't say anything else, he decisively picked up the brushes, and turned his back on her. He heard her breathing, then something close to a sob. He couldn't believe it. He turned slightly to get a glimpse of her, but all he saw was the door sliding closed.

New House

Josh leaned back in his chair, chuckling deeply, after a huge meal with Gregg Ellis and his family. He had been recalling to them his journey to Mount Bryson.

"The last leg was with a family," Josh said, looking the around the Ellis table, "with seven children, eleven in all. That part was...well, let's just say it was interesting."

Gregg was one of the first he'd met when he arrived at Mount Bryson and practically the first thing out of Gregg's mouth was an invitation to dinner.

Now sitting in the Ellis' small kitchen, sipping beer, he shuddered as he recalled that part of his journey. "The old transport seemed to be crammed with children almost everywhere you looked. Their food stocks were not so fresh; smelled up the whole place.

"The father stopped over and over, partly to relieve bladders, but mostly to raid roadside Agristations. It was wild. Each time – after sending his kids into the fields, the dad would say, 'Better than a grocery store – and a hell of a lot cheaper.' I couldn't believe it. One time the station manager sent their security after us."

Gregg shook his head, "I'm glad they went on their way. That kind doesn't settle well; they end up degrading a community."

Josh nodded. He'd seen their likes everywhere he'd been.

Gregg's wife, Marcie, spoke over her shoulder from the sink, "Seven kids! I can't imagine it. Even with two, it's a real strain. Buzz and Ian eat enough for an army."

The two teens were still lingering over their pie.

"Dad, that was great," said Buzz, their oldest. "Can I have another slice?"

"Sure was, Gregg. You outdid yourself." Marcie said, dropping another piece on Buzz's plate.

Josh was surprised. "You mean you that was *yours*?"

"Sure was. We share the cooking in this house. Right, Honey?"

"Sure," Marcie chuckled, "as long as its dessert, he'll help out."

"Well, it was great. I'll have another, too," Josh said, extending his plate.

She paused, pie plate in hand, her wide brown eyes scrutinizing Josh's face. "How it you've never settled down in one place with someone?"

"Good God, Marcie!" Gregg exploded. "You just met the man. Wait a bit before you start your matchmaking." He turned to Josh, smiling, "She's famous for playing cupid."

"I do not interfere. I just like to see people happy. I help them out a bit. So, Josh?" She asked again, providing him with his pie.

Josh had foiled many a matchmaker over the years. He knew none of his answers would satisfy, but he knew how to divert them. "How long have you lived here?" he asked between bits of crust and berries.

"That, Joshua Robertson, is not going to stop me."

"That is all you'll get from him, I'm willing to bet. Let him enjoy the pie. Coffee, Josh?"

Josh's nodded, and before his wife could continue, Gregg asked, "We've heard so much about you, Josh. Just how much have you recorded? Where do you keep the information? I would have thought that much data – how many years? I would have thought it would weigh a ton."

"My original purchase was two-dozen flopticals, the ones that hold 100 zettabytes, and it took me years to fill those. Now I buy more whenever I find them, since they are getting scarce. I have them all in my black bag, except, of course, for the ones I send to my family with correspondence. I'll have to find someone who still deals in them soon, though, as I'm getting low."

Gregg laughed and spoke to his younger son. "Ian, you should see his unit. I don't think I've ever actually seen a tablet notebook, except in an historical context. It must be a hundred years old."

"Seventy-five, actually. I picked it up in Samoa. Traded my watch to an old woman who restored ancient equipment. It was hard to get good equipment there, and I had to take what I could get. I'm not complaining. It's not fancy but it's lasted me."

"Haven't you ever wanted to upgrade?" Ian seemed incredulous. "I know I don't have anything as great as they have in the domes, but seventy-five years?"

"Ian!" Marcie was outraged.

"Sorry, sir."

"That's okay, Ian, you're right. What do you have?"

With that, Ian's eyes lit with fire and he launched into a full description of his equipment. Josh wondered idly where his family had found the GEMs to afford it.

"That sounds great. I know soon mine will break down and I'll have to upgrade to something that uses data mocurs. But for now, I'm happy. What do you use yours for?"

"School work, games; I talk to other settlements, send stuff to my friends, do projects. But best of all, I've been able to…" he paused. "I've been able to tap into the system."

Josh wasn't sure if the boy was just trying to impress him or if he was serious. "Not really?"

Gregg smiled, indulgently, "You know you can't do anything like that."

His brother seemed uncomfortable and exchanged a quick look in Ian's direction.

"No, really, Dad. I've managed to link into GINS and have even…"

Buzz stood up suddenly. "Ian, shut up."

The room suddenly went silent, broken only by the sound of breathing. Gregg glared at his sons. "What have you done?"

"Nothing. Just some fun," Ian said quietly.

Josh knew the system could trace illegal tapping. "Ian, if you are telling the truth, you're in real trouble. Please tell me you're kidding."

"Sure, he's joking." Buzz's laugh was tight and unconvincing. "Tell them, Ian."

Unfortunately, Ian wasn't saying anything. He realized he'd said too much already. Ian's parents looked angry.

"Well, Marcie, this has been really great, but I need to get some sleep. Gregg says he's putting me to work tomorrow." He drained his cup, stood up and shook hands with Gregg. Walking back across the compound, he worried about Ian, who, if he wasn't careful, could get into some real trouble. He'd heard of people getting life for a lot less.

On the other hand, Josh admired the kid's skill.

Min tried calling Alex on her way home, but he was out. She got off the Maglev at the mall just before her condo, as she'd suspended her auto-supplies and only had hydrates. She wandered through the various shops, idly scanning her selections into her RIC. She was just leaving her second food store, when someone called her name.

"Yumin! Yumin, wait."

She recognized the voice and turned to see Asa Ben-Dhari's tall figure moving through the crowd, arm raised in greetings. She stood there waiting for him to reach her. "Asa," she said, smiling "How've you been?" She extended her hand.

"Thank God, you're back." He grabbed her in a hug, "Damn, Min, I'm so glad to see you, but I have to pick a quarrel. How could you exit the domes for two weeks and not even mention it to me? I didn't know anything about it until I traced your return on GINS."

She stepped back. "I'm not accountable to you."

"Min," he said patiently, "when two people are as close as we, it's only polite to inform the other of your whereabouts. I care about you and I was worried."

He was justified in some respects, but she wouldn't admit that to him. "I'm back now. We'll catch up soon, but I'm in a bit of a rush." She perjured herself without the least bit of guilt, as she moved into a clothing store.

"You're not running off? Why don't we grab some dinner?"

"Not tonight. I have things to do."

"Min, wait! Please. It's been so long…"

She relented a bit. After all, he hadn't done anything wrong. He didn't know that her feelings had changed over the last few months. She had never said anything – partly because she hadn't realized how much until just now. "I'm sorry, Asa, I just have so much to do – I just got back, you see."

"Well, I know you can spare some time for *me*." He laid his hand on her shoulder.

For two years, she had welcomed his touch, looking forward to the electric feeling it created. Now his hand felt foreign and intrusive. She moved toward another rack of clothes, forcing him to remove it.

"Min, what is it? You seem upset about something."

"No. Just tired from a long trip. All I want to do is to run my errands and go home."

"I thought you said you were in a hurry."

Oh, damn! "Well, yes, I'm in a hurry to get my errands done. Just give me a call tomorrow and we can make some plans. I just don't want to talk right now."

She put even more distance between them, but he followed her. He grabbed her arm firmly to detain her, "Min, wait…"

She whirled around, feeling the anger flame. "What *is* it? Can't you just leave it alone and give me some space?"

Her outburst surprised him. He took a step back, his face going through a change, as quick as it was comical. He was suddenly all sympathy and sweetness. "I can see you're tired. Yes, you should go home. I'll come over tomorrow night, when you're rested."

"No, I said we'd talk tomorrow; I'll call you. I'm going to be very busy over the next few days."

She could feel him watching her as she walked away, but she didn't turn around. She couldn't explain her feelings to him because she didn't understand them herself.

Alex was eating popcorn and scanning the evening news. An Environ article caught his attention, and it reminded him that he'd told Min he'd review the data again. "Monitor, replay that last article."

This caused James to look up from the remote pad he was reading. "What is it, Dad?"

"Nothing. Just an article. Are you finished? It's getting late."

"Not quite."

The article was more of the hype from Hardy.

Special from JR Hardy (Cincinnati IB) - A call from a distressed family alerted this reporter to the disappearance and probable murder of one Thomas LaFleur of Little Creek, Ohio. The case was filed as a Missing Person report despite protests from his wife and parents. It will probably be closed by the intrepid Cincinnati S.F.

According to the family, LaFleur had been working extra hours to finish an important casting, when he disappeared from his foundry last Saturday. It's unlikely that LaFleur would have simply walked away from a vat of molten metal and disappeared. It doesn't take a genius to figure out that his disappearance is cause for concern.

Cincinnati S.F. have refused comment on the case. What is it going to take to get the S.F. idiots to investigate Environ deaths with some seriousness? This analyst is still waiting for some answers.

"What's the matter, Dad," James said, leaning across the counter, and reading the article on the screen. "Did you know Mr. LaFleur?"

"No. I didn't know him."

"Geez, Dad. Another Scav. Why on earth are you so interested in them?"

What to say? "A friend's son died a few months ago and I got interested."

"Your friend, Dr. Jenkins?"

"Yes."

"But, if his son was so stupid to leave the domes, isn't it his fault that he died? I'm sure a lot of them die all the time. Mom said it's savage out there. Stands to reason."

"What stands to reason?"

James looked at his father with youthful impatience. "It stands to reason that they should kill each other off. Actually, I think the more of them that die, the better. They are such anchors."

Alex looked at his son. God, how did he get this way? "I don't think anyone should be killed, no matter who they are."

James was at least smart enough to look guilty. "No, I guess not."

When Min finally got home, it was almost 10:00 p.m. After leaving Asa, she'd purchased a few more items; then had run into a couple she hadn't seen in a while, so she joined them for dinner. The three had lingered over wine for hours, laughing and catching up on all the news. It had been just what she'd needed.

Collapsing on her sofa, she asked, "Ivan, did Alex leave any messages?"

"There are no messages. Would you like me to try his home?"

"No. Not now." The data was there; she decided to look at it without him. "Ivan, display Environ file." Min's huge living room wall glowed with the columns of data, grouped by common threads – jobs, families, life styles, habits, recent trips, places where they have lived, where they exited – anything that would link them.

"Ivan, fix some tea, double strength." She was conscious of the wine clouding her mind. "And run a percentage on any of the comparisons you've generated."

She went to get her tea and returned to settle into her couch.

Ivan had added percentages to the data; thirty percent here; twenty-two percent there; nothing showing a pattern.

"Ivan, what about ages. Did you extract their ages?"

"That is column ten. Eight percent are in their thirties, five percent are in their forties, three percent are under twenty, and..."

"Okay, enough Ivan." That didn't get her anywhere. "COPI, maybe?" she spoke thoughtfully, then clarified for Ivan. "Is there a commonality with their COPIs? Where or when they were issued?"

Again, there was a scattered pairing, but nothing linking them all. She went back through the victims' backgrounds reading the detail, sure to find something Ivan missed. She was still there reading when morning's gray light stretched into her condo. Frustrated, she told Ivan to encrypt and store the information, sending a copy to her brother, and went to catch a few hours sleep before work.

The man had taken only a couple of days to select the next site. Dwyer had nearly one hundred and fifty Environs. Lots to choose from, but he felt he'd found the right one already. Respected. Lived a little outside of town. Not a big man. It would be an easy dispatch.

New House

But he'd wait. He wanted to follow this one a bit longer. From his camp on the river's embankment, he watched the farm. He needed to find some unique method for this one. After all, Patrick Wedmark wasn't going anywhere.

The next morning, as Josh finished unpacking, he was still speculating on Ian's skill at breaking into the system. People had done it, but using sophisticated tools. This boy did it with outdated and make-shift equipment. Of course, if he kept it up, he would be caught.

He stowed his bag under the cot and pushed open the casement to let in some air. The sharp, light breeze toyed with the curtains. He leaned on the sill.

Marcie was right about this place. While Mount Bryson's immediate appeal was that it was new, its secondary appeal was the location. Nestled in towering Southern yellow pine and overlooking a clear mountain lake, the camp encircled a central, t-shaped limestone structure. This solid building had recently acquired a new slate roof, windows and doors, but the four walls dated back to the twentieth century. This area had once been a national park and it was still beautiful, fresh and unspoiled. It might help get Min off his mind. At least here, he wouldn't picture her everywhere.

There was a light tap on his door. Josh opened it to reveal a slight, dark-skinned man. "Morning, Josh. I'm Bob Whiteagle. I didn't wake you, did I?"

"No. I've been up. Come in," he said gripping the man's offered left hand. He thought it odd, but then realized his right hand and arm hung limply at this side.

"If it's no trouble, Holly wants to meet you. I told her you'd probably be asleep but she said, 'If he is, then wake the lazy bum.'" He smiled lopsidedly. "She's a great lady, even though she talks tough."

They set out across the compound. Bob's stride was marked with a slight limp, but despite this, Josh had to quicken his pace to keep up, the man's energy denied his impediment.

They entered the limestone building by the back door, which opened to the kitchen. The room contained several large, black stoves, with a central, five-foot square chopping block. A woman, whose age was totally unreadable, had been clearly hard at work, cutting and dicing huge piles of vegetables. She was now stirring a huge bowl of batter, pausing to open one of the ovens behind her. Satisfied she lifted a lid on one of the simmering pots, gave it a stir and licked the spoon with satisfaction.

Hearing them, she turned and her tan face folded into familiar smile creases. She put the spoon down, wiping her hands on her apron, and grabbed Josh's hand. "Hi. I'm Holly Zimmer."

"Good morning. I heard that if I had slept any longer, I would have been on your black list."

Her laugh was loud and without any apologies. "You're right. I can't abide lazy people."

Bob had been snooping under lids, "Anything to eat?"

"Get out of here, Mr. Busy-body. It's almost ready."

Bob grabbed a couple of thick slices of bread and sandwiched them around some cheese. "I'm starving." He looked apologetically at Holly, as he slid up onto the counter, "I'll still be hungry for breakfast."

"I have no doubt about that." She resumed stirring the batter. Josh wondered where was her help.

Almost as if she heard his thoughts, she said, "I love makin' breakfast." She ladled batter onto a griddle. "It's one meal you don't need help." She poured coffee into a large mug and pushed it into Josh's hands. "Milk and sugar over there if you want."

"Black's fine."

"Hey, where's mine?" Bob hopped off the counter.

"You know where everything is." Her back was to Josh, but she continued to talk as she flipped her hotcakes. "I've wanted to meet you for the longest time. Can't tell you how many times I've heard your name mentioned. You've made quite an impression with a lot of folks. You talking to people here?"

Bob resumed his spot on the counter, sipping his coffee. Josh slid onto a stool.

"That's the plan. I might even start with you."

"Sure," she roared, "you can come and record how I cook stew. Very grand. Just what people are interested in. Better find someone more interesting than me."

"Don't be too quick. You may have some forgotten recipe that I may want."

She laughed.

Bob laughed, too, saying, "Come on, Holly. You have a lot more to offer than just cooking. Josh, d'ya know she started this whole place? She and the Ellis family were the first here."

"Bob Whitehead, will you get out of here and go help set up the main hall. Ring the bell – everything's almost ready. Josh, you can help too. Reach that stack of platters up there, will ya?"

He put the plates on the block. "What else?"

"Nothing right now. You're in my way. You can go help Bob. Shoo! I can manage this."

He wandered out into the main hall, where several people were spreading out cloths, plates and utensils over the long tables. Bob was outside on the bell rope.

"Did she kick you out too? She gets like that when we talk about her. Doesn't like fuss, ya know?"

"Yes," Josh said, "I know how she feels."

The Robertsons entered Min's office much the same way as they did the first time – Albert lowering himself into a chair, disinterested, annoyed; Chrysta sitting primly on the edge, looking at Min, expectantly.

Min sat down and offered them some tea. Chrysta accepted for both of them.

"Let's get this over with," mumbled Albert. He appeared to be more resentful than before; probably grumbling because they now had to keep their end of the deal.

"She was good enough to go out and find Joshua. We should at least be polite, Bert." Chrysta turned back to Min. "You found him." It was a statement of relief, not a question.

"Yes. At present, he's in Somerville, Tennessee."

"When is he coming home? Did he say?"

"I was not privy to his plans," she lied. The woman talked as if her son had just gone on holiday and was a little overdue. "I have a ROM from him." Min reached into her desk and produced the correspondence.

"How was he?"

"He looked well. And he is very committed to his work."

There must have been something in Min's voice, for Albert raised his head from his bored, inattentive posture. "So you liked him?" he said, his face relaxing slightly.

"Yes. I don't agree with most of his views, and we fought continuously. But, yes, I liked him. There's much to like."

Albert smiled. "Yes," he said simply, with a father's pride.

On the other hand, Chrysta's love seemed to be conditional, a strange mixture of love and disappointment. Min had observed in the two brief meetings with the Robertsons that Chrysta held her family in a tight rein.

After a brief discussion, Min had the system scan their COPI data, and set up an appointment for the others to be scanned as well. Finally, they left, armed with their next appointment and an info-mocur showing various programs offered.

Ten new clients. That ought to make the company sit up and take notice. *Thank you very much, Joshua Robertson.* Then she wondered what he was doing at that moment.

8

Min raced toward the glowing blue circle ten feet up the sloping wall. Her computer-generated opponent was a heartbeat behind her. The magnetic glove covering Min's left hand struck the ring, and a hollow voice resounded in the chamber.

"Hoku. Point for player number one."

"That was good, but I'll get you yet," said her opponent, as she scrambled down the wall towards the yellow ring opposite them. The spherical chamber began to rotate again, pushing the next scoring ring out of reach. Min started to pursue, then let her body slide down the slope of the wall, out of breath and sweating. With her inaction, the referee asked, "Do you wish to pause the match?"

"Yes, wait a minute." Her holographic opponent froze in its last position, and Min leaned her head against the wall. The eerie glow from the multicolored rings was beginning to give her a headache. Once she had pounded her frustration into an impressive score, her energy had begun to wane. She had been so angry at Asa, at his pathetic, arrogant, annoying manner.

He had called her several times yesterday, leaving messages. Finally, when she did talk to him, he insisted they have dinner.

"Can't do dinner, Asa. Lunch?"

"Even better. The Consommé Grill at two?"

"Yes." She had made up her mind that she would tell him how she felt.

Asa had presented a gorgeous picture as he stood in Consommé's doorway scanning the crowd. He'd maneuvered through the tables and sat down. "What a great idea. I love having lunch with you."

She had felt guilty at his cheery nature. *He has no idea what's coming.* She had quietly eaten her lunch, allowing him to recount his last couple of weeks. When he paused to drain his drink, she mustered up her nerve.

"Asa, I think we need to talk."

"About what?" he'd said abstractly, as he signaled for the server.

"About us."

He'd continued to try to catch a server's electronic eye. "Damn, those contraptions. Aren't they supposed to…?"

"Asa! Can you pay attention?"

"Sorry. This sounds serious," he had said sternly, yet smiling through the words.

There – he's doing it again. He acts as if he's humoring a small child. "It is serious. I think we should stop seeing each other."

His reaction hadn't been what she'd anticipated. He'd smiled with genuine amusement. "Min, you'll get into trouble joking like that all the time. Most people don't appreciate your sense of humor as I do." The server had finally come to the table. "I'll have coffee. Do you want something, Min?"

"No." She'd waited until the server moved away. "I wasn't joking, Asa. I can't do this anymore."

"Do you want another drink then?" he'd asked.

"Asa, you're not listening. I don't want anything; not coffee, not a drink. I don't want you!" She had wanted to give it to him softer, but he was either too stupid or too arrogant to listen.

He had sat there stunned. "What are you talking about? We're perfect for each other. You know that; I know that. Why do you want to throw it all away?"

"Asa, this only proves I'm right. You see it only from your perspective; you don't even realize that I get nothing from this relationship."

"What do you mean – you get *nothing?*"

"We've had fun, and I don't want to hurt you."

"Answer me! What do you mean that you've gotten nothing from our time together? There's someone else, isn't there?"

"No, there isn't anyone else; it's just me. I don't love you, and I don't think I will – ever."

"I know there's someone else. Why else would you throw this all away?" His look had turned black and he'd stood rapidly, bumping the table and spilling her water. His dark eyes had lingered on her for a moment; then he'd walked away without another word.

Now it was her turn to be angry. The server had returned with his coffee. Her shaking hands had smoothed the tablecloth trying to steady them. *Well, it was over; for that, I'm glad*; but his abrupt exit had sent her into turmoil. *You gave up too easily, Asa. Argue more, fight for me. After all your protestations of love, you just walk away? Damn you, Asa Ben-Dhari. You didn't even pay the bill.*

Now as she sat in the surreal atmosphere of the Hoku court, she realized she hadn't been truthful with Asa. There was someone else she was thinking about. And she couldn't help comparing them. Asa had been pleasant to be around, never any conflicts, yet there had always been an undercurrent of dominance, his belief that she couldn't make decisions for herself. Josh, on the other hand, had angered her beyond reason, had never missed an opportunity to point out the flaws in her opinions; but when she had been with him, she'd always felt respected, even admired. Sometimes it was in his voice, but more often it was just the way he looked at her. When she had said no to Josh, he'd been gentle, even understanding. Whereas Asa...*damn you, Asa,* she whispered.

The synthesized voice requested, "Do you want to continue?"

"No. Terminate program." The lights dimmed and the opponent faded. Min waited for the court's door to align with the external ramp, then left the court. She used the three blocks to her condo to work up another sweat. At home, she peeled off her purple stretch suit, showered and threw on a thin silk kimono, toweling her hair as she went to her kitchen.

She requested Ivan to prepare linguini with cheddar, and then she opened a bottle of Zinfandel. As she ate her dinner, she decided to look at the data again. She called up the information from the previous night, pushing her plate aside to better view her counter imager. But another hour produced no new conclusions.

This is impossible, she thought, jabbing her fork into her pasta. There was nothing linking the victims' lives, their movements, or their origins. They all lived in different areas, had different jobs. The only thing they had in common was that the families and friends did not believe the accidental death rulings. Then suddenly a brainstorm occurred to her and she forgot her dinner, forgot the time, forgot everything. She was positive she'd found a thread, but after comparing all the records, she didn't know what it meant.

She wondered if Alex had explored this line of reasoning. She wasn't sure if he was even still pursuing the data. She decided to tell him about it anyway, and maybe it would spark another line of thinking.

"Ivan, call Alex's home and leave a message for him. Ask if he can come by in the morning."

"Do you have a particular time in mind?"

"No. Tell him to call before he comes."

She sat back and stretched, smiling to herself. While she wasn't sure where her line of thinking would lead, she was pleased with herself.

As the light began to fade, hard-shelled beetles began their annoying clatter against the broken window and hovered around the glow of his equipment. The man caught one in his hand, smashing it against the wall. He felt some satisfaction in the action. His frustration with his superiors was growing. More and more he wanted to just finish this job and, after taking a long vacation, go off on his own. For one thing, any GEMs he accumulated would be his; none of this 'for the collective good' shit.

He had taken a position in a shed across the road from the Wedmark place, and was just waiting for the right moment. He'd found the perfect method of dispatch, and he was getting excited to get on with it. He realized that he could refine each job as if it were a work of art. Beauty of the dispatch. He might become famous for his creative ways of killing people.

Wedmark emerged from his small barn, carrying some boxes, and went into his shop. He adjusted the reception on his optiscanner. The thermal sensor screen showed Wedmark wiping down one of the counters. As usual, Wedmark was alone in the shop. The woman was on the second floor of the house with the girl. The boy was in the living room.

Almost 2000. Don't want to wait too long. The man emerged from the shed and made his way across the paved road and down the slope into Wedmark's yard. The door to the shop was propped open. He strolled in.

"Hi. I'm about ready to close. What can I do for you?" Patrick Wedmark's gaunt face looked up and smiled; then a puzzled look flicked across his face. "You're new, aren't you?"

The man nodded and pointed to a gun in one of the display cases against the wall. "Let me have a look at that one."

Patrick Wedmark came from behind the counter and went to open the case. "The Ruger. You've got good taste. That one is over one hundred and seventy yea..." As he bent to unlock it, the man's arm slipped around his neck, cutting off his words. *This one was thin, weak – almost like a woman,* the man thought, *like the woman with the wood.* The harder Wedmark struggled, the stronger the man's grip became until without warning the man heard a definite 'snap.' Wedmark went slack, and when the man released him, he slid to the floor.

Damn! I didn't want to do that. The man's heart was pounding and he was sweating even though he hadn't used much effort. He'd wanted it to look so natural – but a broken neck. *Damn!*

He dragged the body to the chair behind the counter. An earlier search had showed that Wedmark kept a moderate stash of high-density cartridges in the shop. The rest of the dangerous stuff was in the barn, well away from the house. The amount in the shop would be just enough to do the job. The best feature of this type of cartridge was that they were clean, neat, and very unstable. A man loading a gun, gets careless, and boom. As long as no one looks too closely, this could still work as planned. He collected one of the guns from the case, and a partial box of cartridges from the cupboard.

He laid them on the counter, along with the two-inch time-activated detonator. He set it with a three-minute delay. *More than enough time to get clear.*

He had just reached the other side of the road, when a low rumble burst through the front wall, shattering the glass and blowing out part of the roof.

A little disappointing. Oh, well, I'll just have to…

A blinding flash, followed by a thundering report shattering the night, cut off his thought. He was thrown into a ditch, and while he lay there, a third eruption shook the ground. His ears were ringing and a sick throb pulsed in his skull. His chest had a grinding pain with each intake of air. Carefully, slowly, he pulled himself over to the lip of the ditch.

All of the buildings were ablaze and the main house and shop were leveled. *Shit, I got all of them. Every last one. Holy Christ, what did Wedmark have stored in there?* As he looked at the spectacular sight, he thought, *God, this is beautiful.*

He also realized that he had to move. He struggled to his feet. Standing straight made him sick, and his shoulder was clearly out of its socket. He stuffed his equipment into his bag and dragging it, made his way to his vehicle.

It was four-thirty in the morning. Min stretched out between the cool sheets, unable to let go of the Environ data in her head. *If we only knew more about the victims. Knowing only one – Buddy – isn't very helpful.* Then she thought, *Josh. Josh might know something about them. Or some of them. If anyone could find a connection, he could. But would he help?* It would mean that he'd have to come back in or she would have to go back out. She tried to tell herself that she wasn't looking forward to seeing him again, but as weariness finally took over, Min's last thought was that her mother had raised no fools.

"You have a visitor," Min's Ivan announced for a second time.

"What?" She'd vaguely heard the first message, but had been unable to bring her mind out of its deep sleep. This time, she opened her eyes, but was still unwilling to move. "Who is it?"

A familiar voice emanated from the wall speaker. "It's Alex. You invited me, remember?"

"What time is it?"

"A little after seven."

"I said to call first."

"Come on, Min. Wake up and let me in."

"Okay, okay. Ivan, admit Alex." She slipped out of bed and pulled on a robe. "Ivan, make some real coffee today. Six...no twelve cups, please."

An hour later, she and Alex were sitting at her counter, with the remains of breakfast pushed aside. Min, after four cups of coffee, had finally gotten her mind to work, and had been explaining the results of her search. "You see, I tried almost everything and nothing connected. Then I called up the records of the reorganization companies nearest each murder. I wanted to see if there was an influx of new clients around the dates of the cases."

"And?"

"After every death the percentage of Environs returning to the domes increased. At first, it was a small percent. Recently, however, the percentage is fairly large. Of course all of my figures only go twelve months back."

"Wait a minute! Are you suggesting that some reorganization company could be murdering people just to get new clients? That's outrageous."

"I know it is. And you're right; it didn't track. Reorg companies are usually limited to a single dome, maybe two. There are laws regulating how far they can recruit people. They would have to be working together for this to be a connection. Let me tell you, these companies are more likely to cut each other out than to join forces. Besides, just because Preservers re-enter the domes doesn't follow that they seek reorganization."

Alex shook his head. "So we're back to where we started. What's the connection? I keep wondering if there is really anything to find. What if the warning was for Buddy's case alone? Maybe it hasn't any connections to the others?"

"You said it yourself. There is too much similarity in so many of these deaths to be a coincidence. Our problem is that we don't know enough about the victims. I've been thinking about that – what we need is someone who knows these people. Someone who knows little bits of information that neither the news services nor the S.F. would know."

"That would help. But there isn't one person who would know everyone. You'd have to visit each camp, interview scores of people."

"No. I think I know someone who may have knowledge of a number of these people." Min said, as she rose to clear away the dishes.

"Oh?"

"He's traveled through the camps all over the world for over twenty years. He has an excellent mind; he could be just what we need. Unfortunately, he's extremely difficult and wants nothing to do with dome life, but...oh...I don't know. Maybe not. He's too impossible."

"Who is this excellent, impossible man?" Alex was smiling in a totally annoying way.

"He was the one I went out to find. He calls himself a true historian, and hates everything we stand for. He probably wouldn't help. He doesn't see anything sinister about the whole thing. I'm sure he wouldn't bother."

"Min, this indecisive attitude is unlike you. Who is he?"

"His name is Josh Robertson and he's more outside the system than anyone I've ever met. Besides, he's annoying as hell. And another thing..." She broke off, remembering other aspects about Josh.

"And you like him?"

"No. Absolutely not." Min was a little too forceful.

Alex laughed. "Someone's finally disturbed that iron calm? This grows interesting. I have to meet him."

"Oh, shut up. I'll bring him in, if I can. But it has nothing to do with my feeling...with what I feel."

"Sure. Okay. Anything you say, Min."

She wanted to hit him, but he slipped out of the kitchen and went down the hall. He was gone a long time and she went looking for him.

"Do you want some more coffee, Alex?" He didn't answer. "Alex?" The door to her spare bedroom was open.

"What's all this?" Alex's voice came from inside.

Her heart sank; she pushed open the door. "Come out of there, please."

"Why? What is it?"

"It's not ready. I don't want you to see it, yet."

"Min, this is ridiculous. What are you working on? You might as well tell me."

"It's a HAM imager." She said defensively.

"A what?" Alex had gone to the control and begun to investigate.

"Here, I'll show you. You'll mess it up if I don't." She slipped a program-mocur into the console, telling Ivan to display Sample #14. A solid green cube appeared before them. " It's a holographic art medium – HAM."

"That's great, Min," Alex said, sarcastically. "You can project three dimensional objects. We've only been able to do that for centuries."

"If you're not interested, say so. Otherwise, shut up."

"Sorry."

Min picked up one of her brush-like tools and requested a 40% crimson, 40% green and 20% white, as she began to stroke one side of the cube. The rich gray hue created a shaded area.

Alex stood fixed to his spot, at first, not understanding the significance of what she'd done. Then all of a sudden, a creative spark lit his face. "Do that again. No wait. Let me try it." Alex walked over and Min handed him the brush. "Let's see. Give me an 85% cadmium-yellow and 15% white," he said, imitating

Min's voice command. When nothing happened, he looked to Min.

She raised her eyes in frustration. "Ivan, please respond to Alex's commands."

The bland voice from her system responded, "I will have to prepare a temporary authorization record. This function is not equipped with multi-user authorization."

"All right. Do it then." Min turned to Alex. "I almost wish I'd gotten a machine like yours. This one is so stubborn. It's just that I can't cook and yours doesn't have the kitchen mode."

"You could have waited. The new I-VN 8000 has eliminated many of the problems with both the 6000 and 7000 models. It's scheduled to come out in a couple of months."

"Great!" she said sarcastically. "I can't wait. By then I'll have this one programmed."

Ivan indicated that the authorization record was complete. "Thank you. Go ahead, Alex."

Alex did and he moved about the image, attacking it with the fever of a child with a new toy. Now it was Min's turn to be amazed. The cube was transformed into a six-sided marvel, each with a different texture.

"I don't believe it. You always make it look so simple." Min realized, with even more surprise, she was a little jealous. She was glad he was excited, but resentful that he'd picked it up so quickly and surpassed her simple efforts. He stood there, his face intent, his eyes glowing with enthusiasm.

"Min, this is wonderful. What did you call it? A ham? How ever did you come up with it?"

She explained how she'd stumbled on to it.

"An accident? That's just like you."

Min was suddenly protective of her creation. She took the brush from Alex. "Okay. You've seen it. Now let's shut it down. I'm not ready to put it on display yet. That's why I haven't shown it to anyone."

"Will you let me take it home so I can play with it?"

"I don't know. I have to admit that my artistic skills are sadly lacking. I've been wondering what you could do with it. Look what you've done in just a few minutes." The image faded as Min removed the mocur.

Alex walked over and wrapped his arms about her, squeezing her head against his chest. "I promise I won't steal your thunder, Min. I know that's the real reason you haven't shown it to me. It's yours. I only want to play with it."

In the end, she handed over a mocur with a copy of the program, two electronic brushes, a couple samples and instructions for setting it up. "Your system will handle it fine."

As Alex left, he leaned down, kissed her cheek. "Thanks, Sis," he patted his pocket. "I can't wait."

"Alex...?"

He hugged her again. "I know. Don't worry. Not a word."

9

Alex arched his back, removing the kinks, and looked at what he had done. He wasn't pleased with it, but it was a start. He also hadn't felt this alive and excited in a long time. God, Min was a genius.

He went to the kitchen to get something to drink and told his system to bring up the news. It was mostly dull and he was about to close it, when his system asked,

"Would you like to review the new articles I have archived in your profile?"

"Yes," he said absently, but the first headline grabbed his interest.

EXPLOSION KILLS FOUR OUTWORLDERS

27 April 2103, 0900 LT, IL (Galesburg, IL local station services)

Apparent ammunition mishandling destroyed an outworlders gun shop Tuesday in a northern Mississippi River community called Dwyer. The shop, as well as the owner's house, went up in the violent detonation. The explosion resulted in the deaths of the owner, Patrick Wedmark, his wife, Kookie, and their two children,

New House

Rick and Amy. This is just another example of the unsafe and unlawful conditions existing in the Environ world.

After a brief investigation the St. Louis Special Forces officer ruled it an accident. No further investigation is planned.

"Monitor, where is Dwyer?"

"Dwyer is not a known coordinate on any map."

"Monitor, did Hardy have anything to say about the incident?" he asked.

"Yes," his system reported. "The Hardy piece is next in your queue."

"Show it to me."

WHEN WILL IT END?

28 April 2103, 1330 LT, Special from JR Hardy (New Chicago IB) –

The Wedmark family of Dwyer is dead and no one seems at all concerned. A brief report out of the Galesburg station this morning indicates that the S.F. in St. Louis dismissed it, as yet another accident. Without even bothering to visit the site, they closed the case.

Perhaps this latest explosion is not connected to the other so-called accidents, but when is someone really going to investigate? How will we ever know what's really going on, if the S.F. refuse to investigate properly? As I've said before, many Environs see a connection and they are fearful. This should not be ignored just because the victims live outside of the domes. When will this end?

Alex leaned back in his chair. He told his system to ring Min, but the quick response back was that she was out. He made a mental note to talk to her the first chance he got. However, the problems of a few abstract Environs seemed less important with Min back in the domes. Besides, he wanted to get back to his new "toy."

Josh stood in the kitchen doorway, doing what had become a habit since coming to Mount Bryson – watching the dawn crawl slowly through the distant trees and spill its long rays over the lake. *Min should be here.* Mount Bryson *would give her so many answers. I wonder what she's doing today.* He'd faced the fact that Min was never very far from his thoughts. Little things kept reminding him of her. He had hoped he would get over her if he moved on, but that hadn't happened. However, once he'd accepted the fact that thoughts of her would not fade quickly, he welcomed them, not dreading their intrusion. It was something he could live with.

Josh had volunteered to help make lunch. An assembly line was busy dicing chicken, leeks, peppers and tomatoes.

Jeannie asked, "How many of these foldovers should we make?" It fell to Jeannie at the end to stuff the little pastry squares with the mixture.

Josh could see Holly doing mental calculations. "Make about sixty," she said with a satisfactory nod. "The older ones will have seconds, I figure."

Jeannie bowed her chestnut head again over her task, her long fingers delicately folding and pinching the pastry. Josh had noticed sadness about her. She worked slowly, smiling and replying if anyone spoke to her, but her smile rarely touched her eyes. She put the next batch into one of the ovens and then started on the next tray.

As Holly went into the main hall, Josh moved close to ask her about it.

Holly shook her head, "Lost her husband recently."

"I wondered if it was something like that. What happened?"

"He just didn't wake up one morning," Holly said simply.

"Dominique Cozens – you know she and her husband are doctors? Well anyway, she said it was something in his brain. That was one time I wished we'd had more sophisticated technology. Dominique said that it would have been detected if he'd had a scan. There are many times I wish for the dome technology."

"You shouldn't wish for anything the domes have to offer."

"But I do. There are so many things in the domes worthy of admiration. Just because there are many things that are not desirable, doesn't make the good things bad."

"No, I suppose not."

"Anyway, we all wished we'd had a scanner that time." She picked up a basket of tomatoes. "It was terrible for Jeannie. She was really out of it for weeks, but she's coming back. This place is good for the soul." Holly had stated it matter-of-factly, but when Josh glanced up, she was looking at him intently. Very perceptive, our Holly.

Josh smiled, taking the basket from her. "Yes, it is,"

"Happy Birthday, Gran." Alex bent to kiss the petite woman standing at his side. "I hope you're enjoying your evening."

She gazed upon the massive assembly. "Yes, I am. But you know me, I prefer more intimate gatherings. Besides, it's a little depressing. I never realize how old I am, until I see how many descendents I have."

Alex laughed. "I'm sure you're just miserable. I know how you hate being fussed over, plus seeing all of your grandchildren and great grandchildren." They exchanged laughing looks. "You're eating this up, you minx. Admit it." He sat on the arm of a chair, bringing him closer to her five-foot height. "You're looking very regal this evening."

"Flatterer!" she said, toying with the simple pearls around her neck, but he could see in her sparkling dark eyes that she was pleased. "By the way, where is Min? I was sure she'd be here."

"She said she was coming. I'm sure she'll be here soon."

Just then, several other guests came up and Alex moved off.

He encountered his father a few minutes later talking with a couple he didn't know, and Alex waited until the conversation paused before speaking. "Dad, do you have time to talk before dinner?"

"Sure, I think the study is free." He moved off in that direction, Alex following, swapping his empty champagne glass for one from a passing tray. The study was small by comparison to the other rooms, but it was comfortable.

Jonathan Villanueva sat in one of the Melbourne chairs, waiting for his son to lower his tall frame onto the other. "So what's on your mind? Has it anything to do with what Karen's been telling us?"

Karen? What the devil? "What's she been saying?"

"About the professorship. She told your mother and me. And, I suspect, anyone else who'd listen."

Alex shook his head. "She's been very upset."

John Villanueva rose, going to the wall opposite his desk and pressed one of the ornamental woodcarvings. The center panel slid aside revealing one of the few gadgets in his parents' home – an automated bar. He requested two brandies. "Get rid of that bubbly shit – here." He pushed the large snifter into his son's hands.

Alex took a sip and let the heavy gold liquid assail his senses. "What's she saying?"

"She wants me to talk you out of it," he said simply.

"Are you going to try? Or are you going to see if you can convince me that it is an opportunity of a lifetime." Alex couldn't help letting irritation creep into his voice.

His father resumed his seat. "You can lower your defenses. I've never interfered in your life and I'm not going to start now."

"Good." He said a bit too strongly. He took a deep breath. Another sip. "I will admit I was looking for some cool discussion on the subject. I'm really confused. I feel my art is stale. And I know I should at least consider the professorship, but with Karen opposing it so strongly…"

"Alex, no one can help you make this decision. Karen will come around if that's what you choose to do with your life."

"I hope so. It's just that I don't want to make a mistake and be sorry later."

"Who's to say that you couldn't teach for a while and then go back to your art? Might give you a new perspective."

"I'm not sure about that. Lumen is always telling me that unless he keeps me in front of the public, I'll lose my standing and would find it extremely hard to get it back. That's why he did this retrospective. On the other hand, another instructor position might not be forthcoming. Then there's…" He stopped. He had started to say something about Min's new HAM, but remembered his promise. It was exciting, but after working with it, he wasn't sure if people would accept it as a viable medium.

Silence settled into the room, pierced occasionally by the gaiety beyond the heavy doors.

His father finally broke the quiet. "Alex, nothing has to be decided now. Go home, and forget it for a while. The right decision will come when you're least expecting it."

"I wish I had your confidence." Just then a group walked close to the study doors and Alex started to get up, "We'd better rejoin the party."

"That's not everything, is it?"

"What?"

"Something else is bothering you."

New House

Alex had thought about using his father as a sounding board for their conspiracy ideas, but saying it aloud with Min sounded ridiculous. He couldn't imagine what his father would say. Instead he said, "Do you remember Dr. Jenkins?"

"Your mentor? Yes, of course. What about him?"

"His son, Buddy, is dead."

"Oh, I'm so sorry. What happened?"

"He died in a fall. It was in an Environ camp."

"What the hell was he doing outside the domes?"

"He had exited a while back. He had joined a community out there and was fairly happy – from what Dr. Jenkins said." He started to say more; then thought better of it. He wouldn't say anything to his father right now. It's too ridiculous.

"What a waste. I feel badly for Dr. Jenkins."

At that point his mother, tapping lightly first, entered the study. "Are you two coming out to join us?" She then smoothly shifted gears, "What about Dr. Jenkins?"

Alex explained to her what had happened.

"Oh, I'm so sorry. I know you liked him."

Alex rose and started pacing the room, finally turning to his parents. "I could use your perspective. I wonder if you'd heard anything about…" but then couldn't think how to continue.

"Come on, Alex. Just say it." His father disliked hesitant, uncertain people.

"I would never have given it a thought, if it hadn't been for Buddy, and seeing Dr. Jenkins that way."

His father was showing his familiar impatience, but his mother sat waiting for him to continue. "I went to see Dr. Jenkins when I found out. He and his daughter, Monica, both feel that it wasn't an accident."

Neither of his parents showed any reaction. His mother said simply, "Well, if it wasn't, the Security Forces will find out what happened. It's doesn't concern you. You have enough to think about."

"But that's just it. The S.F. closed the case as accidental."

"Then it was, most probably, an accident."

His father hadn't said anything; he'd gone to refill his glass.

"Buddy is just one of many unexplained outworlder deaths," Alex continued.

His father turned, "I'm not sure what you are getting at. How can the accidental deaths of a few outworlders be of interest to you? I feel badly for Dr. Jenkins' loss, but people die – outside and in. I'm not surprised more don't die out there."

He said it calmly and rationally, but the words echoed what his son had said earlier. "Well, it does concern me. If you could have seen Dr. Jenkins...well, I told him I'd look into it."

"Alex! How absurd," exclaimed his mother. "What do you think you can do? You're not the S.F."

"Just what I said – look into it. I know I don't have any authority, and I don't delude myself into thinking we'll solve this. It's just…"

"We?"

"Yes. Min and I."

"Oh, Alex." His mother's eyes had taken a hard edge, "Have you dragged Min into this?"

New House

But his father's reaction was different. "Now I see – this was her harebrained project."

"No, I brought it to her." Alex sat his glass down. "Look, I just wanted to know if you'd heard of anything."

"What would we have heard? Your mother and I don't have any S.F. connections."

"I'm sorry. I shouldn't have brought it up."

"No, dear," his mother had processed the situation and was speaking with her calming voice, "I understand you wanting to help. It's commendable. But you have to be realistic – you and Min cannot possibly do anything."

"Listen to your mother. You need to focus on your own life and your own problems."

Alex opened his mouth to say more, but he'd been watching the interest die in their eyes. This was too removed from their lives. Besides, he wasn't even sure himself; how could he convince them. "Maybe you're right."

"Good." His mother slipped her arms around the two men. "Now I can finish my earlier task – Gran has been asking for you two – let's go toast her day."

Gran's dinner was over and Min decided to leave. When she approached the front closet, Alex spotted her.

He asked, "You're not leaving already, are you?"

"I was," Min said, a little defensively. "Are you leaving?"

"No. I was looking for you. I tried to call you last night."

"I was out with friends," she lied. She had been in one of her dark moods and had told Ivan to say she was out.

He didn't seem to notice. "I wanted to ask you something. By the way, I've been so engrossed in your new toy." He touched her shoulder lightly and steered her towards the side garden. "Min, your HAM is fantastic! I've had so much fun playing with it."

She was glad to see him excited. "Thanks," she said through a little chuckle. "I'm glad you like it. But I hope you kept your promise."

"I haven't mentioned it to anyone. And I won't." He flipped up his hand in a mock salute. "Besides, I'm not even sure what to say. That's not what I wanted to talk to you about, though. Didn't you say something about a village called Dwyer?"

"Dwyer? Yes, that's the first place I started my interviews. Why?"

"There was another incident – some people died in an explosion. I would have missed it too, except my system determined it fit our search parameters and extracted it to the file. It showed up yesterday. I can't remember the name...let me think. Whittier or Wetmer; something like that. A whole family went in an..."

"Wedmark?" she asked, in almost a whisper.

"Ah, now that you say it, I think that was it."

She felt sick, and sat down on the nearest bench. *Pat. Kookie. The kids. Oh, my God.*

"Min?" She heard her cousin's voice behind them. "What's wrong?" Phill sat down next to her.

New House

"I'm all right. It's just...oh, God..." Her throat closed off, but she took a steadying breath. "I'm sorry. It's just that I had dinner with them...such a beautiful family." She rubbed a hand over her eyes, pulling herself together. "How did you say it happened?"

"There was an explosion in the gun shop, which took the house with it. The news report said it had again been ruled an accident, but, as I said, my system showed it fit the profile of the others. Also, Hardy linked it to the other killings, which, of course, doesn't mean a thing."

Phill had been looking between the two of them, perplexed. Min and Alex started to explain, when Karen interrupted their conversation.

"Alex, we have to leave." Her eyes turned toward Min. "You'll forgive me if I take your brother home now?"

Alex shook his head, "I'm sorry, Karen. I can't leave right now."

Min thought she noticed an ever-so-slight change in Karen's cool eyes. "The kids need to go home."

"You go ahead. I'll be along later."

Something else passed between them; then Karen slipped back into her well-modeled, social facade. "Yes...well. Good night, Phill. Tell Chauncey I'll call her for lunch. Good night, Min." She turned sweetly back to her husband. "Come home...whenever."

Wow, Min thought. *What's going on here?*

Instead of rising to it, her brother merely kissed her cheek, "Good night."

There was an awkward moment after Karen left, as if they were all embarrassed by her behavior. Then they resumed their discussion. To Min's surprise, Phill fell right into the spirit of their hunt, providing some insight and suggestions that hadn't been addressed. They sat on the patio for nearly an hour, bringing up every conceivable argument against pursuing their search. In the end, even Phill was on board.

"I need to find Josh Robertson. I think he can be of assistance. Phill, can you look at the medical files? Maybe you and your medical team can see something the S.F. autopsies missed."

"I'd just as soon not bring my team into it. You forget, before I became a medical researcher, I was a forensics analyst. I don't think I've forgotten everything."

Min smiled at her cousin. "You've forgotten less than I have learned my entire life."

"I'll send our data over tomorrow morning," Alex said, then turned to Min. "Are you seriously thinking about going out again?"

"Yes. Josh will be invaluable. He will have a totally different perspective."

"Again, be careful – and log in daily, so I know where you are."

The man could hear every footstep on the gravel, every word no matter how softly it was spoken. He could hear when they moved indoors, when they rattled around in the big kitchen. Every sound was so distinct, so amplified. *Must be the mountain air,* he thought. He was encamped in a thicket; invisible to probing eyes, yet where he could easily watch the settlement.

Leaning back onto his pack, he took a deep breath but caught up short. His fingers gently probed his side. It was still tender and the bruises would last a while yet. That last one had been too close. If he'd been a little slower crossing the road, he might not have gotten up at all. His lucky star had been following him that night.

After the blast, he'd gotten to his vehicle and had programmed it for the nearest med-station. Fearing he'd lose consciousness, he put the vehicle on auto. He actually had blacked out a couple of times, but finally arrived and demanded some service. The doctor who attended him had applied a neural wave for his concussion and a fuser on his ribs, and then recommended he be admitted. Against doctor's advice, the man had left and had driven southeast. He'd wanted to put some distance between himself and the Dwyer area.

He again rubbed his ribcage. The cold night air was acting as a numbing agent. *I'm a fast healer; this is nothing.*

His remote coupler vibrated. It was them. He was in no hurry to answer. The RIC beckoned him again; then a third time. He slowly reached down, picked up the unit and slipped it over his ear. He held off answering, enjoying the prolonged tension.

"Receive the call," he said quietly.

The familiar, but overly sharp voice sprang out from the tiny earpiece. "What just exactly are you trying to do?"

"Hello."

"Are you insane? A whole damn family? You're not supposed to make headlines. You have people asking very pointed questions, specifically the S.F. We wanted deaths that could be closed easily. After the Borrellis, we warned you that we didn't want anything like that again."

"LaFleur was low profile."

"Low profile?" The client was almost screaming. "Low profile? They aren't even sure he died. He just disappeared. There was no trace of him. That doesn't do us any good."

"So? I've done others that way."

"You stupid moron." There was a pause. He could imagine the client gathering up his composure. "Look, if there is too much attention, the S.F. might not be able to keep a lid on it."

"The last one didn't go the way I intended. I scouted the place, but Wedmark must have had something stored in his shop that I didn't see. Meant to take him out with a small blast. Instead, I ended up with a couple of bruised ribs and a concussion. And the whole place leveled."

"You were injured? Why didn't you let us know?"

"I took care of it. It didn't concern you."

"Didn't concern us? It's our money, remember? We're in charge."

The man spoke in a cold, dead voice. "No one is in charge of me any longer. I used to do your dirty work and then you sent me out here. I'm doing it and I'll make an effort to keep low profile." The man spoke very slowly. "However, you remember one thing. Anyone gets too close, or if things get wiry, I'm gone."

There were several seconds with only the hum of the active receiver. Then the client asked, "When's the next one?"

"Probably less than a week."

"Fine." Before the client could say more, he broke the connection and laid down the RIC, smiling. He was getting good at dealing with them.

The third try with the HAM was taking shape, but Alex's mind was torn between his new toy and the conversation from the night before. He wondered if Phill would find anything.

Almost as in answer to Alex's thoughts, his system announced a call. "Phill, I was just thinking about you."

"Yes, well, once I got into the information, I couldn't leave it alone. Can I come over this afternoon? I think I've found something in some of the autopsies."

"Really? What?"

"No. I'll come over and we can talk."

Alex decided he needed someone official involved. He called Tami and asked if she could come, too.

It was all he could do to wait until the afternoon. Tami showed up early and ate lunch with Alex. Then while they were finishing, Phill arrived.

Phill helped himself to some mineral water and took time slowly sipping it.

"Well," Alex said finally, slightly exasperated, "what did you find?"

"Yes, ok, yes, well, let me see...yes, here it is." He removed a mocur from his pocket. "Put this in, will you."

The familiar data appeared on the screen, but now there were new columns and it was arranged differently.

"What are we looking at?" Tami asked.

"When I reviewed the medical records on the victims, I turned up eight where the chemical NR2 was detected. Now, I know that doesn't sound like a lot, but only thirty or so autopsies were performed, and of those, eight had the same chemical trace. A very high probability factor."

Tami was obviously surprised. "And none of the S.F. thought that its presence was significant?"

"No, apparently not. It was just listed in the chemical trace as if it were as common as glucose or sodium."

Alex was feeling a little left out. "Ok. Hold a moment. What's NR2?"

Tami and Phill exchanged looks.

"It's a knock out drug," Tami said.

For the second time in a month, Min was exiting the domes. It was strange how different it felt from her earlier trip. This time she was alone – *thank God* – and she wasn't working on a project for the Company. In fact, she didn't even work for the Company any longer.

Min had left a message for Avery, when she'd returned home from Grandmere's party. When his call came in the next morning, she had been packing.

"Sorry, Min, I can't authorize another exit at this time." He must have just gotten up. He was still wearing his robe, cradling a cup between his stubby hands. "We just have too much to do. You have those ten new clients. We have several reports to analyze and action plans to form...well, I just can't let you go now."

"You misunderstand, Avery. My message said I was exiting today, not *may* I exit today. As you can see, I'm packing as we speak."

"Min, there is something else. Belinda has filed a formal protest against you, and I've scheduled a preliminary review to discuss it. You'll have to be here to defend your position. It will probably be tomorrow. So you see..."

Min had been furious. "I can't believe you are listening to that sour-faced woman."

"There's nothing I can do. The protest has been lodged; we have to proceed. I'm sure we'll clear everything up." He had seemed to be almost pleased to have this control over her.

She had filled her lungs, and had let the air escape slowly. It had suddenly become so clear. "Fine."

"Good. I'm sure we'll settle this protest easily, and then, later, if you still want to exit for a few days, we'll see."

With a surprising amount of relief, she'd said, "No. I mean, fine. I quit."

"What?"

"You heard me."

"Just because...?"

"Just because you're willing to listen to a spiteful woman who's aching for a promotion. Because I know the Company will never take anything I do or say seriously, because...oh, damn, Avery. Just because I'm sick to death of that place..." and for a little spite of her own, "...and of you."

Avery hadn't protested. Probably, she remembered thinking, he'd be glad he wouldn't have to deal with her anymore. Only, what would she do now? She thought of her HAM project, which might prove to be something marketable, but that was still a while away. Then she thought of John and Maggie. They wouldn't say, "I told you so" when they heard she'd quit – that wasn't her parents' style. They would be patronizingly sympathetic, which was even worse.

As the Maglev whispered to a stop in the outer perimeter of the New Hope Agridome, she transferred her thoughts to her current task. She rehearsed what she'd say to Josh to make him listen, to convince him to come in and help them. That wasn't going to be easy. She realized her breathing was a little quicker at the thought of seeing him again.

During his time outside, the man had occasionally wondered what the "goal" was. What end result would come from all of these dispatches? However, in the end, he couldn't give a shit. It was 5,000 GEMs for each occurrence; not the number of bodies.

He thought, ruefully, *all those extra dispatches for free. Ah well, next time.*

This next dispatch would be perfect. He watched the target walk across the gravel area towards her cabin. He wanted to do another woman. None of the other dispatches had produced the same sensation. He recalled the exhilaration he'd felt holding the Portland woman against him, feeling her trembling body, her tears, then sensing the energy go out of her.

This woman seemed important, but he wasn't sure what she did. All he knew was that she spoke and moved with a vitality that would give him great pleasure. She would be next.

Min was getting use to getting lost out here. It took three different sets of directions before she arrived in the Mount Bryson settlement. It was mid-afternoon before she passed through the southern perimeter marked by a weathered entrance, which had greeted last century's visitors. The road meandered through the tall pine, continually climbing the mountain. As she rounded a bend, she was surprised to see a very permanent-looking stone building, surrounded by newer structures.

She stopped next to the main building, and suddenly there he was, helping unload a transport. He didn't see her at first, but as her vehicle settled to the ground, he turned his head. He stared for a full half minute, then shook his head and began to walk towards her.

"I don't believe it," he said smiling a lopsided grin.

Min felt she would burst if she didn't do something quick, so she started pulling out her gear. "Yes, I'm back."

"What brings you? Another work project? Don't get me wrong. I'm glad to see you, but it's been only a week."

"No, I'm back on my own account. Or on yours, to be precise."

"My account? What's in that head of yours?"

"Could you hold off grilling me until I've stowed my stuff and had something to eat. I'm starving."

"I wasn't grilling you. It's just that I was surprised to see you. Of course; eat first." He turned and yelled to one of the men by the rig. "Bob, will you see what food you can scrounge up for this woman, while I show her to a cabin?"

"Sure, Josh. I think there is still something left from lunch. Come on in when you're ready."

Josh resisted many impulses over the next hour. First, he hadn't grabbed her in his arms. That had definitely been his first impulse. He also wanted to question her more about her sudden visit, but he held off and continued idle chatter as she stowed some of her things. Once, when she'd turned to ask him a question, he'd shaken off the impulse to kiss her.

The dining hall was now virtually empty, and Min had finished eating. Josh refilled their cups with the strong tea, and asked, "Feeling better? Now maybe you'll tell me what's brought you here. On my account," he added.

She looked down into her cup, as if she were trying to decide what to say. "I don't know where to start. Or how to start."

"Is there something wrong with my family?" he asked casually.

She locked his eyes. "Just before I left the city, I heard something terrible – about the Wedmarks."

"What about the Wedmarks?"

"They're dead. All of them. Killed in an explosion of some sort..." Her voice trailed off.

Josh's mind wouldn't work right. His first reaction had been, *Pat, how could you have been so careless?* Yet Pat hadn't been a careless man, especially where his family was concerned.

He looked up, and saw the pain in her face, too. "When?" was all he could say.

"Last Friday." Min reached out for his hand.

He gripped her fingers, as if he could release some of the pain through her. She must have felt embarrassed by the intimate touch, and released his hand.

Josh pretended not to notice. "Did you come all the way out here just to tell me?"

"No. They were just the deciding factor. I had other reasons."

"Such as?"

"We talked about this before, about all the deaths out here, but you dismissed it. Do you still feel that way?" When he didn't respond, she continued. "My brother first hit upon it, and now our cousin, Phill, agrees. There is something going on out here. The Wedmarks are just one incident in a growing number of unexplained deaths and missing people that we think were murdered."

"I agree that there have been a lot of Preservers dying in the past few months under unusual circumstances. But murder? Why?"

"That's what we haven't figured out. Yet we've identified hundreds of profiles, which qualify as 'unusual.' You know, where the accidental ruling just doesn't fit. We know they're connected somehow; we just can't find a link. Without a link, we can't figure out why."

"What do the Security Forces have to say?"

"Tami – she's Alex's friend in the S.F. – says there is no interest in investigating because they're outworlders. We thought you might come in and help."

"What makes you think so?"

"You know these people. Just as Phill might be able to see a commonality through the medical records, you could look at all of the victims and hit on something we missed."

"Why don't you bring the data to me? Why do I have to come in?"

She was quiet for a moment. "I suppose we could, but I thought if we all brainstormed together, we could make more progress."

He shook his head. "That doesn't wash. With all your fancy equipment, I could easily do it from out here." A thought suddenly occurred to him. "You're worried about me."

"That's ridiculous."

"Admit it. That's the real reason you want me inside."

Min stood and picked up her plate. "I just thought you could help because you've traveled so much. You probably know a lot of the people who've been killed." Then she seemed to realize how that statement would affect him. "I'm sorry. I didn't mean it that way."

He stood up, making a decision. "I won't leave. I'd feel like I was running away just when things got difficult."

"All right – have it your way, but I don't give up that easily. I'll hang around until I've convinced you."

"What about your job?"

"I've quit." She said the words flippantly.

He liked the idea of her staying, but he couldn't resist jabbing at her a little. "You what? You quit? After all of your high-handed statements to me about noble efforts and the good of the people?"

"Why do you always do that? Why do you always try to pick a fight?"

"I just couldn't resist. I'm sorry."

"Okay."

"I'm glad you're here; glad you can stay awhile. But be warned, I won't leave."

Min turned her back to him. "I'll talk you into it eventually."

"Min?" He walked up and stood behind her. When she didn't turn around, Josh pulled her around to face him. "Min, that isn't the only reason you came, was it?"

She seemed agitated by his closeness, but she didn't move away. Instead, she laid her face on his chest. "Damn you."

He lifted her face. As she tried to wipe away angry tears, he bent his head and kissed her. He put every ounce of his being into that kiss. It lasted so long, that she pulled away gasping for breath.

"I don't want to love you," she said, softly.

"I know."

"We have nothing in common."

"You don't think so?"

"Physical attraction, sure." She said the word as if it was distasteful. "I've seen how that dies. My brother was in love with his wife once."

"That doesn't always happen. Besides, we have more in common than that. We both want to change things."

"But we live in separate worlds. And, frankly, I can't see either of us changing."

"We can work it out, if we want to," Josh said, with conviction.

She looked up and mouthed his name. "Josh."

As he kissed her a second time, he felt the passion stir within her as well, responding to his body, to his arms.

A door opened behind them. "Now, this is no place for that."

Min broke away quickly and Josh turned around to see who had come in.

"Holly Zimmer, you shouldn't sneak up on people like that."

Her sharp eyes sparkled with unholy amusement. "Well, you go fooling around in my kitchen, and I will. Who is this? I hope you know her."

Josh turned to see Min's red cheeks. She recovered quickly, reaching out her hand. "I'm Yumin Villanueva. Min."

"I don't know her at all, Holly. I just picked her up off the road and started making passionate love to her."

"Oh, be quiet. Have you no consideration for this lovely lady. I'm Holly. Glad to meet you, Min. I hope you know what you've got there." She nodded her head towards Josh.

Min looked even more uncomfortable. "I'm not sure I have anything." She quickly turned the subject. "We must be in your way."

"Well, I have to start supper for this crowd, so, yes, you are in my way. Are you staying for a bit, Min?"

Min glanced at Josh, who shook his head in a silent *'no, I'm not leaving.'* "Yes," she said. "I'm staying for a while."

"Well, then. I'll see you for dinner. Now you two get out of here and let me work."

Josh and Min slipped out the back door, as Holly began pulling pans off her rack.

"Takin' some air?"

Min looked up, squinting through the sunlight. It was Holly. She joined Min on the limestone slab. "Yes. It's so beautiful here."

Holly slapped her hand on the stones beneath them. "What do you suppose these were for? They don't seem to lead anywhere, so I can't believe they were steps. This whole area all used to be some sort of recreational park, ya' know. But these here stepped walls on the lake shore...well, they don't make sense."

"I don't know. Maybe this was some sort of garden, but what besides trees and weeds would grow through this clay and stone, I couldn't guess."

"I don't figure this was clay a hundred and fifty years ago. You go a little farther south near New Hope Agristation, and you'll find plenty of good soil. Maybe it was like that back then."

"Josh says this place is good for the soul." Min looked up as Holly chuckled. "What's so funny?"

"That's what I told him when he first arrived." She focused her clear eyes on Min. "He was really troubled when he first came here. Were you part of it?"

"Troubled?" Min watched the small waves lap the shore. "He doesn't seem troubled now."

"That's why I asked if you were part of the reason. That, and the way you two were greeting each other. You know that he's in love with you, don't you." She didn't ask the question. She simple stated it.

"I know."

"But you don't know if you love him?"

"No." She looked back to Holly, who was smiling. "I mean, no, I don't know. Could we change the subject?"

"Sure. I'm sorry. I didn't mean to interfere. Just that I've taken a fancy to that boy. And I'm glad to see him happy."

Min decided that Holly was not being nosy. Still, she didn't want to talk about it. "How long have you lived here?"

"Well, since the place began – about four years. Back then, we all lived in that stone building. Plus it served as the hospital, meeting room, kitchen, well, just everything."

"That must have been inconvenient and cramped."

"We managed, but you're right; it was crowded. Now we have so many structures." Her attention was drawn to something on the ground. She reached down and picked up a tiny striped rock. "Looks like a heart, doesn't it."

"Yes. Or an arrow." Then Min realized that Holly was just teasing her. She burst out laughing. "Do you think I should wear it on my sleeve? Or should I just throw it at Josh's head?"

Holly slapped her leg. "Oh, that's good. You'll do him just fine."

The evening shadows claimed Alex's den, but he didn't activate the lights. He sat thinking about the afternoon he'd spent with Phill. Earlier, Alex had asked his system to expand the search. He'd wanted to include all of America's 20 Areas and go back another year.

When Phill had arrived, they'd sat staring at the numbers populating the screen, appalled at the number. This can't be the work of one individual.

Phill had used some medical search criteria on the original files and had applied it to the new data. There was no DNA relationships, no geographic birth connection, nothing that showed any pattern. After several hours, they still had nothing tangible.

Min had called and reported that she'd found Josh, but was having trouble convincing him to re-enter. She'd said she was going to stay a day or so and try to talk him into it. Phill had left shortly afterwards, saying he couldn't think anymore.

Alex finished off his whiskey and got up to get a refill. He'd had three already. He couldn't shake all those thousands of deaths. Horrifying. He took a large mouthful and it burned all the way down.

He was still there in the dark, when Karen came home. "What are you doing here in the dark?" She spoke to their I-VN and the room filled with light.

"Nothing. Just thinking?"

"You're still not considering that offer of professorship? I told you I won't think of relocating."

"You don't have to worry. I have turned it down."

Her face lit up. "You refused?"

"It's more like a postponement."

She gracefully lowered herself into a chair and crossed her arms. Her eyes became suspicious. "How long of a postponement?"

New House

He kept an even tone. "I don't know. Probably years."

Her mood reversed again; she apparently found great pleasure in his decision. "That's more like it. I'm glad your father convinced you it was the wrong decision. I know it wasn't anything I said."

"My father has never tried to force his opinion on me and he's not starting now. The decision was my own."

She got up and moved over to him. "Whatever. I'm pleased with your decision. It wasn't right for us."

"Wasn't right for you, you mean. Rest assured – we'll not move in the near future."

"Oh, Alex, it's just that I hate the thought of leaving my home." There was silk in every word.

He got up and moved to the door. He knew that tone and he didn't want her right now.

She followed him. "Don't rush away. Won't you stay a while?" She slipped her fingers inside his shirt and began stroking his chest. Her lips were next to his ear. "Alex?"

This must be my consolation prize for what she thinks is her victory. Suddenly, he couldn't stand her touch. He took a step back. "I'm tired. I'm going to bed." He didn't have to see her face to know that her false passion had turned to fury.

After dinner, Min walked with Josh along the lake's edge. It was very dark and the wind was blowing up some weather. They walked for a long time in silence, just listening to the water lap the land and the wind click in the tall grass. Then without a word, Josh pulled Min to him.

"I love you, Min."

Josh seemed aware of her feelings. "I'm not sure I want this either. It's just…oh, damn, Min. I've never felt like this before."

"It's just too fast, too much."

"So what are we going to do?"

"This," she whispered, her lips lightly pressing to his.

"But you just said…?"

"Shut up."

Josh's hands removed her top and let it drop to the ground. "Min..." His voice was deep and raspy.

She went down on her knees, pulling Josh down with her. They knelt there inches apart for a few seconds; then Josh reached out and began caressing her shoulders, kissing her face, her neck.

She felt urgency in him; part of her wanted to hurry as well, yet they took great care removing their clothes, as if, with each garment, they were discovering another secret about each other.

Finally, they fell back. She managed a "Josh" between kisses, and then gave into the passion with everything she possessed.

He was so gentle, yet exciting, a combination which Min had never experienced before. She had always felt self-conscious making love, but he released all of that in a spirit of pure enjoyment. After they had exhausted each other, they laid side by side quietly until they fell asleep. A chill drifting over Min's body woke her.

"Josh," she whispered. He stirred beside her. "Josh, I think we'd better go back. There's a storm coming." As if in confirmation to her statement, a flash of lightening lit up the sky, outlining tall thunderheads.

"I suppose." His voice told her that his passion was still close to the surface. He reached for her and they made love again. It was different this time but no less passionate. The storm broke as they were getting dressed, and they ran back to the settlement in the rain.

Don't come into the kitchen, you stupid bitches. The man pressed himself tightly against the wall behind the kitchen door. Sweat dripped off his face. The two women were still talking in the dining hall. They had come in for a cup of coffee, and had sat drinking it for almost a half hour.

"…well, I know it's crazy, but that's what she said."

"I can't believe it. What happened then? Did you let it drop?"

"Absolutely not, and wait – that wasn't all…"

He whispered a silent oath. She was still alive, but unconscious from the knock-out spray. It would keep her out for several hours, but he was counting on the slice in her arm to do the trick, allowing her blood to slowly drain away. Well, shit, these things took time. He hadn't expected anyone to come in so late.

"We can't leave the pot and cups for Holly," one woman was saying. "We'd never hear the end of it for messing up the kitchen."

"Oh, she'll carry on for a while but she doesn't mean it. I'm bushed. Just set the cups in the sink. I'll get here before her in the morning and clean up."

"Okay, I'm willing. It's been a long day."

The door suddenly swung open. He stilled his breath. Through the crack, he watched a woman move to the sink, using just the light from the main hall to guide her. He heard the water come on, cups clinking, water off...all the time the dispatch lying just feet away. The woman moved back into the main hall. Their voices faded.

He slipped from his hiding place and peered through the glass. They were walking across the clearing. He watched them until they were out of sight.

The close call had been nerve wracking, but it also had added a touch to an otherwise flat dispatch. He'd thought just doing another woman would satisfy him, but it hadn't worked out that way. He'd grabbed her from behind, holding her in the familiar way, increasing the pressure on her throat. Instead of struggling or crying, she'd just coughed and went limp. He'd checked her pulse. *Still alive. What gives?* Had he pressed too hard?

To make sure she'd stay out, he'd used his NR2; then had made a large slice in her arm just above the wrist and dropped the knife on the floor next to her. He'd stood looking down at her with an empty feeling. Then the other women had come.

New House

They were gone now, and it was time to go. He checked the dispatch again, then crossed the dim hall and walked cautiously through the door. His eyes quickly adjusted to the lack of light. The storm was over, but there were still too many clouds for the moon to penetrate. No one was in sight and he made his way quickly down the shore to the road.

10

Josh had propped his pillows up against the head of the bed, and ran his fingers lightly through Min's hair. She made him feel at peace. With her, the restlessness was gone; everything made sense.

Min had gone to her own cabin, but shortly after turning out his light, she had been at his door, whispering, "Josh, are you still awake?"

He had raised the blanket and she'd slipped in beside him. She'd been cold and he'd entwined his arms and legs with hers and they had fallen asleep. In the hours before dawn, their passion had rekindled. A wave of such pleasure and satisfaction swept through him, as he remembered the night.

Her head stirred under his hand and she rolled over to face him. "Good morning," she smiled. He bent down to kiss her, and at the same moment she started to sit up. Their heads knocked against each other. "That hurt," she said, rubbing the spot on her head.

"What a way to wake up."

"Just for that, I won't make love to you this morning."

"Is that a threat?" Josh grabbed her, seeking any ticklish spots.

She tried to squirm away, "Stop...stop..." she said through a fit of laughter.

"Shhh. Do you want to wake the entire settlement?"

"I can't...help it," she sighed, out of breath; then started giggling again. "Oh dear," she sighed again. Josh put his mouth over hers to quiet her, but bubbles of laughter leaked out in between kisses.

Suddenly the calm morning disintegrated. A piercing scream reverberated through the air. "What in the world?" Josh said as he rolled out of bed and went to the window. Several people were running.

"What's happening?" Min asked, pulling the blanket off as she stood.

"I don't know. Looks like something's happened at the dining hall. I'm going to see."

"I'm coming too."

They were both dressed and running across the compound within a minute. The screaming was definitely coming from the hall, but it had changed. Another voice, a man's...*Oh my God, my God, oh, no...*

Min and Josh converged with several people outside the kitchen door. Bob came stumbling out, all color drained from his face, his eyes wide with shock and horror. He was trying to support Jeannie Abbott, who was still screaming.

Bob looked blindly at the assembled crowd. "She's dead. My God, the blood. Oh, God. All the blood." Then he bent over the rail and emptied his stomach.

Josh shook Jeannie, "Stop it. Be quiet," but his words didn't penetrate. Min stepped in and slapped her across the face. It shocked Josh, but it was apparently what was needed, as Jeannie slumped to the ground, crying.

Bob still stood anchored to his spot, speaking in a monotone, "There was so much blood...so much..." Josh and several others squeezed through the door and went in.

Paul Cozens got to her first. He turned away, moaning, "Oh...no..."

Josh looked behind the counter. Lying on the floor, surrounded by a large reddish, brown puddle, was Holly Zimmer.

Alex was waiting in his living room for Lumen to arrive, but he wasn't thinking about his agent or his art. He'd just taken a call from Min. The killer was in Mount Bryson and had murdered again. Min had been sure of it.

"Oh, God, Alex. It's so awful. She was so..." Min had turned and reached out for someone. A dark man – maybe in his forties – had stepped close to her and wrapped her in his arms.

This must be Josh, Alex speculated, though no introductions were made. Min had shaken off her tears, continuing, "Holly had a cut on her arm, but there wasn't any evidence that she had been working, and so late? Everyone had gone to bed."

"Min," Alex had said, "come back in... please."

"I will, but I need to stay until after the funeral."

When they had disconnected, he wondered if Josh had agreed to help. Well, he couldn't worry about that now. He had checked the news services but nothing had been reported yet. He needed to tell Tami. Perhaps, if the S.F. got involved early, they'd be able to find something before the leads dried up. The limited investigations of the other cases had occurred long after evidence had disappeared.

Whatever this was, it was getting too close, too dangerous for Min to stay out there. He was standing, staring out of the plexipanel, beating himself up for not being more forceful with her, when his I-VN announced his visitor. He had asked Lumen to come and collect some completed paintings and sculptures.

"Hello, Lumen," Alex said, as the door opened.

"Good morning, my friend," his agent said grandly. "How are you, today?"

"I'm fine," Alex said, without much conviction.

"At your request, I have come to pick up more of your wonderful work." As Alex led him up the stairs to the studio, Lumen continued his prattle. "I have had the foresight to hire a vehicle to carry them back to my gallery."

"I hope you brought something larger than an electrocar. There are quite a few pieces."

"But this is wonderful, wonderful," his hands grabbed Alex's arm. "I am so thrilled you've gone back to work." They entered the studio and Lumen looked around. "My friend, this is most unexpected. You have so many. And they are superb. My friend, you have told me so often about your lack of inspiration. I was expecting something...perhaps...less than perfect?"

"I'm glad you like them. Will they sell?"

"Yes, yes. Of course. And sculptures, too. But they will have to be crated. I will send my assistant for them."

"I was also thinking – what about doing another exhibition?"

"An exhibition?" Lumen was surprised again. "Of course, of course. We could do another. It is not difficult to get buyers to loan their purchases for such a purpose."

He smiled weakly. "Actually, I was thinking that it would be nice to show my new work at the Roanoke Valley Center for the Arts. In the fall, perhaps? What do you think?"

Pleasure showed in Lumen Sandford's face. "I will contact Director Jenkins at once. This is wonderful." He was rubbing his hands together with enthusiasm. "I am sure the Director can fit you into their schedule. He will be so pleased. And you will have more new pieces?"

"I'll want to exhibit something new, yes." He could see Lumen's eyes searching for evidence of the 'new' art. "They aren't ready for showing; I'll show you some in a few weeks."

"But this is cause for celebration, my friend. It is not often that my favorite, but most reluctant client promises to participate in an exhibition." He looked like he expected Alex to change his mind.

Lumen was so absorbed in his future profits and fame; he didn't notice that Alex was far from in a celebrating mood.

Min sat leaning against Josh's chest, his arms comfortably encircling her.

When she and Alex had begun to look into the murders, they had seemed sinister, but distant. When he'd told her about the Wedmarks, she had been shocked, remembering people she'd met and liked. This time, however, it was real. It was in her mind and she couldn't shake it away. She'd seen Holly lying in her own blood, her skin gray and sickly under the tan, her body contorted in a strange angle. It was horrible.

Min turned slightly, watching Josh's face for a few moments. "I'm frightened," she said simply, when he glanced down at her.

"I heard you tell Alex that you were going to go back in."

"Yes. Tomorrow – after the funeral." She paused, brushing her hair from her forehead. "I want you to come with me."

Josh didn't say anything. He just looked off at some distant point on the horizon.

"Please."

He still didn't speak, but his expression was so distressed, she didn't press him further.

"I've been told to stop asking questions about this," Tami said, shaking her head.

Alex had been anxious to tell Tami about the latest news from Mount Bryson and had gone to her home. They were now sitting in her tiny living room, wondering what to do next.

"Then I guess there's no possibility that your captain will investigate this new one?"

"Not likely. She was adamant! Said I must stop all unauthorized investigations; not sure how she found out what I was doing. I was careful to use a scratch code with each search. No trace, you see," she explained, when Alex looked puzzled. "I even encoded all downloads, everything."

"Then how?"

"I've been thinking about that, and I don't like my conclusions. She said the order came from above, so maybe she isn't involved directly; I just can't be sure. Another possibility? Someone tapped into the Security Forces' system and discovered what I was doing. Either way, I can't use that route again."

"Is there anyone whom you can trust?"

"You," she said steadily, with a lopsided smile. "I can trust you."

"I was thinking of someone in the S.F.," Alex said.

"I know."

"Tami, you'd better drop this. I don't want to get you fired, and that's what will happen if you continue. Phill, Min and I can look into this."

Tami was clearly disgusted with Alex's suggestion. "What do you take me for? I thought we knew each other better than that. Besides, what can you possibly accomplish without me? Even though I can't check through normal channels, I still have some unofficial connections that I can use."

"Truthfully? I was hoping you'd say that. I just wanted to give you a way out."

"I know. But don't insult me again, okay?"

"Okay. But where do we go from here?"

"I want to go out to Mount Bryson today."

"What about your job?"

"I have a lot of leave coming. Want to come?"

"Min was coming back in with some man she thinks can help."

"Tell her to stay. We can all come back together."

"I'll call Phill. He might want to come, too."

"No, don't. The fewer people who know, the better."

Josh had roped off the dining hall and kitchen per the instructions from Min's brother. It wasn't difficult keeping people out; no one seemed interested in eating. Alex and his friend from the Security Forces had arrived just before lunch. The S.F. officer had brought some scanning equipment and had spent the better part of an hour in the building. She then walked across the compound and, scanning something on the ground, went toward the shore.

Josh, Alex and Min, as well as a small group of interested people, waited for her to return. She came back shortly, excitement on her face. She'd found something.

"What is it?" Alex asked what everyone was thinking.

"I'll have to analyze the information, but it is clear that someone was here, someone who was not part of this community. There are no prints, nothing except an accidental-looking death.

Except for one thing." She paused for effect, holding all their attention. "It rained last night, but the killer left after the storm. There are tracks."

"Yes, but..." Min said.

Josh couldn't see how that was much of a clue. "Those tracks could have been made by anyone."

"Well, yes, except they lead to a vehicle with a very state-of-the-art signature – even after so many hours I could still pick up the traces. So unless you people have been investing in dome technology, someone from inside killed your friend."

"Is it enough to get the S.F. involved?" Alex asked.

"I'm not sure. Let's get home so I can analyze the data I've collected."

"We can't leave yet." It was Min.

Josh wasn't sure she meant the funeral or his leaving with her, but he said, "Not until the funeral. Holly deserves that." It was clear Alex and his friend weren't going back without Min, so they, too stayed.

The community buried Holly Zimmer that afternoon in a light rain. As one of the men from the group said words over Holly's grave, Josh looked at the faces of the gathered crowd. There with the grief, was anger and fear. The killer is not just taking random lives. He's destroying communities.

It occurred to him that somewhere along the way, he had shifted from disbelief to acceptance. And a rage began to boil, one that was all the more violent because it had no target. He gripped Min's hand.

As they walked back to the settlement, Min turned to him. "Won't you come back and help? Don't you see it has to stop? Whoever is doing this – they have to be stopped. Maybe, between us, we can get some answers."

He walked on a few yards, then turned back to Min. "Yes," he said finally. "All right."

11

Ivan woke Min with the programmed intruder-alert message. Min first reaction was panic. "Location, Ivan?" she whispered.

"Living room, northeast corner."

Then Min noticed that Josh was not in bed. She got up, grabbing the coverlet from the foot, and went into the living room. He was standing by the window, looking out at the quiet street.

"Ivan, he's not an intruder. He's authorized; please recalibrate your sensors again."

Josh turned. "I'm sorry if I woke you."

"You didn't. Ivan thought you were an intruder."

"All the information you've gathered – you've been very thorough, but there's something eluding me. I've been going over and over what I've seen..."

She went up behind him and wrapped him in her blanket. "You're freezing." He turned around and she laid her head on his chest. "Did you come up with anything?"

"I'm not sure. I remembered thinking at Holly's funeral that the murderer was destroying more than the victims and their families. He or she is destroying communities. What if that's what they are trying to do?"

"Destroy preserver towns? Why do it that way? Why not use a bomb or something that would be more permanent. And why do it at all? Besides, people recover from death and disaster. In fact, people have a tendency to pull together, get stronger in the face of disaster."

"I don't know; it was just a thought. There is something else tying some of them...many were brassers – you know, respected leaders."

"I know the word."

"I'm not sure all of them were. I need to look at the files again."

"It still doesn't make sense." Min was feeling frustrated.

"Maybe I'm just grasping at straws, looking to make some sense."

"Well, let's not think about it anymore tonight. Come back to bed."

The next morning Alex looked at the strange group gathered around Min's table. In addition to Min, Tami, and Phill, was this tough outworlder, who softened when he looked at his sister. *Who would have thought?*

He then noticed something odd about the men on either side of Min. Phill and Josh were strikingly similar. There were the obvious differences – Phill was manicured, cultured and calm. Josh, on the other hand, was rough, a little shaggy, with an underlying edginess bordering on anger. Yet they were similar in height, weight, and mannerisms. Even their coloring and bone structure was close enough they could be mistaken for relatives. That might explain Min's attraction – she'd had a crush on Phill since they were kids. Min glanced up and saw Alex watching her. She wrinkled her nose at him and he laughed, but tabled his speculation.

During breakfast, Josh had been sharing some of his thoughts. He used words like "brassers" and "preservers" and other obscure terms, but the meaning was clear.

"This is all fine," Phill said, "but I don't see where it takes us."

"Well, it goes with something I was thinking earlier. What if the motivation is not to kill, but to create that fear?"

Phill asked, "But I ask again – why? To what purpose?"

Tami shook her head, "It's not tracking." She looked at Josh. "You know these communities. Would the whole group disband if their leaders were gone?"

"Well, no, probably not. But some of the weaker ones, the ones who were not totally committed, might abandon the life and go back in."

"Wait." Phill sat upright. "What if someone just *thought* Environs would return?"

"It would have to be someone who doesn't understand Preservers." Josh said, quietly changing Phill's word, *Environs*. "Most are truly committed."

"Who would benefit though?" Min chimed in. "I considered the social-reorganization companies might profit from such an influx, but then ruled them out. They're too competitive." Min looked at the surprise on Josh's face. "Yes, my dear skeptic, I didn't like the idea, but I thought about it."

Alex turned to Tami. "Tell him about your theory."

"Actually, it's a bit more than a theory now. After they told me to quit investigating, I became determined to know why. We have records of organizations that are always threatening to undermine the system with crashes, nano-viruses, some bomb threats to network and communications facilities...you know, terrorist-type activities. So far most are only threats; only a small number have ever actually carried them out."

Phill looked at her. "I've never heard about anything like that."

"No, you wouldn't. It is always quieted very quickly so people don't panic."

"How wide-spread is it?" Min poured more coffee all around.

"And how would any of these groups benefit if Preservers moved back into the domes?"

"I'm not sure, exactly. I do know there's a significant force behind them. One group, the Inner Council, is the most radical. Two other groups are fraternal; the most visible is the Silver Candle. However, that's just it. They're usually overt, and boast about their actions. Our killer goes out of his way to be invisible."

At the mention of the Candle, Alex's heart stopped. He remembered Angel had used that name, but he shook it off and listened as Tami continued. "I asked a retired S.F. friend what he knew about these groups. He gave me some ideas and made a list of people he knew were members. He, too, dismissed the Inner Council."

"The Candle is known outside," Josh stated. "They appear to do a lot of good works, but my grandfather told me tales about them when I was growing up. I couldn't relate back then, but a few years ago, I met a guy who was an ex-member. He had questioned their activities, and eventually went into hiding. He was reluctant to give details, but it was clear that he feared for his family's safety."

Again Alex went back to his conversation with Angel. "Does the Candle operate only on the outside? Or do they recruit members inside as well?"

"From what I hear, the Candle is everywhere, but mostly Scav-class." Tami glanced at Josh. "Sorry. The lower class is most vulnerable to their tactics. Stands to reason. They are mostly descendants from twenty-first century financiers, corporate executives, lawyers, a few politicians – families who used to control society. The 'Silver' refers to titanium which used to back their money base and 'Candle' refers to the light they have promised to keep burning."

Min sat shaking her head. "This is all good, but it still doesn't answer the why."

"Has your I-VN been recording this?" Tami asked.

Min smiled. "Yes. I thought it would be a good idea."

"Monitor, give me a copy." Alex said.

"Authorization for that voice print has expired," responded Min's over-efficient system.

"Good God. I see what you mean about your I-VN."

Min just smiled. "Ivan, please make a copy of the recording, and send it to Alex's home system."

"No!" Tami said quickly. "Don't send it over the network."

"Oh, all right," Min said, puzzled. "Ivan, download copies for all present, and process authorizations for everyone. Don't remove them until I tell you to."

Tami looked around at the group. "We all should take our systems off the network."

Everyone was quiet. One just didn't disconnect from the system! The dome's life-blood was the system.

Tami answered the questioning silence, "Whoever accosted you in the station, Alex, did it right after you visited your friend. I was told to stop investigating after I did a deep-search. Whoever is behind this is getting their information very quickly, so obviously the core of this thing isn't outside, but here. I'd just as soon not alert them that we are still investigating."

"We can't just stop our network connections," Phill said, somewhat irritated by Tami's idea.

"Well, at least go off line while we're discussing all this, and don't send any messages over the system without encrypting them."

"That makes sense," Min agreed. "Ivan, please go off line, now."

"You will lose all network links and alerts, if you choose to go off line," Ivan responded.

"Yes, I understand. Do it."

Josh was at the Maglev station entrance, but paused before going in. He'd made up his mind to visit his family, but now he was having second thoughts. He stood indecisively for several minutes. *Oh, hell, I might as well do this.*

The train slowed for Knightdale Station and a short walk brought him to the old neighborhood. Modernized sections enveloped entire streets, making the older buildings scars on the landscape. A strip shopping mall had given way to large sterile condominium buildings, but further on a faded sign indicated the entrance to Cameroon subdivision. There it was – the apartment building where he'd grown up. He pressed the comlink next to his father's name.

"Yes, what..." then his mother saw who it was. "Joshua?" She turned to speak to someone behind her, "Its Joshua. Oh, my dear God. It is really you."

Then he recognized his father's voice in the background. "For heaven's sake. System, release the door."

Before he could get to the second-floor, his mother was in the hallway. She rushed towards him with open arms, tears running down her face. "Oh, you're back. You're back," she kept repeating. She hugged him, and almost dragged him through the doorway. "Well, here he is," she announced.

Josh took his father's outstretched hand. "Hi, Dad."

Albert Robertson smiled, but Josh caught his glistening eyes, before he turned away with embarrassment.

Josh felt exposed and stupid, as he looked around the room at the small group of strangers, most he figured must be relatives.

The one person he did recognize was his grandfather, who sat in the corner, quietly beaming at him. "Mike," he said heading straight for his chair. "How are you, old man?"

"Not so old that I'll let you address me like that," he said sternly, but his eyes belied his tone. "Sit down."

"No, no, no. I know you two," said his mother, as she pulled Josh toward the big room. "He comes first and says hi to some of the family; then you can huddle down for one of your talks."

Josh turned to the group. It was almost comical – they hadn't moved. And they were all very quiet, as if no one knew what to say or do.

"Well, it's nice to see you all again."

A collective sigh, then a young woman, he guessed to be his cousin, said, "Well, that certainly sounded sincere."

"Oh, my, Denise, you say such things," said his mother on a false laugh.

"Well, Aunt Chrys, you can't make me believe he's happy to see us. He looks more like he's in pain."

For the next few hours he did endure a painful experience. He sat and talked with people, who recalled events that he hadn't shared. He said all the right words to his twin sisters, who just 'happen to drop by' with their families – but who, he knew, were summoned by his mother. Eventually, he got a few moments to speak privately with Mike.

"Still not one for family gatherings, I see," he said as Josh pulled a chair close to his.

"No, guess not. Besides, it's been so long that…geez, Mike. I don't know any of these people. They talk to me like I should know them and care about their lives, but how can I?"

"They're family, Joshua. The only permanence in your life is family – something that will always be there, whatever you do. I was never able to make you realize that." He lifted a thin, wrinkled hand to his forehead.

"Mike, they've only come because Mother called."

"There is that, of course, but you would not believe how many times we talk about you, wonder what you are doing and wish you'd come to visit."

"Oh, yes. If they miss me so much, why have I never received one communication from them? You can't fool me about family. They've come because they are curious or fear what Mother will do if they don't. Or worse, to make themselves feel noble."

"Oh, my boy, you sound so bitter. Tell me. What have you been doing all these years?"

Josh shared with him some of the exciting things he'd seen, the places he'd visited, his adventures. With each question from Mike, though, he imagined he could see disappointment. "Mike, I'm sorry."

"For what?"

"For not living up to what you wanted me to be."

"Crap! I only want you to learn something from your life. Not waste away, like the rest of us. From what I here, you did that."

Just then his mother announced dinner, so further conversation was not possible. As the last of the dishes were being cleared away, Josh rose to leave.

There was the expected "Oh, no, not yet," from his mother. And then there were questions about where he was staying. To these he gave a glib explanation. How could he explain Yumin Villanueva? His mother hung wispily on him all the way to the door. He looked around for Mike but didn't see him. He peeled his mother from his arm and took his father's hands in his, "Good to see you again."

His father's eyes and the tightened grip on Josh's hands, said that his father understood. "I know. Take care."

He gratefully slipped away, regretting only that he hadn't said good-bye to Mike. Then, on the other hand, what would he have said?

When he boarded the train, he found himself in turmoil. He didn't have anything in common with most of those people, except for Mike and his father. If only he could bring them along when he exited.

It was late by the time he arrived at Min's stop. He had just got off the train, still deep in thought, when he sensed, rather than heard, someone behind him. Before he could turn, something hit the side of his head. As he collapsed to the ground, a second blow landed on the side of his neck. He was only vaguely aware of the continued attack as he faded into a well of blackness.

12

Josh heard voices.

"Is he dead?"

"No. I didn't hurt him that much."

"We were told not to kill him. Remember? Why'd you kick him like that?"

"I don't know. I can't stand Scavs. Grew up with them. They were everywhere in my neighborhood."

"Check on him. Make sure he's breathing."

Someone leaned close. Josh could smell his breath, reeking of onions and coffee. "You awake?" Bad Breath poked at Josh's shoulder and a sharp pain shot through his body. Josh started to say something, but it came out only as a moan. It seemed as if his mouth was full of wool.

Bad Breath grumbled, "He's okay. Now what?"

The other voice said, "We're supposed to drop him at some exit portal."

"How do we know he'll leave?"

"I could give a damn. Just following orders. Do the same, will ya? Help me get him into the baggage locker."

Hands started to lift him and the pain shot through every part of his body.

Josh heard a far off voice, "Hey, you. What are you doing?"

"Shit. What now?" The hands tried to drag him.

"You...stop that. Leave him alone. Mac, get some help."

"He ain't worth it. Let's just him," Bad Breath.

There was hesitation with the other one. "Ok. Get in."

A hover engine started and faded; then Josh was aware of quiet. *Quiet is nice.* His head hurt. He tried to get up but found he couldn't move properly. Couldn't even open his eyes.

Hands started poking and pulling at him, carrying him out of the alley. The pain in his shoulder became unbearable and darkness claimed him again.

"Where are you?"

The voice from the man's RIC was high-pitched and tight.

"It's not important where I am," the man responded coldly. "What do you want?"

"There is interest in what you are doing. Too much and from the wrong quarters. I don't know...maybe you should..."

"Are you terminating the contract?" the man asked.

"No...I mean, I don't know. We didn't count on all this. We're trying to deter them, but we're not sure it will work. What's worse, we aren't getting the results we wanted. So many have been done and the numbers are still quite low. We anticipated nearly ten times that many re-entering by now. It will ruin everything..." The voice stopped.

"I don't really care, but if you want more response, I'll have to use other methods."

"We were hoping to not..." A pause. "...might have to," he was saying, almost to himself.

"Are the S.F. getting involved? You said there were no investigations; that they were all closed as accidents."

"Yes, I mean, no. The S.F. aren't formally involved. Just some individuals, but ones with influence."

"Private individuals – are they something you need help with?" he said, liking the idea of returning to the domes.

"No...no. I said...we are taking care of them. You just concentrate on getting the numbers up. Do whatever you have to. We still have several weeks. Just get the job done."

When the connection was broken, the man leaned back and smiled. *More fear? That I can handle. Fear is my strong suit.*

Min was starting to get worried. It was 10:00 p.m. and Josh still wasn't back. He'd refused the RIC she'd offered, so her only option was to see if he'd used his COPI. Reluctantly, she reconnected to the network and did an immediate trace. Nothing.

She put in a connection to Josh's parents. She had resisted contacting them, as she knew it was going to be an odd call.

Josh's father scrutinized her face, apparently trying to discover why this reorganizer would be calling so late, and how she knew his son had re-entered. She passed it off glibly with 'just closing out my report and doing a Company following up' and closing the communication as soon as she could. Yet she'd learned what she needed. He'd left around their house around 8:30 p.m.

Just as she disengaged the call, she noticed her message light. "Ivan, when did that message come in?"

"Because you have been off line," Ivan announced, "the message is forty-seven minutes old." Her system sounded almost defensive.

"Why didn't you announce it? Who's it from, Ivan?" She was thinking Josh, maybe?

"There is no routing address, nor is the message signed. It is text only. Should I display it?"

"Yes, please." It must be Josh, she reasoned. Then she read message with renewed misgivings.

"Now that your Scav friend has returned to his world, you no longer have a need to mess with things that do not concern you."

She sat there, feeling foolish, wondering if Josh had really exited, as the message implied. She didn't like to admit she really didn't know him that well.

Another hour. "Ivan, try again."

Ivan returned, "I presume you mean you want me to place another trace on Joshua Robertson?"

She sighed. "Yes, Ivan, please."

"Negative results," her overly sensitive system responded.

She had Ivan make some more coffee and she waited.

Josh woke up. That was some nightmare, he thought. He started to rub his eyes, but his right arm was stiff and heavy. He raised his left hand to rub away sleep and found his face tender and swollen. Then he remembered that it hadn't been a dream. He tried to focus on his surroundings. He was in a hospital ward. His right arm and shoulder immobilized in a hard, clear substance. He couldn't get a deep breath, and he could feel some type of patch on his head, just behind his ear.

He vaguely remembered two men – *had it been only two* – the attack. He didn't remember much after he fell.

How long has it's been? Josh looked around for the communication panel.

Just then, a nurse appeared. "Our monitors indicated you were awake. How are you doing?" She was looking at the console over his bed.

He opened his mouth to speak, but his jaw hurt. When he found his voice, he didn't recognize it. "You tell me."

"You underwent laser-fusion on your collarbone, arm, jaw, and three ribs. In addition, you have a concussion, a large gash on the side of your head and extensive contusions." The nurse seemed to be reciting the information. "You'll survive, but you'll be very sore for a few days. Do you know who you are?"

"Of course."

"Well, after a concussion like you sustained, it's common for a little confusion and memory loss. Can you give me your name and address, then, for the records?"

He wondered why they hadn't gotten the information from his palm COPI. Then, after so many years without activity, it probably had been archived, even deleted. "Joshua Robertson." Then he hesitated. Did he give Min's address or his parents? "My dome address is temporary. I'm staying with Yumin Villanueva – I forget the number."

The nurse reacted to Min's name and her tone changed immediately. "Oh, my! Let me call the doctor." She activated the comlink and asked for a Dr. Ben-Dhari. "Our John Doe is awake," she said when the doctor answered. "I think you should come around and talk to him." She turned back to Josh. "He'll be here in a minute."

Josh was aware that with the mention of Min, his status changed. He wondered if that was why he chose her over his parents; then dismissed the idea. He hadn't wanted his parents to come to his aid.

"What did the S.F. say?," Josh asked. "Who did this, do they know?"

"The S.F.? We didn't report anything, yet. We suspected, because of your clothes, that you might not be a Scav. But Scavs brought you in, so we couldn't be sure." Josh was surprised at her casual attitude. "I will call them now."

"Could you call Tami Donaldson, Piedmont Heights S.F.?"

"Of course," she said as she hurriedly left the room.

Min had been watching the time click away for what seemed like hours, but in reality, it was just under an hour and a half. She finally made up her mind. Josh wouldn't leave; of that, she was sure. And that odd message...now it seemed more sinister; almost like Alex's veiled warning at the station when this all started. She had her system contact Alex, hoping he, too, had reconnected. He hadn't. However, she knew a way to force an emergency alert, which would bring his system back online. She said the commands, which made her system activate one.

When he answered, he was standing in his kitchen, disheveled and sleepy looking. "What's up? I thought my system was off. How did you get...?"

"Forget how I got through. Alex, he's not back yet."

"What do you mean? Who's not back?"

"Josh. He should have been here hours ago. He left his parents sometime after eight, and he's still not back."

"Hold on a minute. I've an emergency message."

"I think I might know what it says, but go ahead and receive it." She waited while he read the obvious text-only message. When he looked up and she saw his eyes, she knew he'd received the same message.

"What on earth?" Alex was now wide-awake. "You mean, you received one of these, too?"

Min nodded, running her fingers frantically through her hair, "What's going on, Alex?"

"I don't know. Min, do you think Josh would leave the domes without saying something?"

New House

"No," Min said, positively. "I've been sitting here thinking about that, and no," she said again. "He wouldn't. Not without telling me.

"Do you want me to come over and wait with you?"

"Would you?"

Alex arrived just a half hour later, and his calm manner reassured her somewhat. But at 4:00 a.m., she and Alex nearly jumped out of their skins, when Ivan announced another incoming message.

"He's where?"

"Rex-Med University Hospital," said blue-clad nurse at the other end. "He is awake and asking for you."

"Oh, yes. I'll come right away. Please call Dr. Phill Chauquette?"

"Dr. Chauquette is not here at this hour. Besides, he does not treat patients," said the superior-acting woman.

"Please call him."

"Ms. Villanueva, I'm not sure I should…"

"Just do it," Min snapped. "I'll be there shortly."

She looked at Alex. He said, "Let's go."

Josh must have dozed for a while, because he opened his eyes and a doctor was standing over him. "Hello, Mr. Robertson. I'm Dr. Ben-Dhari" he said, checking the monitor. "It looks like you are coming along fine."

"I don't feel fine," Josh croaked.

"I can understand that. You were in quite a state when you were brought in. We are moving you to a private room; you should be more comfortable there." He unclamped and removed the clear cast from his right arm and began checking his handiwork. Josh cringed as he probed the shoulder and arm. "Sorry. I need to make sure the bones are completely fused. The muscles will take a bit longer to heal." By the time the doctor had finished the examination, Josh was sweating.

The nurse came back and said Lt. Donaldson was on her way, as well as Ms. Villanueva. At the mention of Min's name, the doctor stiffened, and the nurse's eyes watched the doctor closely.

"You're doing well enough," the doctor said. "I need to file a report," he said, and left.

The nurse watched him go and turned back to Josh. "He doesn't want to be here when Ms. Villanueva arrives. I think they had a tiff or something. I haven't seen her here in a long while."

Josh was curious, but didn't pursue it. "What time is it?" he asked.

"0338. You were brought in about 2200 – that's 10:00 p.m.," she explained, as if he were stupid. "You came out of surgery at 0200." She fussed over the coverlet a minute or two, as if she wanted to ask something, but then apparently decided against it. "The doctor wants you to rest," she said, as she gave him a hypo spray. "This will keep you quiet for a couple hours."

A soft gray fog filled his thoughts and he drifted into a deep, yet troubled sleep.

Josh could hear Min; she seemed a long way off. "Josh? It's me, Min."

The haze in his brain made it impossible for him to focus clearly on anything, and he pictured her first on a shore, then in a field, then in her condo. "Josh," she kept saying, "it's Min. Wake up."

At last, he forced his way through the drugs and opened his eyes. She was standing over him, relief sweeping across her face. He tried to smile, but his face was too stiff.

"Hi," he murmured. "Did they wake you?"

"Are you nuts? I was going out of my mine."

Again, he tried to smile, achieving a little more success this time. "I, on the other hand, was having a great dream." Josh turned his head to see Alex and Tami Donaldson standing on the other side.

"How are you doing?" Alex asked.

"Better than a few hours ago," as took notice of his private room. He now had a comfortable seating area, a vidscreen, plants and a window. Through a glass wall, he could see the nurse's station.

Tami was a bit more official. "Do you feel like talking? I'd like to contact the locals with some info."

"I don't remember much. They attacked me at the Maglev just as I got off. Two men, I think."

"Did you see either man?"

"No. It happened too fast. They came out of nowhere. I guess they must have been following me." Josh let out a heavy sigh, which made him wince.

"Tami, that's enough," Min said letting go of his hand, only to touch his brow. "We need to let him sleep."

"I guess that's all for now. It's not much, but I'll contact the local S.F. office. If you remember anything else, let me know."

Josh wasn't ready to sleep, though. "Tami, do you know they weren't going to notify the S.F. I guess some homeless people brought me in, and they just assumed I was with them. Does this happen all the time in here?"

Tami looked embarrassed. "I'm afraid it does. Scavs are always getting injured or worse and it's more than the Security Forces can do to keep up with it. Mostly, the techno-medics just fix them up and turn them loose."

Just then, Phill appeared in the doorway. "May I come in?" he asked.

Min walked over and hugged him. "Please. I know the doctors here are efficient, but I want you to check him over and tell me the truth."

"I don't really do everyday physician's work, you know. But I'll check their data."

Phill picked up the nearby diagnostic unit and ran it over Josh, then looked at the readout. "Everything looks normal." He touched Josh's shoulder.

"Don't do that," Josh snapped, as the pain grabbed him. "That other doctor and the nurses have poked me enough. I'll be okay," he said to Min, as she reached out for his hand.

Phill looked concerned. "Do you need another pain treatment?"

"It couldn't hurt," Josh said, oblivious to the pun. Tami, Alex and Phill broke out laughing. When Josh realized what he'd said, he started to laugh, which turned quickly to a groan. *Oh, don't laugh, Josh.*

Min had been trying to sleep in Josh's hospital room recliner, but she couldn't relax. Seeing Josh battered and weak had really shaken her. She was also surprised at the depth of her feelings. He was sleeping now, but fitfully and occasionally murmuring something.

The hospital was quiet. She again leaned her head back, pulling the gray hospital blanket around her shoulders and closing her eyes. She must have drifted off because she became aware that someone was in the room. A moment of panic grabbed her until she remembered the private guard Tami had positioned outside the door. She opened her eyes and saw Asa.

He was just standing over Josh looking down at him. She started to speak, but instead partially shut her eyes so she could watch him. It was strange to see them together. Asa was by far the better looking with dark eyes and curly black hair. He looked very distinguished in his bright blue lab coat. She looked at Josh, bruised, tousled and with a day's growth. No comparison.

Asa suddenly seemed aware of her eyes and turned to her.

"You're awake." No question, but a simple statement. "He's doing fine." He'd lost his possessive assurance; he was awkward. She couldn't really blame him. He'd been so positive about their relationship; it must have come as a blow when he realized where Josh was staying.

"Thank you, Asa. You've been very good in arranging everything."

"Well, I have some other duties to attend to. If you'll excuse me."

"Yes. You can leave him in my hands."

When the glass door sealed with a click, Josh murmured, "Oh, Lord, I'm doomed." He opened his eyes and she forgot all about Asa.

The next day the same group, who only days earlier, were in Min's condo, were now comfortably ensconced in Alex's den. Josh, stretched out on the thick sofa, seemed surprisingly fit for having been so immobile just a day earlier. Alex found Josh an interesting man, but he never expected someone like this to appeal to Min. She seemed softer, more pliable.

"So where do we go from here?" asked Josh. He'd remembered more from the attack, of waking up and hearing bits of a conversation. *"...isn't dead..." "...told not to kill him..." "...dropping him at an exit..." "Leave him..."* His memory was returning but it was sketchy. One thing was clear – they hadn't wanted him dead, just out of the way.

Phill said, "I suggest we turn everything over to the Security Forces and let them run with it."

"That would be okay with me," said Josh, showing discomfort, as he shifted his position.

Tami gathered up another sandwich, and plopped into a comfortable chair. "It would be the logical way to go," she said, wiping away bits of rye and ham. "Except that I can tell you the S.F., for some reason, aren't investigating anything. I turned my report over to the locals, who at first showed interest. This morning I was told that it will be listed as just another mugging."

"What?" Min said, jumping up. "What's the matter with them? It's clear that it wasn't a mugging, especially with those strange warnings that Alex and I received."

"Don't bite at me. I'm just telling you what I was told."

"Is it because I'm an outsider?" Josh didn't seem to be offended by the idea, but Min clearly was.

"It couldn't be that. They wouldn't!" she said, her voice raising an octave.

Phill walked over to Min, laying a hand on her shoulder. "Min, I don't think that's what Tami's saying."

"I'm saying that someone high up is blocking every attempt to get into this. I had my suspicions before, but this confirms it."

"So what do we do?" Phill asked.

"I say we finish what we started..." Alex said, sipping his drink. He looked around at the group; they were all starring at him. "Let's just finish our investigation."

Tami smiled at the suggestion.

Alex went on, "We have all we need right here – Security Forces contact, medical expert, outworlder experience, and systems expert."

"And what are you bringing to the team, my dear brother?" Min said with a jab at his stomach.

"Whatever is needed. For now, I'll make some more sandwiches."

"And second, you can bring up that report." Tami said, putting the last bit into her mouth. "Wait, I'll help you. I'm still hungry." Tami followed Alex into the kitchen, "Alex, what's with Min? I've never seen her like this. Is she in love with that guy?"

"Love? Min?" Then he realized that was a close description. "I guess. All I know is that since her first trip outside, she's been acting weird."

"He's seems nice."

"Yes, but my folks will erupt," Alex said with a grin.

They both laughed, but Alex was dreading what his family would say about Min's new love.

Just as the man expected, they needed him to deal with the problems inside. They gave him the target's name.

"I thought you were handling this nuisance factor?" the man asked. He had no trouble with this deviation, but he wouldn't let them know – he liked them thinking he was unwilling. It made it easier to plump the contract.

"It didn't work; the job was interrupted. We've decided that he needs to be eliminated."

"Is the original contract terminated?"

"Of course not; this is just a little deviation. We'll pay you extra, of course. Once this person is out of the way, you can re-exit."

"Whatever you say. But I want triple for this new dispatch."

"Triple? You're kidding"

"It's that or I don't do it."

"Okay. Make it quick, then, and, if possible, accidental."

"Quick and accidental aren't always possible. Accidents take time."

He tapped off his RIC without a word. *Stupid jerks.* The triple bonus would make the trip worthwhile, he thought, as he checked the Maglev schedules to The Triangle.

13

Alex's mother was busy, getting ready for her World Senate rotation. Her assistants were fussing around trying to look busy, yet succeeding only in getting in the way. Alex watched from a comfortable chair across the room, waiting for a break when they could talk. He sipped his coffee and rehearsed what he wanted to say. Robert, her chief assistant, was holding a RIC pad and trying to get her to sign the document.

"Yes, yes," his mother was saying. "I'll deal with that later. Now, leave please. I want to talk to my son."

As if being pulled by an invisible rope, the assistants withdrew. His mother stood, smoothing out her skirt and twisting her back slightly. "What a day. Those three will drive me insane one day. Would you like more coffee?"

"No, I'm fine."

"Robert," her voice rose barely above normal, but Robert suddenly appeared on the scene.

"Yes, ma'am?"

"Please get me some hot tea – then I don't want to be disturbed."

"Certainly." He disappeared.

"So what's on your mind?" She sat down opposite him.

"I started telling you and father about it the other night."

"Oh, Alex. You're not still trying to solve Dr. Jenkin's son's death?"

"It's more than..." he started, but was interrupted by a girl bringing in the tea.

"Thank you, Phoebe. We don't want to be disturbed."

Alex waited for the door to close, then said, "Mother, please listen to what I have to say before you interrupt."

She leaned on her hand lightly, saying, "All right. I'm listening."

"We have a problem and I'd like a little advice on how to proceed."

"First, before you go any farther, tell me who the 'we' are. There are others besides Min?"

"Yes, Phill is helping and so is my friend, Tami." Alex had decided it was not the time to mention Josh; this was complicated enough. He decided to pose a question – a trick he'd learn from his father. "What would you say if I told you we've discovered conspiracy to murder outworlders?"

Margarite Villanueva's face held a mixture of surprise and interest. "Go on."

"As I said earlier, I first got involved when I learned about Buddy Jenkins."

"But what has Buddy to do with outworlder plots?"

"He left the domes to live outside as an Environ. His death was reported as an accidental fall, yet Jerry Ray was – is convinced he was murdered. My visit to Jerry Ray was disturbing to say the least; he talked at some lengths about other deaths, of conspiracies…well, I was curious and had my system do a search on Environ deaths."

"Alex, why on earth would you listen to the rantings of an aggrieved father?"

"It wasn't just that. Min, on her recent trip outside, also learned many of the same things. She didn't pay much attention until someone she had met out there was also 'accidentally' killed." Alex was leaving huge gaps in his story, to be filled in later, if needed. He first just wanted his mother to listen and take him seriously.

His mother held her saucer in one hand and took a sip of her tea. Then very slowly put the tea down, stood and walked to the window. "I'm not sure what you want me to do."

"Ask around, find out if the S.F. are hiding something; ask some of your colleagues about possible investigations into subversive groups."

"Alex, be realistic. If there is an investigation going on, it will be confidential and whatever I learn, I won't be able to share with you."

"Oh, I suppose I knew that, except I was hoping…"

"Alex, what you are doing is very dangerous. You are in way over your head. My advice is the same as before. Drop it. If there is something going on, whoever is doing it, will not appreciate you're meddling." She turned to face him. "Please, Alex, give this up before one of you gets hurt. Let the officials handle it."

"But the officials aren't doing anything. Most cases are closed like Buddy's. Either they don't want to solve outworlders' deaths, or they can't be bothered or someone high up is stopping them."

"I don't believe there's corruption in the Security Forces. You must know how hard it is to investigate anything outside the system. They live in a very dangerous environment; one expects violence. However, if you insist on pursuing this fool's game, look to some of these subversive groups." She got up and went over to her desk. "Security, Margarite V," she spoke, then laid her hand on a scanner imbedded in the surface. A small safe opened on the side of the desk, and she pulled an electronic pad from it. She handed the pad to Alex. "This doesn't leave this room, you understand?"

Alex nodded and read. The report contained details on several different groups that were under investigation. As he tapped through the report, he saw lists of people suspected of belonging to one or more of the groups, plus incidents that either they acknowledged or that were attributed to them. The incidents included explosions, Maglev derailments, power shutdowns, and the worst – system infiltration and manipulation. "I never dreamed…" he looked up and saw his mother watching him carefully. "Why don't we hear about this? I read the news everyday and have never…"

"Alex, do you know how fragile our society is? I don't think you do. I can't tell you everything; but I want you to be careful. These groups are very determined and dangerous."

"But what would such a group have to gain by killing Environs? Outworlders seem to be aligned with their thinking."

"Most of these groups don't care who they hurt; their goal is to stir up trouble. And, unfortunately, someone close just might..." she left her sentence hanging, allowing her anger to show.

"Who...?" Alex started to say, but he knew she was referring to Angel. "Do you think he's in deeper than any of us know?"

"Lately, you know him better than I do." His mother gracefully moved around the room, touching objects, picking them up, setting them down. "Who do you think has gotten to him?"

"I don't know. He really doesn't talk to any of us."

A furrow pinched her brows. "I have a few ideas. My best guess would be that annoying Silver Candle. If I had to look somewhere for a conspiracy, that's where I'd start." She took the pad and returned to her safe. Then she faced her son again. "Alex, I don't demand anything from you. I believe you have to make your own decisions. But, just this once – for me – please drop this."

Alex wasn't sure what to say. His mother never asked him anything before. He wondered vaguely what she would say about the warning and the attack, or if she saw the information they'd compiled? Would she see the need to continue? Would she include some of their data in her report to the Senate?

"What are you thinking?" His mother had been standing quietly watching him.

"Just that you're probably right. I'm sorry I bothered you."

"It's no bother. System, please send Robert back in." She settled back into her desk chair. "When is your next exhibit? I hear that you have quite a number of new pieces."

He vaguely wondered how she knew he had new pieces. "Yes, I have finished some; Lumen wants another exhibit soon."

Robert came in, "Yes, ma'am?"

"Please cancel my appointments for the remainder of the day."

"But ma'am..." he began.

"Robert," she smiled, with a note of finality, "You know there is nothing important on my calendar. And tell the kitchen that Alex is staying for dinner."

"No, Mother, I can't. Thanks,"

"Very well, but will you go for a walk with me?"

He gave into her gentle command, and spent the next hour walking in the gardens, discussing his art career.

On the way home, he thought about what he'd read. At first, she'd dismissed the idea of outworlder plots; but when he pressed, she'd revealed her information on subversive groups. That was a real admission. Perhaps, she feared her children's involvement would weaken her position in the World Senate. That was a very real possibility. He wished she'd been able to talk more about what she was doing. He was also comforted to know she, too, was worried about Angel. He resolved to call his brother soon. Tomorrow. He'd call Angel tomorrow.

The man had waited by the run-down apartment complex for nearly a day. This place was perfect for a staged accident. However, a whole day and night went by and the target was still a no-show. He checked the address for a second time. It was correct. He'd just have to wait.

After another day, it was clear that he wasn't coming. He activated his RIC and looked up the alternate address his client had given him. *Well, that's a switch. This Scav has really moved up from his roots.* He went to the Maglev and checked the schedule for Piedmont Heights.

"Does anyone here think we're crazy?" Phill had gone to the bar, and had stopped mid-action, turning to the group.

Min had been thinking that very thought for the past hour. They had reconvened at Alex's house, but after hours of working, still didn't know what they were doing or how they should proceed. They had sorted all of the data every possible way. The current list was by date and Alex had his system connect the incidents in order. It revealed a jagged, yet identifiable trail – but one that got them no closer.

"I've been willing to go along with this because you all felt so strongly. Yet it's crazy to think we can do anything. Tami can't even use the S.F. system any longer for fear of detection."

They were all quiet for a few moments.

It was Josh, who finally broke the silence. He was walking around, testing his stiffness, "I know I was the last to believe in what you were all doing. Min had to drag me forcibly back in to face this. But now I feel something horrible is happening and I need to do everything I can to stop it."

"Me too," Alex said, telling his system to dim the screen, "but if you feel you need to leave, Phill, no one will think badly of you."

"Oh, I'm not quitting. I just wanted us to think about what we're getting into. Look at what happened to Josh." He took his drink and sat back down, showing his willingness to stay. "We need to think about each step very carefully."

"I can't agree more," Tami said.

"What we need is something drastic." Josh said it quietly, as if the thought had just formed and he was trying it out.

"Like what, Josh?" Min asked.

"I think we need to set a trap."

"A trap? What would we use for bait?" Tami was clearly interested.

"A Preserver. One who is trying to make a lot of trouble for whoever is doing this." Josh looked around the room, smiling.

"Oh, really?" Min asked sarcastically. "Well, I won't let you. Tami, this is stupid."

"Josh, I think the idea of a trap is good, but I can't let you do this. I can get some of my fellow officers on this. Some I trust."

"Tami, think about it," Josh argued. "This killer is very smart. He won't trick easily. He must have studied the victims, learned their habits. You can't just put in a Security Force officer and expect him to take the bait."

"Now *this* is crazy." Min said.

The issue was debated for another hour, nothing concrete coming out of the conversation. Tami said she would call in some favors and they would get something worked out. Tomorrow morning, she said, as she left. Phill, too, had to get home, and Alex's kids were due.

Min and Josh, at Alex prompting, stayed for dinner. Min noticed that they didn't wait for Karen. She was going to ask Alex about it, but decided against it. Throughout the meal, AnneJuleé kept eyeing Josh, and finally curiosity got the better of her.

"Who *are* you?" she asked in her innocent way.

Alex sighed, "I told you, honey. His name is Josh and he's a friend of Aunt Min's."

"Yes, but who are you? Where do you live? You talk funny."

Min and Alex glanced at each other, but Josh answered. "AnneJuleé, I live outside the domes. You could call me a historian. I'm..."

James' fork clattered loudly onto his plate and he eyed Josh, disgustedly. "Oh, God, you're a *Scav*."

"James!" Alex was outraged.

"I'm a Preserver," Josh continued as if he hadn't been interrupted. "That's what we call ourselves, because we preserve old ways."

"Oh, that's nice," AnneJuleé said, satisfied. "I'm glad you came for dinner."

It was clear that James wasn't. He sat sullenly staring at his plate. Min was surprised at her nephew's attitude.

New House

As they were finishing, Karen came in. "Oh, I'm sorry. I didn't know we had company." She said with polite coolness, "Min. How have you been?"

"Fine, thanks, Karen. Josh, this is my brother's wife. Karen, this is Josh Robertson."

True to her well-bred ways, she came over and extended her hand, "How do you do, Mr. Robertson. I'm glad…"

"He lives outside the domes, Mommy. Isn't that snaggy?" AnneJuleé caught Karen mid-sentence and she froze. She pulled her hand away awkwardly, not knowing what to do.

"I promise you, it isn't catching," Josh said through a crooked smile. Min wondered why he wasn't getting upset.

"You'll have to excuse me. I have a lot of work to do." She turned stiffly and left the kitchen.

"May I be excused, too, Dad?" James didn't wait for his father's answer, but rose and followed his mother.

"I'm sorry, Alex. I'd better leave." Josh, too, rose from the table.

"Absolutely not; this is my home and I want you to stay a while. Kids, don't you have things to do?" Alex said, as he gathered up some dishes.

Min followed her brother into the kitchen. "Alex, how can you endure her?"

"Min, let it go." They went back into the dining room. "I'd like to apologize, Josh. I knew how she would react to an outworlder."

"It's okay. I'm used to it."

"It's not okay." Min was more annoyed with Josh for not getting angry, as she was with Karen. "She was rude and unbelievable. So was James. Lord, Alex..."

Min suddenly saw the painful look on her brother's face, so she let it drop. Later, though, when Min and Josh were heading home, she started to apologize again.

"It's not important. After a while you grow immune to that type of reaction."

"Well, I never will." Then she realized that in her own way she'd been prejudiced against outworlders. She'd always thought of them as the lowest class of people, beyond reclamation. Until she'd exited. Perhaps, it was guilt that caused her fierce reaction. Or maybe it was just because of Josh. She slipped her arm through his, protectively.

Alex rarely visited Angel, but each time he did, the neglect of this area depressed him. Angel had lived in the same place – the University Quarter of Ashville – since he moved out of his parents' house. This had once been an elitist university; now it was just another renovated community of apartments, condos and shops.

Instead of using the Maglev, he'd decided to drive, giving his little-used craft a spin. The trip had taken a little over an hour. He pulled into Angel's drive, noticing with satisfaction that his vehicle was there. The system hadn't been able to tell him if Angel would be home. He got out and requested entry.

New House

"Who's there?"

"Well, look at your vidscreen, idiot."

"Alex. What are you doing here?"

"Can I come in?"

"Wait – just a…"

He could hear muffled voices as Angel turned and spoke to someone. Then there was a long silence before Angel's face reappeared and he said, "System, admit Alex."

"Thanks," Alex muttered sarcastically. As he entered the apartment, he could tell someone had made a hasty exit. "God, Angel, you're a slob. Don't you ever clean this place?" Angel himself looked ragged and in need of a shower.

"What do you want? Did you just come to criticize?"

"No. It's been months since I've been out here. Can't I just come and visit my brother?"

"Without calling first? I don't think so."

"Got a drink?"

Angel looked as if he wasn't going to offer, then unbent and went to his kitchen. Alex followed.

"Want a beer?"

"Sure, I can engage auto cruise on the way home."

Angel's I-VN synthesized two beers, and he handed one to his brother. "So, what do you want?" he asked again.

"Let's go sit down. We need to talk."

They went back into the living room, but Angel didn't sit. He said, "If you've come from father, you can just as well go home. It's none of his business what I do with my life. Nor yours."

"Father didn't send me. Actually, mother mentioned something that made come." It seemed as hard to talk with his brother, as it had with his parents. "I'm into something where I could use your help. Actually, Min, Phill, Tami and I are working on this together."

"You intrigue me. What could I possibly offer to such a distinguished group?"

"Look, Angel. Can you lop off the attitude?"

He shrugged and sat down on the sofa.

Alex explained, sticking just to the high-level points, as he had with his mother. Angel sat stone-faced, but as Alex got into the subversive groups theory, his face started showing signs of anger.

"Now I see what mother said. She thinks I'm involved, doesn't she?"

"She thinks you know more than you tell any of us, yes. Are you involved with some of these people?"

"I'm just supposed to sit here and discuss this with you calmly – just admit that I'm working with subversive groups? You're so goddamn civilized, it makes me sick."

"I gather that means you are."

Angel's once gentle blue eyes, now flashed at him. "That's none of your business." Then he turned back to the window, saying more quietly, "Go home."

"Angel, this is serious. If you've gotten yourself into something, tell me."

"Do you have any idea what happening out there?" Angel asked. "And what makes you think I would help you?"

"If you won't discuss it, how can I begin to understand?" Alex sat his beer down, "Come on, kid, talk to me. At least, help me find who hired this assassin. You can't want that kind of thing."

"No, it's a senseless waste of life; nothing we'd ever do."

Alex was appalled at the "we." It was a clear admission.

But, after three beers and a couple hours, he was just glad that Angel was talking to him. A lot echoed the report his mother let him read – sabotage of network stations, bombs in selected buildings, organized rebellions in public places. Yet it was always clear that their intention was to disrupt the network and raze structures. Nothing indicated they directly wanted to harm anyone.

"Angel, I don't want to keep repeating myself, but you're into something that is not only illegal, but extremely dangerous. How deep are you in?"

"I didn't tell you all this so you could preach. You need to realize that our group…"

"Would that be the Silver Candle?"

"How'd you know that name?"

Alex had been just guessing, but he'd hit it. "Come on, Angel. Last time we talked, you mentioned it yourself. And I've heard about it from others – one a Security Officer."

"We're a secret society, and I thought we weren't that well known. But it doesn't matter – we have a function and a goal."

"What? To destroy all that we've built?"

"Are you proud of this life? Our society is as elitist as the one it replaced. We are tracked and controlled. We exclude a whole portion of society."

Alex didn't know what to say. His brother was almost a stranger. "Angel, I have to go."

"Have I hit a nerve?" He got up and paced the room.

"It's not that. We're not going to accomplish anything here. Someone is out there killing outworlders; we need to stop it. You tell me that none of your people would do this, so I'll take your word. But it also means I'll have to look elsewhere."

Angel then said something unexpected. "Do you want my help?"

"Really?"

"I have some contacts. They might know something."

"That would be…yes, thanks."

Alex's drive home seemed long and tedious. With auto cruise engaged, he had a lot of time to think about his brother. It really scared him.

"Would you like some brandy, sir?" asked the efficient waiter, as he swept away the remains of an excellent meal.

"Yes, brandy. With some cappuccino," the man responded. That was what he liked about the Putnam House – they had real waiters, not those fucking robotic things. He had lingered over several courses, confident that he'd conclude this dispatch quickly and be back outside soon – more the pity.

New House

He leaned back in his comfortable chair and looked out the window. Situated on a ridge over the Crabtree River, the Putnam provided him with an excellent view of the City. The Triangle Dome wasn't the man's favorite area – it was too artsy for his taste – but it was way better than outside.

He thought about the next dispatch. The client only wanted him to do one, even though there was continued reference to 'them.' Well, that was their business. The urge to walk away swept over him again. *But no. Can't do that. If I want to go out on my own, credibility is important.* He'd finish, first; then he'd go. He tossed off the last of the golden liquid and ordered another.

This is a strange place, Josh thought. Consuelo's Restaurant implied a Latin cuisine, but the place was very eclectic, with a clearly Anglo owner, red hair and all. Josh noticed that Min's brother was very familiar with the restaurant's owner, who, after a brief conversation with Alex, closed off the back garden for their use. Connie – Josh assumed it was the derivative for Consuelo – stayed out of sight and let his "Robbie" served their drinks and food.

Within an hour of their arrival, several co-workers of Tami had joined them. They'd been discussing the data and reviewing Tami's ideas for trapping the killer for the past hour. One idea was to leak information that Josh was continuing his investigation into outworlders deaths. The officers would rotate and cover Josh at all times during their off-duty hours. It sounded plausible, and while Josh was nervous, he knew this was the best course of action.

Josh looked around. Someone was missing. "Where's Phill?" Josh asked Min.

"He had an appointment but said he'd meet us later. He isn't comfortable with all this. For that matter, neither am I." She turned to Josh and laid her hand on his arm, "Josh…"

"Don't do this. We have to find out what's going on, and it appears that I'm a target. If we uncover something concrete, the S.F. will have to start an investigation."

She got quiet and was lost in thought; then she turned back to him. "Let's go for a walk. There's not much more we can contribute to their discussion."

"Okay."

They exited the restaurant and strolled down the street. Finally, Min asked, "When are you exiting?"

"Tomorrow. The sooner, the better. I'd like to get this over with and get back to my life."

"I meant what I said. I'll leave with you."

"Min, no."

"You don't want me?"

"Yes, I do, but…" He wondered what they were going to do. "Let's just get through this next part and then we'll figure it out."

"Well, I'm coming with you when you exit. I can be one more set of eyes looking out for you."

"No, that's out." Josh said adamantly.

New House

They went back into the patio.

The man had it set. These units were isolated from one another with gardens so there shouldn't be any fallout to another home. The capped charge would make it look as if the home fuel container merely exploded in the garage. It should be easy, but he had one problem. The woman hadn't been going to work. She and the target were always together. He wondered vaguely whether there would be repercussions if he dispatched her as well, then decided he better not. They had been very specific about not touching the Classé-riche and he wanted to be paid.

Then he saw him. He was alone. The woman's place was dark, so she wasn't inside. It was now or never. He watched as the tall figure made his way up the path to the door and went to the security entrance that separated the house from the garage.

The man put his finger on the tiny transmitter and was just about to detonate, but stopped. The target came back out. Something was wrong. The target walked down the pathway a few yards and hesitated.

He was close enough to the garage that it still might work. No. He had to be sure. He thought briefly of putting him to sleep, but they trace NR2 more closely in here, so he watched some more. The target was talking on his RIC, laughing at something the wavering holo-image was saying. He then walked back to the condo's entrance. He spoke into the security console, the door swung open.

The man pressed the button on the transmitter. At first, it sounded like a firecracker. However, as the charge burned through the garage's fuel container, the real explosion pushed through the garage wall into the breezeway. He waited for the usual excitement to stir him. When it didn't come, he shrugged and drove away, content that the dispatch was complete. Now he could get back to completing the original contract.

Walking home from Consuelo's, the small group realized that, despite having spent hours in a restaurant, no one had eaten anything and they were hungry. A lively debate ensued as to what they would make. Min kept suggesting things she knew she had at her condo.

"Whatever it is, don't let Min cook it." Alex said with a laugh.

Josh made a grimace. "I know what you mean."

Min punched Josh on the arm, and saw him grimace. "Oh, I'm sorry."

"It's okay. It only hurts when someone beats on me. Just don't let it happen again."

They continued their banter as they roamed through the market, and deciding on steak, Min purchased five, thinking Phill might want one, too.

They headed back to Min's, but as they got close, they saw the sky lit with flames and flashing emergency vehicles. Min

New House

suddenly realized it was her place engulfed in fire. She just stood there, numb.

Alex yelled, "That Min's place."

"Oh, my God," Tami exclaimed, "though it looks like it's mainly the garage. Look! They have the condo under control. Min...?"

A wave of immense cold swept over her, and she began shaking. "Oh, God...oh, my God. Phill..." Her voice trailed off. Suddenly she was on her knees retching.

14

The hospital staff said there wasn't too much they could do except wait. Alex thought it unbelievable that with all the technology and science today, they couldn't do more. While they waited, the S.F. officials interviewed everyone. They asked Min how she knew Phill was there. She told them mechanically that he'd called her...had gotten there early...needed a code. She was devastated, and neither Alex nor Josh could comfort her.

Phill's wife, Chauncey rushed in. "Where is he? I want to see him."

Alex went over to her. "He's in a bad way. He took the explosion almost head on."

"What explosion? What was he doing at Min's anyway?" She whirled around at Min, who sat huddled in a chair. "What have you gotten him into?"

Min raised her dark, hollow eyes and shook her head. Alex touched Chauncey on the shoulder. "We were working on something which is very important. He wanted to help."

"All I know is that he was worried about something and wouldn't talk to me about it." She brushed her hand over her eyes, "If anything happens to him…" She turned finally and she walked off to consult with the physicians.

Min, suddenly coming to life in an explosion of energy, began pacing the floor. "He didn't want to do this. Remember? He said it was getting too dangerous."

Tami came back from talking with the other officers. "They said it looked like some materials stored in the garage ignited. Could be accidental, they said, but they are continuing to investigate."

Alex looked around at the assembled group, "Has it dawned upon anyone here that Phill was most likely not the intended target?"

They all looked at him, but Tami nodded. "Yes," she said. "I've been thinking that ever since it happened. Considering what happened to Josh, they might have mistaken Phill for him. I'm not sure about anything anymore. I do know that we need to get you two safe."

"What about Alex? And his family? And you, Tami? What about you?" Min's voice was near hysteria, and Josh attempted to calm her, but she pushed away and resumed pacing.

Tami was so calm, that to anyone who didn't know her, she appeared not to grasp the urgency of the situation. Yet, Alex did know her. Calm amidst the chaos – which is what made her a great Security Officer.

"I've already thought about that," Tami said, signaling to three of her friends from earlier in the evening. "They will escort all of you to a safe location, and we'll have you disappear. Alex, do you have a safe place where you can take your family?"

"Karen's mother lives in Cincinnati."

"I was thinking of some place where they wouldn't think to find you." She said, then turned to Josh, "What about you? Where can we escort you?"

Josh shook his head. "I'm going back out, but I don't need any cover. I think we can still make this plan work. And besides, I can move more effectively out there."

"If you're going, I'm going." Min said, moving up to him.

"No. I can't protect you and do what must be done."

"I'm not going to argue with you," Min said.

Alex heard the familiar tone in her voice and knew what was coming; but Josh clearly misunderstood. "Good, I'm glad you see it my way."

"No, I mean, we aren't going to discuss it. I'm just going. I'm a far better shot – besides being in better condition."

Before it became a full-blown argument, Angel walked in. Alex wasn't surprised; after all, it was a family emergency. However, Angel wasn't there simply to check on Phill. His brief nod to Alex indicated that he wanted private conversation and the two walked down the hallway.

"What's up?" Alex asked when they were out of earshot.

"How's Phill?"

"We'll know in a couple of hours. It's not good."

"I'm sorry, but he shouldn't have gotten into this. None of you should have.

"Don't start, Angel..."

"I have some names."

"What do you mean – names? You mean leads?"

"I don't know if they are leads, but the head of our group gave them to me. Actually, one is a former Candle member, but they kicked him out for being too radical. His name is Preston Rockefeller."

"That's sound familiar."

"It should. Teresa Rockefeller was honored two months ago at the Wilmington Conference for her work with the Scavs."

"Right. And this Preston is related?"

"Her brother."

"Who are the others?"

"Here, I have them on my RIC." Angel pressed the transmission light, sending the names to Alex's unit.

"Why are you helping?"

His brother looked surprised. "What do you mean?"

"I mean, this just seems awfully convenient."

"I said I'd help. Now, more than ever." Angel looked offended.

"Okay, I'll give this to Tami and let her investigate."

Angel put his hand on Alex's arm, "Don't tell her where you got them, OK?" Then he walked back to rejoin the family.

Phill's parents arrived, along with Phill's brother plus Alex's parents. After another unbearable hour, the doctors, accompanied by Chauncey, came down the hall, all dressed in blue scrubs. They had their heads together deep in conversation. Chauncey looked up, when they reached the crowd waiting for news; the clinical researcher in her had taken over, governing her emotions. She was able to greet her husband's family outwardly composed.

"He's stable," she said, as she hugged her mother-in-law. "He had major contusions and breaks in most of his skeletal structure. It's amazing he survived it at all. We've blocked the internal bleeding and fused the more severe breaks and set the rest." She pushed the blue cap from her head, looking suddenly weary. "If he survives the night, he has a chance. We won't know for several hours. There's more." She looked hard at Min. "He may have brain damage."

Margarite Villanueva went over to her son. "Alex, has this something to do with our discussion? You didn't stop, did you? And what was Angel telling you just now?"

Alex avoided the last question. "None of us ever thought it would result in this."

His father's face was turning a dark red, his eyes blazing. "Your mother told me what you were trying to do. I want you to stop immediately. Do you understand? I won't have anyone else getting hurt."

"Father, we can't…"

"I won't say it again, Alexander. Let it alone."

He didn't wait for a response, but turned, taking his wife's arm, and walked toward Phill's room. Alex felt his aunt and uncle quietly watching him, before they turned and followed.

Min sat in the S.F. vehicle, while Josh and Alex had a brief discussion with Tami. Then the three were chauffeured to Alex's house. Tami stayed at the hospital for a while longer. She then was going to her office to file the report and check the names Alex had given her.

"I'll come in the morning," she'd told Alex, "and get you people good and lost."

The three sunk into the chairs in Alex's den, not feeling like talking. That's how Karen found them when she came downstairs.

"I didn't hear you come in. How is Phill?"

"He's stable; that's about all they will say. Chauncey is making sure everything is being done."

"Well, you now need to stop this – whatever it is. Min, you can get yourself into all sorts of trouble if you want, but keep Alex out of it."

"Karen, please, we are tired. Can you make up one of the guest rooms?"

Min saw the surprise on Karen's face, as she pulled Alex aside. Min also noticed, though, that she kept her voice loud enough for them to hear.

"Surely they are not staying here? I will not have it. First, she involves you in her little schemes; now she brings one of those into this house. This is where I draw the line; they are not staying in my house."

Min could see Alex stiffen. "This is my house and she is my sister. She and Josh are welcome here. They're staying." It was apparent that Alex was reluctant to tell Karen about their exiting. *Just as well*, Min thought. *I'd just as soon not to be around when he did.*

Karen turned and looked at Min, ignoring Josh completely. "You can stay the night, but I want you out in the morning."

When she'd left the room, Min followed Alex, who had gone to the living room plexipanel and was staring out angrily.

"Alex, we didn't mean to cause trouble."

"The trouble was there long before all this started." The pool lights made eerie blue shadows on his face. "Long before." He raised his eyes to Min. "I'm sorry for what she said," then turned and include Josh in his apology.

Josh got up and joined them. "The sooner I leave the better."

"Well, not tonight. Let's all get some sleep," Alex said, as he went to make up the guest room.

"Here you go." Tami produced three sets of IDs, with new COPIs embedded into the millifilms, and the various account-mocurs. Alex would become one very dead Quentin Rathburne; the other two sets for Min and Josh were also of deceased people. "I've reactivated these, plus transferred some funds from my travel account. I'll need to replace it later."

"That's good thinking. Don't worry about covering the withdrawal later. I'll transfer the GEMs for you right now."

Tami smiled wryly. "Thanks, but that would sort of defeat our purpose. You are trying to hide. Remember? If you access your account, the transfer could be traced."

"Glad, at least, you are thinking."

"I do this for a living."

"What. Forge IDs and disobey your superiors?

Tami just smiled. "Where's Min?"

"She and Josh will be right down. Tami, thanks for all this. I know you're risking a lot."

"Where else would I be." There was a moment, quiet and unspoken. It was gone quickly, with Alex pouring two cups of coffee, and handing one to his friend. He'd known her for such a long time, but now something had changed.

Just then, Josh came into the kitchen. "Min will be down in a few minutes. Any news from the hospital?"

"Still no change. He's in a coma."

"The S.F. are taking it very seriously," Tami said, "especially considering who Phill is. I spent the better part of the night at the office. Everything is very grim."

"I think I should take offense." Josh smiled.

"Take offense to what?" Min asked, as she came in.

"I was injured, and got dumped into a ward. Phill was injured and they call out the troops."

Tami looked like she was going to explain, but Alex cut in. "He's just running with you, Tami." Min and Tami exchanged looks with Josh, each sharing a different level of understanding.

"Tami was just explaining how we use – or not use – these COPIs and mocurs."

They brought Min up to speed on Phill's condition, then Tami went through the explanation on how to moisten the microfilm and place it over the COPI in their palm. "As soon as you and Min get to where you're going, send a message to the ID we discussed – don't give details; just say 'It's okay now.' I'll understand. Alex, you do the same, when you get to wherever you're stashing your family. Have you decided yet?"

"The only place I can think of is Cincy. To Karen's mother."

"As I said, I'm not sure that's the best place. Don't you have some place where people wouldn't think to look for you?"

"Outside," Josh interjected. "They could stay at some community outside."

"If you think I'll get Karen to exit for a Preservers' settlement..." Alex raised his eyes to the ceiling. "No way. She's already fuming. I don't want to stir up anything more."

"God, Alex, grow some and stand up to her. Even *she* must see the urgency." Min said over the rim of her cup.

Alex grimaced, but shook his head.

"Well, if that's the only place, we'll have to put tight security on them. My guess is that they won't be bothered, but you need to hide somewhere else, Alex." Tami said. "I want all of you stay hidden until we catch this killer."

"How do you plan to do that?" Josh asked, but didn't wait for a response. "Tami, I'm convinced this killer was trying for me. That means I'm still the best bait to dangle on your hook." Josh had said it flippantly, but Alex could see that he was serious. "You have no clues as to who or where this person is. The only thing you suspect is that I'm a target. Ok, then use me."

When Josh suggested Min hide with Alex, she said, punching his arm, "Oh, no, you don't. If you're determined, then I'm going with you. That's final."

Alex had a thought. "When I get my family settled, I'll join Josh and Min."

Min smiled maliciously at Josh. "Oh, boy, now you're in trouble. You're going to have both of us."

Josh laughed as he dropped the dirty dishes into the disposal. "Tami, we'll stay hidden until you give the word. Of course, I'll want you to show up quick, with plenty of big, armed individuals."

"I'll be there with the troops, don't you worry. Well, see you soon. Safe travels." She smiled, and was gone.

The room was quiet after Tami's departure. Alex picked up the micro-film COPI of Quentin Rathburne. "Let's just hope that Rathburne didn't have any enemies who might want him dead again." A good laugh covered the tense moment.

When Karen came into the kitchen, they were all still sitting around the counter, laughing. Alex noticed that Min and Josh, the traitors, disappeared quickly. Alex took a breath and explained to Karen what they wanted her to do.

"You want me to do what?" she asked, indignantly.

"I'd like us all to exit for a while to a…well, sort of a resort." He should at least try and get them to an isolated location. Josh had mentioned a new camp in the Pennsylvania mountains. Alex began to describe it in more flowery details, but she immediately perceived where he was taking her.

"You want me to go to a Scav camp. Are you insane?"

"Look. Phill's injuries weren't an accident. We have gotten involved in something that's dangerous and I'd like you and the kids to be safe until it's over."

"*You're* involved. *You'd* feel better. Well, I didn't sign up for this and I'm not going to exit for you or anyone."

Alex fell back on his original plan. "Well, if you won't exit, will you at least go visit your mother?"

She glared at him. "What have you been doing?"

"Please, Karen, just do as I ask."

She was rigid and white, her eyes burning with a fury that startled him. "I'll go, but this is it. I really can't stand this anymore – you or your insane family."

"Mom?" James was standing in the doorway. "What's going on?"

"Go and get your brother and sister. We have to pack for a trip." Then she did something surprising – she began to cry.

The man couldn't believe it; he'd made a mistake. It had happened before, but long ago, long before he'd honed his skills. The client's anger, though, was out of proportion. "You imbecile, you…moron! You were supposed to take out the Scav. Not only did you hit a Classé-riche, but you did it at the home of another Classé-riche. What if the woman had been there? Would you have taken her out, too?" There was a long pause filled with tension. "God, how could you have been so stupid?"

The man just waited.

"Are you still there?" the client asked.

"Yes. Everything, though, is correctable. However, if you'd like, I can terminate the contract."

"No, no. I was just...oh, hell. There is too much at stake to quit now. But you have to be more careful. The man's condition is bad, and he might not make it. If we are discovered, everything would be lost."

"Why you worrying about this guy, even if he is a Classé-riche? If he was making trouble, he deserves what he gets. The message was delivered at any rate."

"But because he is a Classé-riche, the S.F. are investigating. So far, we can manage them, but I don't know how long we..."

"You've got someone in the S.F.?"

The client went silent. He seemed to regret what he'd said. He became all business. "Forget the Scav. I need you to escalate outside."

"You know me. I don't leave a job unfinished. I'll take care of him before I re-exit."

"No. I'll give you half the GEMs promised for the Scav dispatch; just go back out. Besides, we're not sure where the Scav is now. They wouldn't return to the condo. He isn't at any of the logical places he would go and he's not using his COPI. It would take too much time to track him down. No," he said emphatically, "exit now."

"An unfinished dispatch is bad for the reputation."

"Just do as I say, or we won't make any more payments."

Shit, he said to himself, as he disconnected. *No one tells me how to run a dispatch.* He began tracing connections of the woman who owned the condo. *Someone knows where he is.*

Josh and Min ran onto the platform, just as the silvery, sleek train raised on its bed of air and disappeared down the tube.

Min flopped onto a nearby bench, out of breath. "I'm sorry, Josh. I really couldn't have hurried any faster." She dropped the bags with newly purchased clothes and personal items. "I couldn't have exited without some things. I don't know about you, but I can't wear these clothes another day."

"It's okay," he said, sitting next to her. "We can wait for the next one." He was just glad he finally had Min at the station.

Min turned to him, laying her hand on his arm. "I have a thought."

"Oh, Lord, you're thinking again...always a bad sign."

She slapped his arm. "Listen. It's quite a while until the next train. Let's rent a terracraft and drive over."

Josh smiled patiently, "By the time we got our vehicle and got on the road, the next train would be here. We'll do better if we just stay here and wait. Besides, Tami warned us that there wasn't that much on these mocurs."

"Well, you can at least buy me something to drink."

"Oh, okay."

They gathered her packages and wandered off in search of a food vendor.

Alex went into the bathroom. He dampened his hand and applied the nano-foil as Tami had instructed. It felt slippery at first, but soon began to dry and conform to his palm. Funny how Tami was so knowledgeable about criminal tricks, but then, S.F. have to know how to cheat the law to catch the crooks. As Alex walked into the front hall, he slipped his hand into his pocket. Even though it was nearly invisible, he felt conspicuous.

"Are you ready?" he asked his silent wife.

"Dad, where are we going?" Adam asked, looking between his parents.

"You're going to visit your grandmother Sarah."

"Must we go, Daddy? I want to stay with you." AnneJuleé hung on her father's arm. "Please, Daddy?"

"No, sweetie, I want you to go with your mother for now. I have a couple of things to do. I'll come and get you soon."

James stood tall and stiff. "Dad, is this about that Scav who stayed here last night? I knew it would be trouble. I think you should come with us."

"I am coming with you. All the way. It's just that I have to come back here after I drop you off."

Karen picked up her bags. "Get your things, and stop talking. We're going."

At the station, Alex allowed the system to scan the false COPI. Karen started to put her hand up, but Alex pushed her arm away. "We don't have time for that. I scanned for us."

She looked at him a little puzzled, but said nothing.

On the train, everyone was silent. Karen was still, her arms clenched, her face turned to the window. The kids seemed afraid to ask any questions; and Alex – well, he just didn't know what to say to any of them.

They arrived at Sarah's. She received them with a smile and hugs all around for the children. However, with a closer look at their faces, she began to ask questions.

"Don't Mother," Karen said wearily. "Just don't."

Sarah looked at Alex, but he could only shake his head.

"Well, kids. Looks like from all your bags that you'll be staying for a while. I'll show you where you'll be sleeping. Then I'll make you some snacks. I'll bet you're hungry."

Alex waited long enough to see the kids settled, trying again to reassure AnneJuleé and Adam. James was distant and refused to talk to him. As he headed back to the station, he vowed to find a solution for all this. He couldn't imagine his life without his kids.

By late afternoon, Josh had Min safely in Mount Bryson. Min had wanted to call the hospital from the exit station in Ashville, but Josh reminded her they were to minimize the ID's use.

They settled into the cabin Josh had occupied earlier.

Min sat on the edge of the bed. "Now what?"

"We wait."

"I wish we hadn't come back here. I see Holly everywhere."

"I know. So do I. Yet, it makes sense the killer won't return. That was one thing we did determine – he never repeated the same location."

New House

"Josh?" He didn't look around immediately, so she said his name again.

He turned. "What?"

"Josh, I want to tell you something. In case…"

"Nothing is going to happen, Min."

"You don't know that. Let me finish, please."

He went and sat by her. "Okay. I'm listening."

Suddenly, she seemed unsure. She raised her eyes. "I love you."

"I sort of figured that already."

"No. I don't just mean I love you the way people say it when they are making love. I really love you – I need you."

He was quiet, not because he didn't know what to say, but because he had longed to hear her say it. He took her in his arms, and lying back, they fell asleep.

Josh woke up and the room was dark. Min was still curled up against him, warm and vulnerable. All of his life he'd run away from relationships, and now all he wanted was to protect and care for her. As she stirred, he said to himself, *it was worth the wait, old man.*

By the time Alex arrived at the South Lake Industrial Domes in Virginia, he was exhausted. The last few hours had taken a toll; enduring Karen and James' hostility, and AnneJuleé and Adam's questions…and just the fact that he left them, and didn't know what the next couple of days would produce.

He now had his rented vehicle, but couldn't face any driving. He decided to take a room at the exit-portal hotel. *Just for a few hours*, he reasoned; *that can't hurt.*

Checking in with the false ID, he was again thankful that Tami had been so thorough. He went to his room. It was not fancy, but it was clean and quiet. He lay down on the top of the coverlet and exhaustion overcame him.

The next time he opened his eyes, it was dark. The room was shadowy and unfamiliar; then he remembered where he was. There wasn't any way he could go anywhere tonight, so he contacted the desk and told them to wake him at 0500. He'd be up with Min and Josh by mid-morning.

The man didn't know where the Scav had gone. The brother's place in Piedmont Heights was dark.

Now what? The man decided to wait, but after a while, he gave up. He went to the second one on his list, but this wasn't right either. This estate said it all – old money and influence to boot. Not a place for a Scav to hide.

He'd already had run a trace on the owners. Jonathan and Margarite Villanueva. *He thought the name sounded familiar. What the hell was a Scav doing with them?*

Yet somehow, in his gut he knew that if he could find one of these Villanuevas, the Scav would be with them, as unlikely as that sounded.

"Check travel for Alex or Yumin Villanueva?" The system listed the last travel record for the brother – two days ago. The woman was several days earlier, a return to the Triangle. *Both must still be here.*

"Scan for addresses on other Villanueva family members." His RIC refreshed with the needed info.

Another brother – *over near Ashville* – and a grandmother, some assorted cousins, aunts, uncles. A lot of places to check. Throughout the night, he traveled from address to address, but found no sign of the Scav.

Towards dawn, he caught some sleep, but woke with a sudden thought. *They're amateurs? Where would amateurs hide?* In-laws. People always think they are safe with the in-laws.

"System, location of Alex Villanueva's wife's relatives?" The system came back with a list, and at the top was a surviving mother-in-law in Cincinnati.

"Scan the trains from Piedmont Heights areas yesterday traveling to Cincinnati," he queried his remote system. The response was negative. No Alex or Yumin Villanueva. No one named Josh Robertson, either. He asked for the full lists of passengers, and while the RIC transmitted the data to his mobile reader, he speculated on another course of action. They might have traveled in their own vehicle, but probably not – not this family. More than likely, they just didn't scan in, which was why he got a negative.

Shit. They are smarter than he thought. Frustrated, he went for some coffee at a local café, where he sat sipping it, reading the list of passengers again. Suddenly, a name jumped out. Quentin Rathburne. *Well, well, well. Quentin, you've risen from the dead.* One of them was using a COPI from one of his earliest dispatches. He didn't know which – but he didn't care. Find one, find them all.

He tapped his earpiece, "Trace Quentin Rathburne," he instructed. He remembered Quentin very well – a simple arm-bending, which went too far. It was the first time he remembered feeling the rush. He hadn't set out to become a dispatcher; just an enforcer. Yet once he felt that rush of finality, of a life slipping from his embrace, the choice was clear. He began to look forward to the intricate planning and execution, the same way others appreciate a beautiful landscape or piece of art. It filled him with a sense of life.

His RIC interrupted his thoughts, "That individual is currently registered at the Meade Gap hotel at the South Lake Industrial Domes, Virginia."

The voice for the wake-up-message sounded in the room. "Mr. Rathburne, time to wake up. It is now 0500." The name didn't register with Alex. Consciousness, however, pushed away sleep and he remembered that he was supposed to be Rathburne. He acknowledged, and the message terminated.

Within a half hour, his rented vehicle was on the winding road to Mount Bryson.

The man was at the station, checking the schedule to Virginia, when it occurred to him that he would be too late. *He'll be gone before I can get there.*

"Keep an active trace for Rathburne's movements," he queried.

His RIC responded, "The ID has a rented vehicle."

"Destination?"

"The destination is the Triangle."

That didn't make sense. Why go through all the effort of hiding and then come back here? And why rent a vehicle when he could take a train? Despite his misgivings, he went back to the brother's house. His uneasiness was reinforced when the brother didn't show. *What's the deal?*

An hour later, the man requested another trace. Still nothing. *Shit. Where are you going?* He hated delays; hated not having things go right. He pounded his forearm against the door. "Damn!" Then he took a deep breath, willing himself to focus.

He activated his RIC again. "Give me a read-out of the Villanueva's close friends and colleagues." The list filled two pages on the mobile reader with several columns on each screen. *Christ! Do these people know the whole world?*

"Eliminate the colleagues." The list was considerably smaller, but still sizeable. For a moment, he thought of just going to Virginia, trying to trace him from there. Yet deep down he knew it would be a waste of time. He read the shortened list again. He was trying to determine where to go from here, when his RIC announced Quentin Rathburne activity.

"The ID in question has purchased food at a station in Clovis Cove, North Carolina."

"Display a map of that area." The map came up on his reader. It was out in the middle of nowhere. Then he noticed something. It wasn't far from his last dispatch. Mount Bryson? *It couldn't be.*

15

Min was with Marcie Ellis, pulling weeds from the vegetable garden, when she saw Josh waving to her.

She stood up and stretched her back, "What?" she mouthed to him. He was too far away and she couldn't hear what he was saying. She shook her head again, and indicated that she would come. "I'll be right back, Marcie."

As she rounded the building, she saw Alex standing next to a dusty vehicle. She hurried over to him, giving him a brief hug. The worried feeling dissipated, replaced by mild annoyance.

"Well, you weren't in any hurry to get here. Have trouble leaving the family?"

"I just wanted to see them settled. By the time I exited in Virginia…"

"Virginia? Why did you go such an out-of-the-way route?"

Josh looked at her. "Min, for an intelligent woman, you can be really obtuse."

"Oh." She smiled, "Okay, okay, I get it."

"Can I finish? When I finally exited, I was so tired. I rented a vehicle, but decided to sleep for a while which ended up being all night. I would have called but, well, for one, I didn't want to risk a direct communication. No telling who is monitoring."

She hugged him again. "I'm just glad you're here."

Some of the people had begun to clear out from the breakfast crowd; they joined Bob Whiteagle at one of the tables. "Welcome," Bob said as they sat down. "Josh told me what ya'll are planning. I think you're crazy, but I can help."

Min moved closer to Alex, "How's Phill? Have you heard anything?"

"Nothing yet, but Tami will call when she has something."

"How are we going to draw him out?" Min asked, looking around the group.

"*We* aren't," Josh said. "You are staying in here until he's caught."

"We talked about that," Min said.

"We did and I decided you aren't coming."

"Alex, tell him," she said to her brother.

"Actually, I agree with him, but I know you. No use arguing."

"Smart, my dear brother, very smart. See Josh, so stop fighting it?"

Josh laid his hand over hers. "I'll be worrying about you, instead of focusing on what needs to be done."

"Well, I'm sorry for that, but I'm coming."

A deep appreciative laugh shook Bob. "Stubborn, isn't she?"

"Yes, I'm stubborn. And now that we're beyond that discussion, I get back to my original question, how are we going to draw him out?"

"Tami said that, if Josh is a target, the killer is tracking his movements, and probably has an open trace on his COPI. If Josh uses it, the killer will be alerted. However, Josh will not be alone. Tami will have her army waiting to grab him."

"It sounds too simple. Besides, Josh didn't use his COPI when he was in the domes. It hasn't been active for years, so why would he start using it now?" Min said.

Alex looked surprised. "What?" He turned to Josh. "Why didn't you mention that when Tami gave us the false COPIs?"

"I didn't think it would matter." Josh shrugged his shoulders. "Does this wreck all the plans?"

"I don't know. I'll wait and see what Tami thinks."

Just then, Alex's RIC hummed and he tapped the earpiece to open a connection. Alex could tell there were others with Tami, but her imager captured only her.

"Are you alone?" she asked.

"Go ahead. We are among friends."

"We're all set. I don't have many officers, but..."

Alex interrupted her, "First, have you had any news about Phill?"

"He's stable for now. He's not conscious, but his wife is making sure he has the best care."

Min pictured Chauncey bossing the hospital staff around. *He has to make it. He has to.*

Tami went on, "How are things up there? How's the family?"

"They're fine, no troubles." Alex said. "We might have a hitch."

Min saw Tami grow intense, "What?"

"It's Josh's COPI. He didn't use it when he came back in."

"Why are we just learning about this now?"

Josh looked a bit defensive, "I didn't see how it would matter."

Tami was trying to keep her patience in check. "Wouldn't matter? Don't you think that anyone who murders for a living would get all sorts of warning signals if you suddenly started using it? I'm figuring he's fairly smart, or at least has smart people telling him what to do. He'll realize that there's only one reason you'd use it, and that's to draw him out." Tami turned for some discussion. This went on for a while.

"Well?" Alex finally asked.

Tami wasn't through and snapped back, "Give me a nano, will ya?"

The small group at the table waited patiently, and finally Tami turned back to her RIC tablet. "We'll have to rethink this. We need to find some other way to alert the network to your location, Josh. Using your obsolete COPI would just scream 'trap'!"

Min sensed relief in Josh, "What now?"

"Give me a day to work it out. For now, it looks like you're safe. Stay put; I'll be in touch." Her image faded.

"Damn," Alex said.

"Sorry," Josh shook his head.

"What do we if Tami pulls out?" Min asked.

"She'll come through." Alex moved towards the door. "She'll handle it."

New House

Min hated waiting.

Josh had slept fitfully and woke just around dawn. It was still dark, but he could hear doves cooing, so the sun wasn't far off. He turned so he could watch Min. She was lying with her right arm across her eyes, her breathing regular and deep, so deep that she snorted occasionally. It wasn't a real snore, just a funny little sound.

She is stubborn, he thought; *one of the things I like about her.* As he watched her, the passion rose up in him. He reached out, running his finger over her lips, down her neck and began caressing her breasts. Her breathing checked and she moved her arm. "Good morning," Josh whispered, pulling her close.

"I really hate people who wake me this early, but in your case, you're forgiven," she murmured as she responded to his urgency.

The man had parked at the Exit Portal #20 near Eflin about 0100, dozing when he could. The larger vehicle exits closed after midnight, and he didn't want to hire a new transport at this point.

Tomorrow is soon enough. He'd go to Mount Bryson and see if his hunch was right. He knew they had to be together. It made sense.

He was still disgusted with everything that had happened in the Triangle. He must be slipping to make so many missteps. But he had watched the woman's place for days and the only people in or out was the woman and the Scav. How was he to know that someone else would show up – someone looking like the Scav?

They had all slipped away too cleverly. Someone was helping them. That's the only explanation for their disappearance. That made him nervous, but he was also feeling the excitement of the hunt. The job would be longer, but it would also be more interesting. His vacation would be a long way from Scavs.

The first threads of light began to filter in through the dome. He could see people moving about in the office. He started his vehicle and moved toward the exit doors.

Alex was still sound sleep, when Tami called. "Alex, I have really bad news."

"Hang on. Let me get focused." He raised himself up on his elbow and rubbed his face of sleep. "Ok, what's up?"

"Phill didn't make it."

Alex's stomach tightened, "Oh, God, no. Oh, geez, poor Chauncey."

"She called me just a bit ago. How'd she know to contact me?" Tami asked.

"That's my doing. I left your name if she couldn't reach either Min or me. Min...oh, geez," he said again, "I have to go tell her."

"Wait, Alex. There's more."

"What?"

Tami looked down, thoughtfully, then back up to Alex. "I'm not sure how reliable it is, but it changes things. Michael came to see me this morning."

"Our Michael? Whatever for?"

"He overheard Ellen talking with a couple outside of Consuelo's yesterday just as he arrived."

"So?"

"Well, you know Michael. He has to be involved in everything. He hung about and heard you're name was mentioned."

"How is that relevant? We all talk about each other at times."

"It's just that Ellen quickly quieted the other two, and they left. He had a funny feeling and decided to check it out. He said he found out that several people in Ellen's family are suspected Silver Candle members."

"What? Snobby, elitist Ellen is a Candle? Not possible."

"Well, I don't know if *she* is, but Michael checked into the two with Ellen. They are definitely members. He recognized their faces in his files."

"His files; what files?" Alex swung his feet off the cot, shaking his head. "I feel like I've fallen into a different world, Tami. Phillippe is dead, and a killer is hunting us. Now you tell me that our friends are not who we thought them to be."

"Alex, you have to focus. I know this all bit hard to take in, but we have to make some decisions."

Alex took a breath. "Ok, ok. How does this change our plans? Is it off?"

"I'm not sure. It's all getting so complicated. And I don't know who to trust."

Alex straighten up. "You know who could help? Angel. He practically admitted to me that he was a Candle member."

"Oh, now you've surprised *me*. Where else has this group infiltrated? And, also, that settles it. You are all coming back in until we can figure this out. I can put you all in a safe house."

"Ok, I'll talk with Min and Josh, and get back to you."

"Right. And Alex?"

"Yeah," he said through a yawn.

"Be safe."

Alex watched as Tami disconnected and, in those brief seconds, he realized again that their friendship had deepened. Maybe it was just the closeness people experience when they are in a dangerous situation. It would probably disappear when this was all over and they'd go back to the old camaraderie.

There's the Scav, the man said to himself. He'd left his vehicle farther up the road and had walked through the woods towards the buildings. As he watched from behind a shrub, he realized the target wasn't alone. A woman – *must be the sister*, he reasoned. *Interesting. The Classé-riche likes slumming. No problem. Eventually the dispatch will be alone.* He felt a smug satisfaction that he'd been right.

Just as the couple approached a building, a second man approached. He said something, and the woman screamed, "No!" and leaned against the Scav. He watched as the three people huddled together for a bit and then went inside.

Damn! Now what?

Something had happened, and he just knew it was going to complicate things even more. But he had no choice; he had to wait.

He needed a hiding place closer to the settlement, so he gathered his pack and gear, and keeping just inside the woods, he made his way around near a storage shed. He had a good view of the compound, and he settled in.

Min looked around at the people gathered in the room. Alex was there. There was a determination on his face, something she'd not seen before. Josh was arguing with him about something, telling Alex that he wouldn't do something. She heard their voices clearly, like a play on the network – hearing it all, but not retaining it, filtering it in and out impersonally with no reaction to anything.

She took a breath, but her chest felt it would explode. She tried to listen to what was being discussed, but Phill kept invading her thoughts, filling her eyes again and again, giving her such a headache that she put her head down on the table. Phill...more a brother than a cousin. Phill who had died because of what they were doing. The voices in the room grew, until finally she got up and left the building. She stood in the fresh air and shakily filled her lungs.

"Are you all right?" Josh had followed her out.

"I just need to take a walk. I can't breathe in there."

"Do you want me to come?"

"No, I'll be okay. I'll be back shortly."

"You're sure?"

She nodded and walked a few yards, when he called to her.

"It'll be dark soon. Take a lantern." He stepped back into the building and emerged with a light.

"Thanks." He gave her cheek a peck and she walked towards the lake. She found her way to the stone steps where she and Holly had sat a short time ago. So much death; so many good people. And now Phill. My poor Phill. The pain and sorrow she'd been holding in finally let loose.

She cried so long that her throat and eyes ached and she was drained. Then as she sat there, she felt her pain being replaced by something new. She drew a deep breath and knew that she'd have to focus. If they were going to catch this killer, she'd need all of her faculties. And she did want to catch him; catch him and kill him. She stood up.

Josh had been right. Although the sky was still light, the sun was gone and the terrain was too dark to see her way. She flicked on the lamp and headed back towards the buildings.

The man pushed through the thick shrub and could tell immediately that she had sensed something. She paused, swinging the light in his direction. The beam did a couple of quick arcs trying to penetrate the foliage; then the beam began to bob up and down. She was running. And, as with most spooked quarry, she was running in the wrong direction. She was headed deeper into the woods. The man quickened his pace.

She was a fast runner, and agile. He was breathing rapidly now, in part from running, but mainly from the pursuit; his senses stirred to life. He'd discovered that he liked the ones who refused to give in. It made the victory all the sweeter.

She appeared to be doubling back. He couldn't let her reach the encampment, but he lost sight of her momentarily. Then the light; she had found a clearing, and had paused, expecting, he guessed, to see something familiar.

As the man caught up to her, she swung the lantern towards his head. He was as quick as ever, ducking under the swinging object. He caught her wrist and pulled it back over her shoulder, removing the lantern from her grasp. Her other fist, landing on the side of his neck, took him by surprise.

Damn, she's strong.

He punched her stomach, and she doubled over. He didn't want her dead – not now, at least. He had formulated a new plan.

With her out of action for a few seconds, he easily slipped around and caught her from behind. She straightened up, still coughing. She tried to kick him, but he side-stepped her attack.

"Okay, stop struggling, little girl." He whispered in her ear.

Her words came out in jerks. "Go...to...hell."

"I don't want you or your brother, just the Scav. And you're my bait." He knew ultimately that he'd have to dispatch her – he couldn't have anyone around who could identify him.

While he was looping a fiber snare around her wrists, he nearly lost her. She pulled an arm free. His foot twisted around her ankles, causing her to fall face down. The snare tightened around her wrists and he turned her over to face him.

He grabbed her up, pulling her against him. "You like to fight?" She continued to struggle, kicking and twisting, landing a few bruisers, which only aroused him more.

"You...bastard. I'll kill you. I'll kill you." She screeched, and her spit caught him in the eyes. She reared up and knocked her head hard against his.

Shit! He'd had enough – it wasn't funny anymore. He struck her on the jaw, and she groaned. He hit her again and again until she was limp, and threw her back to the ground. She lay quietly, and he thought she was faking it, but when he turned her over, there was blood trickling from her nose and mouth, and a cut over her left temple. *Damn it. Hit a rock.* He kicked it away and slumped onto the ground to catch his breath. Finally, picking her up, he tossed her over his shoulder, heading to his vehicle. He hoped she didn't die too soon.

Alex walked into the compound and found Josh standing there, looking around. "What are you doing?"

"Trying to decide where Min went. She left over an hour ago and I haven't seen any sign of her. I'm getting worried."

"She probably just needs some time alone. She and Phill were really close."

"That's what she said, but she also said she'd be back shortly. I've got a bad feeling."

"Well, let's get some lamps and go look for her."

They headed in the direction Josh saw her take, but after looking for a half hour, found nothing.

"Okay, now I'm worried." Alex said. "Let's get some more people and widen the search."

The man's RIC beeped, announcing an incoming message. He debated on whether or not to answer, but the way this dispatch is going, he thought he'd better. He let the woman slide off his shoulder and onto the ground. She didn't stir. He reached into his vehicle and put the remote in his ear.

"Yes, what is it?"

"First, where are you? We haven't seen any new ones in days. I thought we told you to escalate the agenda."

"I'm taking care of your other problem."

"You're what?! We told you to discontinue. Why are you still pursuing it?"

"I told you. I finish what I start."

"Leave it alone, do you understand? That's assignment is over. There have been other developments."

"Why am I not surprised."

"*Listen.* Your last mistake has the Security Forces making waves. The man died and everything's in an uproar. I need you to escalate the deaths out there."

"When I finish with Robertson."

"You don't understand. We have a deadline."

"What deadline? What's going to happen?"

"Not important. Get back to the original job."

The man was silent. He was tired of them. He wanted to get paid and get the hell out. They could find another dupe for their work.

The client was clearly annoyed he hadn't answered, "Do you understand?"

"Which word did you think was unclear?"

"I just want to make sure. You made one mistake. No more. If you can't manage to finish the job, perhaps we should terminate."

"Go ahead and threaten. You and I know that you don't have time to find someone else."

"You aren't the only..." the client started to say, but someone in the background silenced him. "Just do the job."

He tapped off his remote, and realized that he might not be the only one out here. It never occurred to him that they would have others, but now it made sense. They were attempting something global and he'd only been in the Americas. His bargaining chip just evaporated.

He looked down at the woman, still motionless. He was in a dilemma. *What to do with her?* If he wasn't to do the Scav

Robertson, then he'd taken her for nothing; but then, he couldn't let her live either.

He logged into his account to check the balance. They had made all payments to date, except the Robertson one. Well, he couldn't expect any payment for that. While it wasn't what he thought he'd have to strike out on his own, it was enough. Maybe they'd throw in that last payment if he actually did dispatch the Scav. At any rate, Robertson was a loose end. He decided he was working for himself now; look out for number one and forget the rest of them.

He dragged the limp form into the vehicle's rear compartment and scanned her vitals. She was okay, just unconscious. Just for good measure, though, he redid her hands and secured her feet, before closing the lid.

I might even hang onto her for a while, he though, remembering his excitement as she struggled against him. He'd never been bothered much by sex, either male or female, but the thrill of the hunt – that was something he had discovered he couldn't live without. And she was a worthy quarry.

Alex contacted Tami, and she immediately became aware of the anxiety on his face. "What's wrong?"

"Min's missing."

"What do you mean 'missing'?"

"I mean she went off a while ago…"

"It's been closer to three hours," Josh said as he came up next to Alex. "And we've searched the woods. Nothing."

"Could she have fallen? Has she gone off before?"

Typical Security Forces questions, Alex thought annoyed. "Tami, you know Min. You know this isn't like her. Something's wrong."

"Have you used your own IDs for anything?"

"Don't be absurd," Josh answered. He was barely controlling his agitation. "This is a waste of time. What can Tami do from inside? We need to find Min."

It was Alex's turn to get angry, "Well, Josh, we've looked everywhere. What do you suggest? I want to find her too, you know."

"Sorry." Josh stepped back, letting Alex go back to his conversation with Tami.

However, Tami wasn't at all helpful. She shook her head at Alex, "Unless she uses one of the COPIs, I can't trace her – or any of you – especially out there."

One of the men searching ran up, yelling to him. Alex said, "Hang on, Tami, something..."

"We found this." A young man Alex knew only as Martin, held out a lantern.

"That's the one I gave Min," Josh said, snapping it up. "That's clear. It doesn't take skill to figure out who has her."

Tami was calling to them, "Hey, you guys. Fill me in."

Josh held up the lantern. "Min had this. They just found it." He turned towards Martin. "Where?"

"About a quarter of a mile further down the lake, near a clearing."

Tami was showing her frustration, "Fan out. Look for her; but be careful. I'm coming as fast as I can."

16

"You're crazy if you think I'm going to do anything but look for Min." Josh was tired of people trying to get him to 'listen to reason.' His reasoning was telling him to find Min. Suddenly the RIC Min had given him, started vibrating. He stepped away from the group. *Oh, thank God,* he was thinking, as he slipped it into his ear and tapped to receive the signal. No image appeared, only a garbled voice.

"Evening, Scav. Want your woman back?"

Josh looked over to where Alex and the others stood near the building.

"Don't call them. They can't help you." The voice continued. "Come down the main road; take the first right fork. Keep walking. I'll find you. By the way, bring anyone else and I'll kill her right away." The link went silent.

Josh was frozen. He glanced again to Alex, who turned and raised his eyebrows in a "what" expression. Josh shook his head, but Alex started over anyway.

"What's up? Was that Min?"

"Nothing. Stay here."

"What's going on, Josh. Who was that?"

"It was him. And he wants me for her."

New House

Alex stopped dead in his tracks.

Josh turned and headed in the direction of the main road. "Where are you going? Josh, stop...Josh..." Alex grabbed his arm. "You can't just go to him. You'll both end up dead."

"He's watching. Don't talk to me or she *is* dead."

"Well, make like you've forgotten something and come back into the building. We'll figure out something."

"No. I'm going. Give me that lamp. I'm not suicidal. When I'm gone, follow with as many as possible. I'm going to need a large rescue squad. Just don't follow too close and don't make noise."

As Josh walked down the road, he just prayed that Min was all right.

The man watched the Scav start to obey, then someone started towards him and they talked. Looked like the brother, but he couldn't be sure. *Damn. Why didn't I bring my scanner? What are you thinking, you dumb Scav? Those people can't help you. Can't help the woman. Just do what you're told.*

He started to move in closer for a better look, just as the Scav flipped on his torch, and started walking.

The man shadowed his target from the dark of the hedgerow, glancing back occasionally to make sure there weren't any reinforcements following.

Okay, good little Scav. Keep moving.

Min moved her head. It felt like a lead weight. *Damn. What a headache. Where am I?* Then, like a dam bursting, all the memories came flooding back. The man. His hands, his breath...hitting her, knocking her down. Of falling and nothing.

She opened her eyes, but only one opened to take in the blackness around her. The other was swollen shut. She tried to sit up but banged her head on something metal. She realized she was in the storage compartment of a vehicle. His vehicle. She knew she had to get out, to warn them. They didn't know he was here already. Yet, with her arms secured behind her back and her feet tied together, she could barely move. She twisted and strained at the tethers for a full five minutes, ending only with raw, bloody wrists and no closer to freedom.

It's funny how the mind works. She suddenly remembered as kids – siblings, cousins – they would all show off their weird talents. Angel could wiggle his ears; Phill could sneer; another could burp on queue...could she still do her 'one big trick?'

She inched her joined hands down her backside and under her torso until they were against her thighs. She was breathing hard and her muscles were throbbing. She wasn't as flexible as she'd been as a kid.

Keep going. Do it slowly, one inch at a time. She worked her knees up until they were almost touching her forehead. Nearly crying from the pain, she crawled her heels into her palms, then another inch backward...her shoulder joints felt like they were being ripped from the sockets... *a little farther.*

Suddenly she did it; she had her hands in front of her. Her "Little Houdini" nickname still held.

Rest a nano... but resting only brought the pain to the surface. Instead, she focused on her binds. They were cutting into her wrists from all the contortions. She reached down so she could feel the cord around her ankles. It was some sort of zip-binding that, once secured, had to be cut free. Cautiously, she began to feel around for something to cut them. Her hands touched on something fabric.

A bag? She dragged it closer but it contained nothing sharp, only some more cord, a couple of small boxes, some cloth...and one bonus, a weapon. Careless of him to leave it here, but she guessed that he didn't expect her to wake up.

She carefully lifted it out, trying to determine its type and model. It was larger than a normal pistol, very heavy, probably some sort of light-charged type. *Perfect.*

She laid it down, emptied the bag and pulled it over her face. Then, feeling for the weapon again, she pointed it towards the latch. Her hands were numb and she nearly dropped it, but eventually managed to get a charge off. It missed the latched and blasted a large hole in the metal. She decided to risk it without her face covered. This time the silent burst of light exploded the latch, sending fragments everywhere. She felt a couple hit her face, and one on her arm; but it did the trick – the lid sprung up. The cool night air flooded into the compartment.

With the thin moonlight, she could see her bindings. There was some space between her feet; she hoped she didn't miss.

She swung her legs over the side of the vehicle. With her feet straining wide against the bindings, she let off a charge. The beam severed the cord but also grazed her left ankle and the side of her foot, and the fiery pain that followed almost made her faint. She retrieved the cloth from the bag and wrapped it around her foot to slow the bleeding.

As she slid out, her legs wouldn't support her and she grabbed the vehicle, steadying herself. Now, she did another search of the compartment, unearthing electronic equipment, dried foods, vials, and some items she couldn't identify, but still nothing, which would work on her wrist binds. She gave up the search; she didn't know how long she had. She grabbed the weapon.

She went about twenty paces, stopped, confused and disoriented. She held her breath and strained to hear something familiar. *Damn, which way?* Her final direction was based on pure instinct.

With each labored breath, the pain battled with her consciousness. She leaned against a tree. The salt from her tears stung her face. She righted herself and pushed on, tripping on logs and underbrush, punishing her already injured foot. Part of her tried to turn off the pain; she had just one focus – to stop him. No one else was going to die at his hands.

Josh knew he was there a second before the arm came around his throat. He shifted quickly, but it was too late. There was something in his hand. A vial. Josh grasped the wrist, forcing it away. It snapped, the fine mist exploded and drifted away. The two continued to struggle, hitting up against a tree, swinging out, then back.

Josh's wind was being cut off, but he had a height advantage and he used it, leaning forward, lifting the man off his feet. The arm and legs of the violent man only wrapped tighter. Josh clawed and dug at anything he could reach, trying to unseat the leech on his back.

Josh had been sliding his chin down until he managed to get his mouth around the arm, his teeth cutting into thin cloth and finally flesh. A sound like a grunt came from the man and the arm relaxed momentarily. Instead of trying to twist out of the grasp, however, Josh doubled over and the motion brought the surprised attacker flying through the air.

Josh ran to the man and slammed his foot into his stomach; then towards his face. The man grabbed Josh's foot, which was poised for another kick, and pushed him over backwards.

Then suddenly he was on top of Josh. "Nice fight, but it's over."

He strained to again dislodge the man, but he wasn't successful. He heard a low chuckle, a strange sound for such a death struggle. He saw the man reach into his pocket for another vial. Josh figured, it was the drug Tami had mentioned.

Josh saw the man take a deep breath. He did the same, just as the spray hit the air. It seemed to descend in slow motion, and he shut his eyes. Just then, he heard voices and footsteps running up the road. The man heard them too. He swore, leaped up and disappeared into the trees.

Alex was beside him, "Josh, are you okay?"

He rolled away from where the mist was still drifting, breathing in deeply, coughing. He managed to choke out, "Get him, dammit."

Alex jumped up and followed the others who were in pursuit.

Min could hear voices, branches breaking, people moving through the brush. She headed in that direction and saw some figures, their lanterns scanning the trees. She figured they were looking for her, until she saw him. All she could see was his silhouette, but she knew. He would pause behind a tree and then move on, always careful to avoid the lights.

She was a little ahead of him, but he suddenly turned and headed straight towards her. She thought he'd seen her, but he was still looking over his shoulder. She raised the weapon, steadying it with both hands. Exhaustion was making her legs feel like lead and each breath was painful, but she held tight. By the time he realized she was there, he was only fifteen feet away.

"Well, Classé, how'd you get out? Resourceful, aren't you?"

"Shut up."

"If you want to fire that, you'd better hurry, or the others will be here."

"You're right. I want to kill you."

"Hurry. What are you waiting for?"

Min, suddenly faced with the decision, hesitated. She'd been so sure she wanted to kill him. It had been that vision which had kept her going. But, now, facing him...

He taunted her, "I thought, of all people, you'd be able to shoot."

"I said, shut up." And she fired a beam at his feet. The silent round exploded a log and sent fragments flying. She realized he had been slowly moving towards her. "Stay there." She fired again. "I said don't move."

He crossed the distance so fast it surprised her and she jerked off another round. He was caught in the left shoulder, but he didn't cry out. Instead his arm swung out wildly and knocked the weapon out of her hand. It flew off into the brush.

The others heard had heard the commotion. "Over there." "Hey, that's him." "Come on."

The man pushed Min into a tree and ran past, moving swiftly into the darkness.

The pursuers were close, as Min struggled back to her feet.

Then they were around her, a harsh light catching her in the face. Alex yelled, "Min? Oh, thank God."

The man could barely stand. The hole in his shoulder was bleeding profusely. *Not much farther...get to the vehicle...get away.*

He could still hear people in the brush, their beams penetrating the foliage. But they were stupid. He'd crouched in a bush and allowed them to pass, then circled around behind them. He'd be away soon, if he didn't pass out.

How did everything go wrong? How had the woman escaped? And then the Scav got the better of him...and, well, shit, just everything. I owe that Classé-riche bitch, but not today. Focus now. Just get away.

His vehicle was a welcome sight, until he saw the trunk. It made sense now. Everything was scattered on the ground. He picked up the duffle. It still contained the first aid kit and a couple of towels. He wrapped the towels around his shoulder, and threw the bag on the passenger's seat. He'd attend to the wound later. He started his vehicle and moved off.

17

Josh poked his head into the shadowed upstairs bedroom; Min was still sleeping off the meds. Even though it sickened him when he looked at her, nothing was seriously wrong.

They hadn't been safe after all, despite all their precautions. Tami was still trying to determine how he'd found them. It was clear this man was a pro, and now, worse, he was wounded and loose. That's why Tami had installed them in a safe house, and no one knew where they were.

Not even me, Josh thought as he looked out the upper hall window. The safe house was a large two-story structure situated on a slight rise overlooking the Atlantic coast – near Wilmington, he figured, or further south, maybe.

Back in Mount Bryson – *had it only been yesterday?* – Tami had arrived with reinforcements after everything had settled down. She'd been furious that they had done something to give themselves away. Alex and Josh tried to reassure her, but without much success. She'd said her officers would wait for more light to do a thorough search. Tami had seemed frustrated to a point where she'd said she was moving *"you damn Villanuevas"* to a safe house immediately. Josh had presumed she meant him, too.

Tami had deposited them at the safe house shortly before midnight, but left shortly thereafter. Now, it was just before 5:00 a.m. Josh wandered back downstairs. Several of Tami's officers were on the grounds somewhere, but when he looked out the front door, he didn't see anyone. He knew one of officers – Aaron – was on the widow's walk where he could spot anyone coming from a distance. Josh and Alex had taken turns checking windows and doors.

"Morning?" Alex's voice startled him. "Sorry."

"Geez! I thought you went to catch some sleep."

"I couldn't. How's Min?" Alex said, as he poured some coffee.

"Still asleep."

"Good. Hopefully, she'll sleep most of the day. How are your new bruises?"

Josh smiled, "You know, I'd almost forgotten about the other attack. It seems like such a long time ago."

"I know. Have you given any more thought to how he found us?"

"No. You?"

"Not a clue," Alex said, shaking his head. "I haven't used my real COPI since I left the Triangle."

"What about Karen? Did she scan out?"

"No, I wouldn't let her," Alex said, shaking his head. "Besides, that would have led him north, not the Mount Bryson. It's something else."

"Tami will have something more this morning, I'm sure."

New House

She showed up around 8:30 a.m. Josh, Alex and Tom, one of the outside officers, were starting into the second pot of coffee, when she kicked on the kitchen screen door. "Give me a hand, will ya?" Her arms were filled with bags and a satchel was slung over her shoulder.

Tom jumped up, looking almost guilty. "Sorry, Lieutenant," he said. "Let me take some of that."

"Here," Tami barked, handing him some of the grocery bags. "Shouldn't you be outside?"

"Just going," and with that Tom started to slip out the door. "Wait, Tom," Tami smiled, lopsidedly. "There are a couple carafes in there. Why don't you fill them and give them to the team. Later we'll do rotation on breakfast. I'm sure you're all tired and hungry."

Tom nodded and went about his task.

"Can you pour me one of those? It's been a long night." She slumped into a chair. "We couldn't find any trace of his trail. One good thing – we have some of his stuff," she said, nodding to the satchel. "When Min freed herself, she must have pulled a lot of the trunk items onto the ground. Apparently, he didn't have time – or couldn't find everything – before he made his escape."

"Did I hear my name?" Min came into the kitchen from the front hall, looking swollen and stiff. "Hi, Tami. What were you saying?" Her words were a little slurred.

Josh went over to her, gently kissing one of the undamaged spots on her face. "I didn't hear you come down. You should go back and rest."

"Stop bossing me around, please?" She softened the words by slipping her arms around him.

"Ok, but rest, will ya? Want some coffee?"

She settled gingerly onto one of the kitchen chairs, smiling, "Oh, yes, please."

Tami was looking mildly annoyed. "May I continue? One of the items we uncovered was a RIC unit; very sophisticated and extremely secure." She produced the unit.

Alex was surprised, "You still have it with you? I thought you would have deposited it with the S.F. evidence lock up. In fact, isn't all of this evidence?"

"Yes. I didn't want to leave them."

"Still don't know who you can trust?"

Tami shrugged.

Josh picked up the RIC. "What's on it? What does it connect to?"

Tami sipped her coffee, as if it was a restorative elixir. "As I said, we don't know. It has major security. We might crack it, given enough time, but I have a strong feeling that's one thing we don't have much of."

"What do you mean?"

"A bomb went off in one of the GINS substations last night, just outside the Ashville Dome. We're tracking the source, but we think it's just the beginning. No one is taking credit for it, yet, but some indicators point to the Candle." She took another sip, shaking her head. "This is getting so crazy."

Josh had been watching Min, who had leaned back with her eyes closed, but at this, she opened them and straightened up. "How's a substation bombing linked to these murders?"

"That, Min, is what I still don't know, but I have a hunch that this little unit," she tapped the screen, "will give us some answers."

An idea came to Josh. "I know someone who might help."

Min watched in fascination as the teen worked. She remembered him from Mount Bryson. He was Ian Ellis – one of Gregg and Marcie Ellis' boys. Sitting at the big kitchen table, Ian had connected the assassin's RIC to another unit – a unique piece of equipment, built by the boy and running his own program. It appeared that Ian Ellis had the gift, and he had perfected it by breaking into other systems.

Tami, on Josh's suggestion, had gone up to the settlement to retrieve Ian, and the whole family had ended up coming. *Good thing this is such a big house*, Min had thought when they'd all burst through the door.

Now Buzz was watching over his brother's shoulder, making unwelcome suggestions. Per Tami's suggestion, Gregg and Alex were in the living room, scanning news services for any new unusual activity. Marcie was busy feeding the large group.

Josh, Min realized, was watching her every move, while pretending to be engrossed in Ian's work. She wished he would relax and stop worrying about her. It was true that she looked a mess and hurt all over, but she was okay. Okay, except when she slept, and the dreams came. Or when she'd wake, imaging him in the room. She wasn't used to being afraid or vulnerable. It nagged at her, that she hadn't stopped him when she had him in her sites. She wouldn't be all right until he was dead.

"I got it!" Ian suddenly yelled. "I'm in!"

Everyone moved closer to have a better view. Min wasn't sure what they were looking at. Each file, according to Ian, had its own code, though, so there was a lot more work to do.

At the thought of the man, Min shivered and Josh was immediately at her side, "You should lie down."

"I'm fine, really. Just a chill." She pulled up a chair next to Ian. "Maybe I can help."

Alex had always been impressed by his sister's skills, and he was equally amazed at this young man. Between them, Min and Ian had been working for more than six hours, deciphering and decoding volumes of data. Some of the lists Tami recognized as suppliers of equipment, electronics and other useful items. "This list," she murmured, "is remote links; I have a hunch what they are for."

There were also files with names – lists similar to the one they had built – of victims. This man kept impeccable, but gruesome records; with details on how and when each occurred, the planning behind each one, how he felt afterwards. There was one comment next to Phill's name – *a mistake.*

Alex noticed the assassin's numbers didn't come close to the list Alex had generated. Maybe some they had generated weren't part of all this after all.

"There!" Tami said, pointing to the screen. "That's how he found you. Quentin Rathburne." She shook her head, "That's my fault. When I choose terminated COPIs, I never figured Rathburne had been part of all this. The assassin must have spotted Rathburne's COPI activity and followed it."

All of a sudden, Alex took in a sharp breath. He looked around to see if anyone had noticed. No one had. A number in one of the access lists jumped out at him. *Oh, God, no.*

18

The man managed to get to a doctor who had helped him before. She had been a 'techno' years ago before she'd lost her license for lending her services to the highest bidder. She worked quickly and quietly in her back room, cleaning, and then fusing the wound.

"I won't ask how you got this," she said as she applied thermal gauze. "This will dissolve in a few days but don't do anything to tear it or you'll start bleeding again."

"Thanks." There was little else said, except when the man asked how much.

"I don't want anything; don't want any record. Just don't come back. I have a husband and am respectable now."

The man laughed sarcastically, "Sure, doc, respectable." He carefully pulled on his clothes.

"You're still weak; lost a lot of blood. You shouldn't travel too far."

"No, not far."

The man was shaky, but he still had to finish this business. He knew – if he was any judge – that they would hide now and it wouldn't be easy to find them.

New House

Occasionally, when he was in the domes watching for the Scav, he'd noticed a woman who looked like she was Security Forces personnel. He'd already figured she was the one helping them. If he could get a trace on her...but he didn't know her name. He did another search on friends of Alex Villanueva and found only one that would fit the bill.

He regretted leaving his RIC behind. They might find it and, if they were clever and had enough time, they might get into his information. However, when he was finished with this assignment, he wouldn't have anything to do with that group again, so he could care less. He just needed to tie up the loose ends. It took him most of the day to get to his closest stash, and, picking up a replacement RIC, he started an activity search for Lt. Tami Donaldson.

Min was lying on the deck still at the safe house. The sun's warmth seeped into her bones; a light breeze clicked the tall grass and the ocean lapped at shore just past the dune. It was wonderful.

It had been five days and there had been no sign of the assassin. Tami sounded rueful when she said she suspected he'd died of his wounds or he'd gone so far underground they'd never find him. Min guessed the S.F. wanted him alive for questioning.

Meanwhile, Ian and his family had gone back to Mount Bryson; he'd done all he could. Tami insisted that Alex, Min and Josh stay hidden for a bit longer – just to be sure. However, security had lightened on the house. Only two S.F. officers remained with them, wandering somewhere on the grounds. Alex and Josh had gone for more supplies. With so many people, they'd quickly run through what Tami had brought.

Min got up and went inside to refresh her drink. She was still in the kitchen wiping the counter, when she heard a sound outside. She hadn't heard a vehicle, but she was glad they were back. She still didn't like to be alone.

She went back through the living, and onto the deck. She sat her glass down by the chair, stretching out like a cat and closing her eyes. *This is wonderfu...*

A hand clamped over her mouth at the same time another slipped around her neck. With a sinking feeling, she knew instantly who it was.

He dragged her off the chair and was down beside her, his mouth close to her ear.

"You here alone? Blink twice for 'yes.'"

She refused to respond, simply staring at him. He shifted his hold by placing his knee on top of her left arm, further restricting her movements.

"Never mind. Been watching, and I figure there were only the two S.F."

At the mention of '*were only*,' her expression must have changed, because he smiled. "Yes, my little Scav lover, you appear to be indeed alone."

His tone was smooth, as if he were discussing the local news – sociably, calmly, in a low voice close to her face. She was so repulsed, that she exploded with fury and tried to kick him in the back. He was like a snake and wound himself even tighter around her.

She realized that her actions only aroused him more, so she grew deadly calm, and closed her eyes.

"Givin' up already? Too bad. I liked your fight, but I guess we can't have everything, can we? Should I dispatch you now and do the others later? Or do you want to wait and go with them?" He chuckled.

Her right hand was slowly feeling for the glass she'd set down near her chair. She knew it was close. Her fingers touched something damp. *Moisture from the glass? Yes, that's it.* She opened her eyes.

His returned stare was, at first, puzzled, but then he smiled. "Ah, so you do still have fight? Good. I don't like..."

The glass crashed into his face with every ounce of her strength. He was thrown off balance, and she pushed him off with her knees and rolled away. Getting to her feet, she ran towards the house. She could feel shards of the glass under her bare feet – but he was getting up and she had to move fast. She reached out and grabbed the nearest object that would qualify as a weapon – the broom she'd used to sweep the deck.

He reached for her just as she whipped the long pole into his legs, then she swung it back in the opposite direction. He fell against the living room window, smashing through it with some force. He didn't move. She stood there looking through the broken opening, panting, fearing he was faking it. She waited, breathing heavily from the exertion, panic. Still nothing.

She ran past him, back into the kitchen, ransacking the cupboards for something to secure him. She found some rope under the sink, but when she went back to where he'd been, there was only a dark bloody stain. *Oh, God.*

She picked up the broom again and, holding it in front of her, carefully moved through the house.

"Min, where are you?" It was Alex's voice coming from the side entrance.

"Alex, he's here!" She ran back into the kitchen. "Where's Josh?"

"What? Who's here?" As he put the groceries on the table.

"That man! I hurt him but..."

"You're right, I'm still here," the man said as he came into the kitchen from the door by the stairs. He was holding a weapon and was pointing it first toward Alex, then Min. His shoulder was crimson and blood was oozing from cuts on his face and arms. Yet, he seemed unaffected. "Let's go into the living room and sit down. Please answer her, Alex. Where's the Scav? When will he be back?"

Alex sat beside Min on the sofa. "I don't know. He dropped me off at the grocers a while ago."

"Where is he?" he said angrily. For a moment, he seemed unsteady, as he moved behind a chair in the corner. Min noticed he had positioned himself to have a full view of anyone coming from all three entrances to the living room. He saw Min staring at him, and looked squarely back. "I don't kill that easily, huh?"

"I wish my aim had been better."

He laughed. "I'm sure." He fell into that conversational manner again, looking about the room. "This is quite a come down from your homes inside." He tugged at his shirt, pulling it away from his wounds. "You..." He pointed at Min, "...get something to stop this bleeding."

"Let me do it. She is still not well," Alex volunteered.

"Don't give me that. I was just struggling with her; she has enough strength."

Min went up to the bathroom for the first aid kit. She looked around, too, for something she could use against him. He was weak and she might get the better of him again. She found in one of the drawers an old communicator – battery dead, of course, and in another a bottle of sleep aides. If she used enough...? She poured the bottle's contents into her pocket.

"Here!" She said, returning to the living room, tossing the kit and some towels into his lap. She went over to her brother, "Alex, are you hungry?"

No, Min, Alex's eyes were saying. She nodded slightly.

"Good idea," the man said. "Get me something and a drink too. By the way, we'll have your brother test it first."

Damn, Min thought, *he's guessed.* She went into the kitchen, her mind still searching for a solution. And wondering where Josh was.

Alex knew his sister was planning something. He needed to figure out what, so he could help, or come up with a plan of his own. Occasionally, the man's body shook, and he'd slump forward. Nevertheless, each time Alex moved even an inch, the man would sit up straight.

"Don't even think about it, Classé."

Min seemed to taking a long time but finally came back with a beer – still with the cap in place – and some sandwiches.

"Good. Now take a bite, brother. If she's trying to poison me, we'll know soon enough."

Min sat down, "I didn't poison you. I want you to suffer; poison's too fast." She turned her head and looked at Alex, "You okay?"

She was trying to tell him something. "I'm fine," he said.

"Well, at least for now," the man said, smiling in that irritating way. As the man ate his sandwich, he settled back, "Now we'll wait."

When Josh and Alex had gotten to the grocery depot, they had agreed that Alex would do the shopping then walk home; Josh would go in search of generator fuel. Neither wanted to leave Min alone for long. However, Josh was discovering that his task was harder than expected. He had to go to three places before he found the type of fuel they needed.

It was nearly sunset, when Josh finally headed back to the house. He parked in the worn spot they used as a driveway, and unloading the heavy container, walked up the path towards the house. As he passed the shrubs near of the front porch, a hand grabbed his arm and dragged him down. "What?!"

"Be quiet," Tami whispered.

He crouched close to her, "What's going on?" he breathed.

"He's in there – he has Alex and Min."

"How do you know?"

"Min got off a message about an hour ago – it was all binary, but clear enough. Not sure what she used. At any rate, we've done a thermal scan and they're in the living room."

"We've got to get in there." Josh started to get up, but she pulled him back down.

"No. I think he's waiting for you. It's probably the only thing keeping them alive. If you blunder in there, it's over."

"I can't just sit here."

"That's exactly what you'll do," Tami said in a harsh whisper. "We're moving in; sit tight."

"Then give me a weapon or use me as bait...something so I don't have to just sit here."

Tami put her face close to Josh's ear. "I do have an idea, but it will require perfect timing on your part. I will let you go in, but only on my signal. My teams will enter from the front and back doors – you from the side by the drive. You following me?"

"Yes," Josh whispered back.

"Good. Here's a RIC. I want you to stand just outside the door, and when it blinks three times, you go in. But *quietly*. Give me about ten seconds before you make yourself known. Got it?"

Josh nodded. *'Now?'* he mouthed.

Tami shook her head and held up five fingers, as she moved over to some of her people. Those five minutes were the longest of Josh's life. Finally, she came back.

"Okay, but make your way around to the side staying behind that hedge row. I don't want him spotting you early."

Josh crossed the front yard staying low as instructed, positioning himself just outside the side door. It took all of his energy to stand there and wait. Finally, the small light on his RIC blinked the signal and Josh took a deep breath. He quietly opened the screen door and moved into the dark kitchen. From his shadowed position, he could see Min and Alex on the sofa, but the killer was out of site. He wasn't sure where the man was, but knew he was close. Josh figured Tami's people were in place and it was time to let them know he was there. "Hi," he said cheerfully, "I'm back."

Min looked up and saw him, crying, *"No, stay back!"*

As Josh moved to the archway, he saw the killer standing behind a chair in the right corner.

"Finally," the man said, moving around the chair and leaning on a table. Something caught in his hand. "Shit," and he brushed it off against his leg.

That's when Josh noticed that shards of glass covered the table, as well as the floor, and the window overlooking the deck was broken. That would help with the surprise to come, Josh thought smugly.

"Oh, God, no," Min was mumbling over and over, almost in tears.

Josh just smiled at her. "It's okay."

New House

At that moment, everything broke. Tami and another came in from the back; two others burst in from the front hallway. The killer was fast too, though. He ducked behind the chair, and shot the one who came in with Tami; then pulled off another couple of shots towards the front. Two of her people managed to take cover behind the doorway; one other went down, not moving.

"Stop shooting, everyone," Tami yelled, as she peered around the kitchen doorframe, where she'd taken refuge, pulling Josh back with her. "Let's talk."

The killer's answer to Tami was two more shots in her direction. Then he spoke to Josh, "Now you, come out here" as he started to stand and take aim.

At that same moment, Min moved. Josh couldn't believe it. She sprung up from the sofa, practically leaping over the chair. There was a knife in her left hand; she was aiming its long blade at the man's back.

Tami screened, "No, Min," and rushed through the doorway, grabbing Min's free arm, just as the knife found its target.

The man spun around from the blow, and for a split second, Josh couldn't tell what was happening. Everything was chaos.

Alex had seen Min race toward the assassin, swinging her arm, something shiny in her hand. Then Tami had burst in from the kitchen. In the struggle, both fire arms went flying, Tami was knocked backwards onto the floor and Min, releasing the knife, had fallen to her knees. As the man reached back for the knife, Josh dragged Min towards the kitchen.

With the killer busy, Alec saw his opportunity to help Tami, but he moved too late. Alex felt the knife slip under his chin and an arm slide across his chest, pulling him tight against the killer.

"Everyone..." the man's voice was close to his ear. "...hold it." *Pant.* "...now...you two in the front hall," he said, indicating the two remainder officers. The man was breathing in short jabs. "You..." he coughed slightly, and Alex heard something bubbling from his mouth. "...throw your weapons...away."

No, Alex thought. Out of the corner of his eye, he thought he saw Tami move.

The man started backing towards the deck door, dragging Alex with him. Each time they moved, the knife nicked his neck. The next few seconds seemed like hours. When his eyes met Tami's, he realized she had reached one of the weapons and was taking aim. *God, Tami, don't miss.*

With a strength he didn't know he had, Alex pushed the knife away, leaning with it, just as blue light burst from Tami's position on the floor. It seemed to take forever, but the assassin's forehead exploded, sending a warm spattering over Alex.

Unbelievably, the man stood for all of five seconds, his arm still clutching Alex, before he slowly fell backwards, pulling Alex backwards with him. Alex rolled into a sitting position and with his sleeve, wiped the killer's blood from his face.

19

Min's mother, Maggie Villanueva, opened the huge front door. She was elegantly dressed as always. "Alex! Min! What a surprise?"

Alex asked, as he, Min and Josh entered the hall, "How is everyone holding up? Chauncey? How's she doing?"

"I was just on my way to see her. She's hiding her feelings. It'll probably hit her soon, but for now, well…" Maggie seemed to sense the undercurrent. "That's not the reason you've come, correct?"

"Is father in?" Alex asked.

"In the study. Why?"

"We need to talk to you both," Alex said, as they walked down the hallway.

Her mother fell into step with them. "What's going on? Why are you all acting so mysteriously? And who, pray tell, are you?" she said, finally acknowledging Josh.

As no one answered her, and she knocked lightly on the study door.

"Come." Her father's strong voice resounded through the door.

As the group entered, Min saw her father look up. The light from the window was behind him, so she couldn't read his expression.

"What is it? I'm really busy right now."

"We need a few minutes of your time, father," Min said formally.

Alex went to one of the two chairs opposite his father's desk. "Dad, we need to show you something." He handed him a small screen. "This is some of the data we've downloaded from that assassin's RIC." He paused as his father looked at the data. "See that one? That ID code? It's part of a block reserved for our family. I tried it but it's secured. What is it used for and why did he have it?"

His father looked again at the screen in his hand, laid it carefully on his desk, and stood up.

Min was impatient with Alex's gentle approach. "Well, father. What *was* that man doing with it?"

"Min, there could be a hundred ways the assassin could have gotten it," Alex said quickly. "We're just trying to eliminate some of them." He turned back to his father. "Dad, I was thinking, do you think Angel could have been using it?" He didn't want to believe his brother had fallen to this level. "I know he's in a bit of trouble, but this? Is it possible?"

"No."

"How can you be so positive?" Min asked.

"Because there are only three people who have clearance codes to this particular account – your mother, me, and Robert, who uses it when he handles some of our communications." He took a deep breath.

"You're saying Robert used it – *on his own?*" There was more than a little sarcasm in Min's voice.

Her father turned on her, angrily. "What are you implying, Min? Do you think we had something to do with this mess? I don't know how it found its way into that man's system, or why anyone would want to implicate either of us."

"Father," Alex said sadly, "please, call Robert. We need answers. Tami cannot hold off the authorities for long."

John Villanueva asked his system to locate Robert.

"That won't be necessary." Min's mother had been standing with her back to the door, watching the scene. "System, please tell Robert that he is not needed." She looked around the room; then continued. "Robert used it...but he was following my instructions."

Everyone displayed vastly different emotions.

"I'm not sure I can explain it to you," she went on with a hint of sadness in her voice. "We've lost so much order and control the last few decades, we had to do something to regain our stability." She seemed unsure as to what to say next. She went to a chair and sat down on the edge, very straight, very calm. "Imagine if the number of people outside became larger than the number of people in the domes? What if they found a better life out there? Can you understand what it would do to the carefully constructed world we've created? We've been struggling with the question of how to get Environs back into the domes – into the system. Our propaganda wasn't working – especially when we saw even upper classes leaving the domes.

"Our position was that we would make their lives out there less desirable. The Candle and other subversive groups were already stirring things up. We would just use them to further our agenda. More often than not, they actually took the blame for our activities; sometimes more than one group would claim credit for the same thing. I suppose they though it made them more powerful and feared."

When Alex spoke, he was unable to keep the shock from his tone, "Mother...why?"

"We knew we had to do something dramatic – before the '2103 Public Order Act' came before the Senate," she said.

"Maggie," John Villanueva asked, "what has all this to do with that legislation?

"We anticipated that the huge influx of new Scavs would create havoc. This would bring about a cry for more force and control. Parts of the Act would give us that leverage we need to regain our equilibrium." She shook her head. "I still believe in that Act, just not the solution we took to get there."

Josh had a thunderous expression. "So you're *dramatic solution* was to hire assassins to murder innocent people?"

"Not in the beginning. It was only suppose to be scare tactics. In fact, I didn't know about that part, not until later. However, when so many suspicious accidents started showing up, and I started asking questions, it had gone too far; and too many people were involved." She looked at her husband. "You must believe that."

When no one responded to her, she slapped her hand on the arm of the chair. "Dammit. Can none of you see it? By disrupting the lives of those outside, by driving them back into the system, we would almost assure the passing of the Act. We were hoping to do what Cloward and Pivan couldn't do back in the 20th Century. It failed then, but we thought it was possible now with our global networking."

Min's father stared at his wife. "Their theory was to create turmoil, anger and distrust. Is that what you wanted, Maggie?"

Maggie stood up, agitated. "That's wasn't all they wanted. Overwhelming the system's resources so people would demand governmental action was their ultimate goal. That's all we wanted to do. I couldn't...I wouldn't let myself be blinded with details, because I knew we were right. We would have succeeded, too; the plan was working. Then people started snooping around, making trouble. Annoying reporters like Bannister and Hardy were trying to turn public opinion against us...trying to defeat the legislation."

Alex had been pacing. "And us? Were we also annoying and in the way?"

"You'll remember, I did tell you to stay out of it."

Min held her hands tight against her sides to keep from shaking. "What about Josh? Did you have him beaten to make your point? Was that warning from you? Did you really think we'd stop because of a threat? I thought you knew us better than that." Then her eyes filled with tears. "You blamed me for Phill's death, but it had been you all along."

She didn't answer at first, but then said quietly, "Yes, I will always regret Phill's death. But I still say it was your fault for keeping on with your ridiculous investigation when we warned you to stop."

Alex was standing by the window, looking out. Min could tell from his bent shoulders that his world was crumbling around him. He and mother had always had a special relationship. Min could barely hear him when he asked, "I still don't understand; when you found out, why didn't you report it; stop it?"

"Robert said no one would believe that we weren't part of it from the start. I hated the way we did it, but it was working," she said again, as if that made everything all right.

Min's father had been leaning on the desk, as if holding on for dear life. "My God, Maggie."

Maggie rubbed her forehead. "We need to contact the authorities. I'm ready to tell them everything. Actually, I'm almost glad to be able to tell everything."

No one had been looking at Josh. He took several strides in her mother's direction, his hands stretched out as if to grab her. She backed away, surprised, falling back into the chair. "You're glad to be able to speak up? Where the hell were you when a whole family blew up; when a beautiful, gentle woman bled to death? Damn you…" He curled his arms into his chest, controlling his instinct to lash out. Min was sure that if Maggie had been a man, he would have hit her.

When her mother looked up, tears were running down her face, but her voice was calm. "I am so sorry. I know nothing will bring back those people. Believe me – I am so sorry." She stood and cleared her throat. "System, please contact the Security Forces."

Alex suddenly came to life. "Mother, no. Tami said to contact her and she'd handle it."

John Villanueva went to his wife and laid a hand on her shoulder. "Leave us now." He didn't look at his children, but they knew when to drop it and leave the room. Josh, however, wasn't ready to go. Min and Alex, however, convinced him to leave.

Min looked back briefly at her parents. Her father was crouching down and holding his wife. And to her surprise, his shoulders were shaking. Min had never seen her father cry and it embarrassed her. A part of her would never forgive her mother, but at that moment she felt sorry for them and what lie ahead. She quietly closed the door and walked down the hall.

C.E. Anthony

Epilogue

In the summer and early fall of 2103 several articles were reported on the GINS, some widely commented on, some passed almost unnoticed.

CONSPIRACY UNCOVERED

27 May 2103, ET, Security Forces Special Reporter (NC, IB) – The North Carolina Information Bureau reported that the Triangle Security Forces filed a report on a far-reaching conspiracy to terrorize and force Environs back into the system and resulted in thousands of outworlder murders.

The motivation is still unclear, but certain unnamed members of the Classé-riche and Security Force officials are among those linked in this heinous crime. During an attempted arrest by the S.F., an involved assassin was shot and killed; all attempts to uncover his identity are proving futile. The investigation has been escalated to the Global Courts and arrests are imminent.

OUTWORLDER CONSPIRACY STILL UNCLEAR

2 July 2103, ET, Hardy (Chicago IB) – This reporter has learned that a certain new legislation before the Global Senate last year was at the core of this recent outworlder conspiracy. Today that legislation, the 2103 Public Order Act, was defeated. If passed, it would have created a mandatory COPI scan for all citizens. This legislation would have also extended to the outworlders, forcing strict laws and controls over Environs and their communities. Support for the legislation dissipated rapidly once it was associated with the conspiracy. Sources told this reporter that a key information source has been Maggie Villanueva, renowned matriarch of the Villanueva family. While it is unclear as to her involvement, the Security Forces have said she is providing valuable information. She will begin formal testimony next month in the Geneva Global Courts.

VILLANUEVA EXHIBIT OPENS

7 August 2103, 1330 ET, (Roanoke IB) – Roanoke Valley Center for the Arts – The Villanueva name is not unknown in the art world or in conjunction with this Center, so it comes to no one's surprise that a new exhibit debuts today by Villanueva. What might surprise some is that it is a dual exhibit, featuring art by Alex Villanueva, and a new medium created by his sister, Yumin.

Dr. Jerry Ray Jenkins, Director of RVCA, will give the dedication at a reception today, starting at 1300 Eastern Time;

it's by reservation only. The exhibit, entitled "A House Revisited," opens to the public starting tomorrow at 0900 Eastern Time; additional access on GINS at rvcaAHouseRevisited.co.

MARGARITE VILLANUEVA DEAD

22 August 2103, (Triangle IB) – Margarite Villanueva was found dead at her Umsted Park estate yesterday. The coroner and the S.F. have not released a formal statement. Ironically, it was one day before Villanueva was to begin testifying before the Geneva Global Courts to expose the recent outworlder scandal and related legislation.

Villanueva was the aunt of Phillippe Chauquette, who also died recently in an explosion, also rumored to have some link to this conspiracy.

Margarite is survived by her husband, Jonathan; her sons Alexander (Karen) and Angel; and her daughter, Yumin; mother, Joline Huan Villanueva; her sister, Marie Chauquette; and 3 grandchildren. Services will be held Friday on GINS.Villanueva-m.bereavement.nct and are closed to the general public. Pre-registration will be required for attendance. Her remains will be taken to the ancestral vault on the following day for entombment.

The world will miss this great and respected leader and we look to the next generation to carry on in her excellent tradition.

In vain we build the world, unless
The builder also grows...

Made in the USA
Charleston, SC
02 April 2011